GOING HOSTILE

GOING HOSTILE

BARRY DAVIES

BLOOMSBURY

For Yvonne

First published in Great Britain 1995
Bloomsbury Publishing Plc, 2 Soho Square, London W1V 6HB

Copyright © 1995 by Barry Davies

The moral right of the author has been asserted

A CIP catalogue record for this book is
available from the British Library

ISBN 0 7475 2185 9

10 9 8 7 6 5 4 3 2 1

Typeset by Hewer Text Composition Services, Edinburgh
Printed in Great Britain by Clays Ltd, St Ives plc

Many novels take as their starting-point the author's own life experiences. The events and personalities in this book are no exception, but I must leave it to readers to decide where truth ends and imagination begins.

CONTENTS

1

The Fire of Youth

O*man, southern Arabia, 1943*
      As the boat lurched dangerously on the tide, Ali
bin Mohammed al Dhuhoori's ancient, bony hand
tightened around the ragged bundle on his lap. Its weight,
combined with the hardness of the wooden seat, numbed his
skinny legs. He eyed his fellow travellers apprehensively. He
was afraid not of drowning – an acceptable risk in this small
dhow – but of being robbed. Robbed of his wealth, and thus
his status, he would become a nonentity. He carried with him
an elderly musket. True, it would allow him only one shot,
and that would probably miss; nevertheless it afforded him
some comfort. Ali shrank back against the side of the dhow
in an effort to make himself invisible, and in the fading light
of the setting sun kept watch.

Another lurch of the boat compelled him to turn his head,
and with a sense of relief he saw in the distance the faint glow
of the village lights. Not far now, he thought, his bones aching
for the comfort of his bed and his heart longing for the safety
of home.

This trip had been most profitable. For a money-lender there
were good pickings to be had, even for a small dealer like
himself; but they could not be had without travel, and that was
hazardous. Business in his own village of Taga was minimal,
and Ali had long since discovered the riches to be reaped from

1

a monthly boat trip down the coast to Aden. The rich coastal towns of Salalah, Rakyhut and Aden itself were populated by people who needed money, but the journey itself was fraught with danger. The life was lonely, for even the moneylenders were suspicious of each other, but he didn't worry about that; and he had grown inured to being called 'bloodsucker' and 'leech' when it was time for his clients to repay their debts. No, it was the bandits and robbers picketing the overland routes that caused him concern. The mountainous route to Aden ran partly down the Dhala road, which was flanked by the Radfan mountains. Here the dreaded Quteibi tribe augmented their meagre income by collecting 'taxes' from merchants and travellers alike. This was why Ali travelled by boat. Only in the winter, when the sea was very rough, would he consider travelling overland. Twice now when he had done so he had been robbed of all he possessed. The 'taxes' were one thing – accepted as inevitable, albeit resented – but to lose everything was quite another. The last robbery was carried out in the name of freedom: 'A donation to the rebel cause,' they had said.

Foolishly, he had reported the incident. Travelling on to Salalah, the capital city, he had thought to find assistance in recovering his money by informing the Sultan's soldiers. But far from being helpful, they had questioned him closely. Why had he been so easily parted from his money? Why had he not resisted? After all, had he not had a rifle with him? Why did he not put up a fight against the Sultan's enemies? His excuses seemed futile, and eventually Ali realized that he was under suspicion of actually supporting the rebels. Fortunately, help was at hand in the shape of a dignitary to whom Ali had lent money. Quick to seize his advantage, the official had negotiated a huge adjustment to his repayments and at last Ali was free to go, reflecting ruefully on his double loss.

A warning cry from the dhow's owner jogged Ali's thoughts back to the present. He braced himself as the small boat washed up on the tide and hit the sandy beach. Gathering up his heavy bundle, Ali stepped stiffly off the vessel and struggled inland. Following the well-worn path that guided his steps in the darkness, twisting through the wind-battered palm trees that grew parallel to the shoreline, he came at last to Taqa.

Little had changed throughout the two thousand-year history of this village of small, flat-roofed dwellings made of wattle and mud. It was protected on the southern side by the Arabian Sea and walled in to the north by the high mountainous plateau of the Jebel massif that rose out of the desert and towered above the coastal villages. The Jebel was a refuge for wild, ancient tribes, bandits and dissidents. In summer it was a place of beauty: lush green grass rippled in the cooling winds, tall trees gave homes to birds and small animals, and occasionally larger game could be seen. To the tribesmen who lived there, it was a place to raise sons and breed cattle. A proud people, they exulted in their freedom, and from their breezy plateau they looked down disdainfully at the towns and cities sweltering in the blistering summer heat.

Ali trudged through the village streets. As he neared his own modest dwelling his thoughts turned to what might await him there. Surely she had given birth by now — it had been so long.

A son, a son: he would give anything for a boy child! The vessel that would give form and flesh to his vision was but fourteen years old; he had purchased and married her a little over nine months ago. Ali already had two other wives, but one was barren while the other had produced two daughters — both murdered at birth, as was the custom with unwanted female children. He kept both wives as mere chattels, to cook, clean and occasionally endure his diminishing sexual urges.

As a money-lender Ali's status fell somewhere between that of a boat-owner and that of the Sultan's tax-collector; he was tolerated by those who owed him money, and hated by those who did not. But with a son his social position would be different. He could plan a future, school the boy, walk with him to the mosque and be respected. A man could be proud when he had a son.

Almost a year earlier his longings had been intensified by a twist of fortune. He had been visiting the neighbouring fishing port of Mirbat in connection with the repayment of a loan long overdue. The recipient had bought a boat with the money and thus was able to fish in order to support his growing family, but times were hard and he could not repay the loan. Ali, however, had steeled his heart. Was he not also entitled to live?

'No more time!' he had snapped. 'The money now, or the boat is mine.'

Ali had closed his ears to the man's entreaties and insisted upon his rights.

Emotionless, the man had turned to his son. 'Get the girl!' To Ali he had continued, 'We have no money to pay you. The fish we catch is barely enough to feed us.'

The boy had returned, pushing in front of him a girl child.

'My youngest daughter,' the man had announced. 'Allah be praised. May He grant you the son I know you hunger for.'

Ali had stared at the child who stood before him. Her slim body was covered from head to toe in the traditional black abayah; only her eyes were visible, a look of incomprehension in them. But even in the all-enveloping garment the curve of her small but prominent breasts promised future delights, and Ali's head was swimming already with thoughts of carnal pleasure. Dumbfounded by this turn of events, but not wanting to lose mastery of the situation, he had said, 'What makes you think that she will produce a son for me?'

The father had not replied. He had seen the weakness in Ali's eyes and his heart went out to his daughter. 'May Allah forgive me,' he had prayed silently.

Ali, his thoughts and his blood racing now, had hardly been able to contain himself: the words had leaped from his mouth of their own accord.

'The debt is settled. See that she is in Taqa by the end of the month. The wedding will be simple.' With that he stood up and swiftly departed.

On the day of the marriage, minutes after the wedding ceremony Ali had legally raped the young girl. It was the custom. Taking her into his home he had thrown her, like a rag doll, face down upon the mattress. Despite her muffled cries, Ali had fallen upon her and penetrated her from behind, forcing his withering penis into her vaginal channel, ripping her flesh and destroying the flower of her youth forever. Moments later his seed had entered the fertile young body, and with a grunt of satisfaction Ali had rolled away from her. Ignoring the girl's distress Ali had left the room, taking with him the small white towel from under her body. Then he had danced in the street, waving above his head the bloodstained cloth which proclaimed to all that his wife had been until that moment a virgin and that he was still a man.

Thinking back to that moment, Ali smiled to himself. It had been well done, and now her time was near. Would she deliver a son or disgrace him with a daughter? He was impatient to find out. But suddenly a voice disturbed his day-dreaming.

'Peace be with you.' It was his neighbour, the village baker, who greeted him.

'And with you let there be peace,' Ali replied impatiently, not wishing to be drawn into conversation so close to home.

'A pleasant and profitable trip?' the man enquired.

'By the grace of Allah.'

'And what is the news from Aden?'

Ali's monthly trips were a source of interest to the villagers. He acted as a messenger from the outside world, keeping them informed about events of which they would otherwise be ignorant. But today Ali was in no mood to gossip.

'Very little news, by the grace of Allah,' he replied. 'It is late and I am weary. Perhaps tomorrow.' He could delay no longer. His son called and he hurried on.

At last Ali reached the two-storey clay dwelling, a symbol of his wealth, which occupied a prominent position overlooking the village square. 'Allah be praised, to be safe in my own house,' he said, giving thanks as he entered. The room was in darkness, but through the connecting doorway he saw the dull yellow glow of lamplight. The house was silent – too silent. Ali stopped in his tracks, listening, and knew that something was wrong. The smell of death hung in the air. Dropping his bundle and his rifle, he crossed the room swiftly and opened the door.

He took in the bareness of the room, the eerie shadows cast by the small kerosene lamp, the two figures in black – his older wives, one holding a bundle in her arms. Then he looked at the mattress on the floor and put his hand to his mouth as his stomach heaved.

There lay the still and lifeless body of his young wife, her abayah pulled up about her waist to expose her parted legs which were drenched in blood. Blood soaked the mattress and ran on to the dirt floor. Ali felt faint. He leaned against the wall and stared with a morbid fascination at the dead girl. He had never before seen her private parts in this manner; their copulations had been sordid affairs as Ali had fumbled with her body in the darkness of his room.

His mesmerized gaze was broken by the movement of his eldest wife and the cry of a new-born child. Holding out the small bundle, she said simply, 'Your son.'

Ali trembled with emotion. Was it true? He took the bundle and let the swaddling cloth drop. There was no mistaking the maleness of this lusty infant. The old man's eyes moistened with tears of joy and he laughed as he carried the child outside. In the village square he held his naked son aloft and shouted for all to hear, '*Al hamdu lillah* – a son, a son.'

The two wives turned their attention to the corpse lying on the blood-soaked mattress and set about preparing it for burial before the heat of the following day. They felt no sense of loss for the dead girl. Her burden was ended – she was the lucky one. They now had the added task of looking after her offspring.

Ali bin Mohammed al Dhuhoori named his son Mahmud, and as the child grew there was a warmth in the house that had previously been lacking. The boy captivated the two older wives who took great delight in rearing him even though he was not of their flesh. Mahmud was a sturdy child, with a large head which was crowned, right from birth, with a mop of glorious black silky curls. Ali worried about its size but his wives quashed his fears, assuring him that the body would grow to match the head as the boy matured.

Life in Taqa was easy and uncomplicated. During his younger years Mahmud spent much of his time playing with the other village boys, and the only schooling that he received was at the mosque or from his father. Teaching the boy was a task that Ali was eager to undertake, for the young Mahmud's bright and inquisitive mind was a constant source of joy to him. In the cool of the evening they would climb the steps leading to the flat roof of the house and in the glow of the setting sun they would sit and talk. It was here that Ali taught Mahmud to read and write, and occasionally told him stories. Ali's knowledge of the Arab world was excellent for, unlike most of the villagers, he had travelled far and wide. The young boy was enthralled as he listened to his father's tales, and a bond of affection was forged between the two.

One evening, shortly after returning from a trip to Aden, Ali summoned his son to the rooftop. They talked for a while, and as usual Ali's spirit was warmed by the closeness of the boy, who was now taller than his father and almost fourteen years old. Ali stretched out his arm, indicating the village.

'Here in Taqa, my son, there is nothing for you. We have no schools and your young life will be wasted here.' Ali paused and a look of despondency crossed his face, for Mahmud's existence gave purpose and meaning to his life and he would miss his son badly. 'I have done what I should have done two years ago,' he continued. 'I have made arrangements for you to go to school in Aden.'

'Aden!' Mahmud exclaimed, his eyes shining with excitement. He stood up and punched the air with joy, and Ali forgot his grief momentarily as he was caught up in his son's enthusiasm.

GOING HOSTILE

Aden 1957

From the deck of the dhow that sailed monthly along
the coast Mahmud saw Aden for the first time. Gigantic
steel ships filled the busy port, which was overshadowed
by huge buildings some ten storeys high, and the dark,
rocky background of an extinct volcano towered above
the place. It was a long way from the clay hovels of the
fishing village that had been his childhood home. Mahmud
surveyed the scene with mounting excitement, and as the
small boat sailed into the bustling harbour the strange
sights and sounds set his nerves tingling with eager anticipation.

Back in Oman the ruler, Sultan Said bin Taimur, denied
his people every aspect of modern civilization. There were no
schools, hospitals or proper roads. His rule was absolute, and
protest was ruthlessly punished. To disagree with the Sultan
would bring swift reprisals. It could mean a village well being
filled in with cement and all weapons confiscated. Deprived
of water, the villagers would suffer a slow and painful death.
Now Mahmud had put that life behind him. But its memory
would remain with him for all time, and would shape his future
in ways as yet unknown to him.

School was difficult at first. New boys were always
bullied, and as the son of a money-lender Mahmud was
singled out for special attention. He was fast growing into
a powerful young man with a well-muscled body, but his
abnormally large head with its crop of dark curls still made
him a figure of fun.

At the back of the classrooms was a small courtyard and it
was here, one bright morning, that Mahmud turned the tables
on his tormentors. A gang of eight boys had him cornered and
were jeering and taunting him.

'Is it true that your mother died because your head split her
in two?' one boy shouted.

'No, it's because she saw his ugly face,' another jibed.

At the mention of his mother, Mahmud's blood rushed to
his head. No one had ever spoken to him about her, and his

father had quickly changed the subject whenever Mahmud had questioned him. But Ali was well known in Aden, and rumours must have spread. To hear these boys joke about her death angered him, and he stood in the corner seething at the insults.

Normally, Arabs do not fist-fight as Westerners do. At moments of conflict they shy away from hard physical contact and resort to slapping and words. Not so with Mahmud. One boy, Ahmed Said, braver than the rest, moved to slap him round the head. Swiftly, Mahmud reacted. He grabbed the boy's arm and punched his own balled fist into his assailant's face. The boy yelled as he staggered backwards, his nose spurting fresh red blood which soiled his white robe. In that moment of shock Ali took his advantage and, roaring like a bull, launched himself at his persecutors, lashing out wildly, light-headed now with the power he had unleashed. Thinking better of any attempt to resist, the boys fled, screaming.

The hullabaloo brought the teachers running, and once again, like an animal at bay, Mahmud faced his captors. But as suddenly as it had engulfed him the rage subsided, and, panting with his exertion, he was led back to the classroom. His punishment was a severe beating with a leather strap, which he endured proudly and without a whimper. News of his indiscretion was sent to his father, and Mahmud spent some time in isolation awaiting his fate. Only Ali's offer of a large sum of money enabled his son to avoid expulsion and remain at the school.

The incident was a turning-point for Mahmud, who had discovered within himself a power that until that moment had remained hidden. He became a natural leader of his peers, and to the younger ones he was a hero. One small boy in particular, Dhardir, became like his shadow.

At the age of twenty Mahmud finished his schooling and returned home to Taqa. But now, after six years in the big city, he found village life stifling. He endured it for some months, but then, despite his father's entreaties, decided that he could not stay there any longer.

'I grow old, my son,' Ali pleaded. 'I am afraid to carry money around and I grow weaker. I need you to help with the business. You will have enough travelling, I assure you.'

But Mahmud was not assured. 'I will not lie, father. I do not know my destiny, but a money-lender – no! You did not educate me just for this. I need more from the world.'

Ali knew in his heart that Mahmud was right. There was nothing in Taqa for him – after all, that was why he had sent his son to Aden in the first place. He was being selfish, for he would miss Mahmud: that, he acknowledged to himself, was the real reason for his reluctance to see him go.

Mahmud, too, could see that his departure would be painful for his father, so he compromised. 'Give me two years, Father. If in that time I have not found what I seek, I shall return and do your bidding.'

Two days later Ali walked with his son down the path that led through the palm trees to the beach. He glanced at the young man who strode beside him and felt proud to be his father. Mahmud had grown tall and strong, and his leonine head sat well on his broadened shoulders. He had an air of confidence – a man among men, Ali thought.

Stopping at the water's edge, they stood side by side in silence. As the cool breeze gently ruffled their robes they shared one last peaceful moment. The dhow on which Mahmud was to sail was anchored a short distance from shore. As the ferry boat returned one last time for Mahmud, his father spoke.

'Do for your life on earth as though you will live forever, and do for your end as though you are dying tomorrow.' Ali repeated the old Arab proverb with feeling.

Mahmud smiled. 'Why blame a man for resembling his father?' he responded.

Now it was Ali's turn to smile. Inwardly he thanked Allah for giving him the one thing he had most desired, a son.

''fi ammanillah, I leave you in the protection of Allah.'

'Ma'a salaama.'

10

For over an hour Ali stood at the water's edge, watching the dhow sail out of sight. With Mahmud had gone the warmth of his life. He shivered. Cold now, Ali bin Mohammed al Dhuhoori walked back to the village. He would never see his son again.

Aden, 1964
Aden was now a bustling commercial city. Under British control since 1839, this port at the southern tip of the Red Sea had developed into an important refuelling facility for shipping using the Suez Canal. It had also become a vital military installation because of its strategic position on the sea route between East and West. There had been a British military presence during Mahmud's school years, but recently their numbers had risen dramatically and armed soldiers now patrolled the streets.

So it was a changed city to which Mahmud returned, and there was a tension in the air that he had not noticed before. Once settled in the home of his old school friend, Dhardir, he questioned him about the new assertiveness of the British army. Although his father had often talked of rebels and revolution, Mahmud had taken no heed.

'Why should the British restrain us?' answered his friend. 'Are we sheep to be driven here and there by foreigners?'

Mahmud was shocked by the venom in Dhardir's voice. He remembered him as a gentle and good-humoured youth.

Dhardir reached out across the table and laid his hand on Mahmud's. Their bond of friendship was strong, and Dhardir had a secret to impart. 'While you were away I joined the People's Front for the Liberation of the Occupied Arabian Gulf.' The organization sounded more important when given its full title.

'Am I to understand, my brother, that you have become a rebel?' Mahmud's jesting tone ridiculed his friend. The grip on Mahmud's hand tightened and the eyes of a fanatic looked into his, compelling him to listen.

'You are not stupid, my brother. Look around you! The

11

British exercise control over the Arabian Gulf. With their warships and soldiers they stifle our growth and deny us independence. It is time to cast off the oppressor. Look at your own country – the British keep in power that old man who treats you like slaves.'

Mahmud was bewildered, not so much by the outburst as by its content. At school Dhardir had excelled only at football and had shown no academic inclinations, let alone an interest in politics.

'It seems to me that this revolution is keen on words and indoctrination,' he said. The comment was uttered in jest, but even as he spoke Mahmud realized that he knew little of the political situation in Aden. He was aware, however, of the problems in Oman, and Dhardir's words rang true.

'Tonight you shall see for yourself. I have advised our cell leader of your arrival,' Dhardir remarked. 'He is enthusiastic about meeting you. He still recalls the bloody nose you gave him.' There was a mischievous look on Dhardir's face.

'You mean to tell me that Ahmed Said is in charge of the revolution?' Mahmud threw back his head and howled with laughter. 'This I must see!'

'No, no! He is only my cell leader. But you must come tonight for another reason too – it is an important meeting. They are to select people for special training.'

'I cannot refuse my brother's wish.' Mahmud was still grinning. 'I will come. Now tell me more of this revolution.'

The delight showed on Dhardir's face. He stood up, pushing back his chair. 'I will,' he said, 'but first let us eat. My father and brother await our presence.'

The rebels assembled in an upper room of a small café in a narrow side street which ran north from the Crescent, a tourist shopping centre. As he entered with Dhardir Mahmud looked around the overcrowded room and saw many familiar faces from his schooldays, including his one-time enemy Ahmed Said.

Stiffly, with an officious air, Ahmed approached them. He

checked Mahmud's attempt to greet him in traditional Arab fashion, by a kiss on the cheek, and held out his hand in Western style.

'Mahmud, it is indeed a delight to see you again, comrade. We have need of strong, capable men. I hope you will join our movement.' Without waiting for a response, he turned and walked away. Groups of men sat at tables drinking and talking animatedly. The snippets of conversation that Mahmud heard excited him. There was a vitality in their voices, and the spark in their words that night ignited a fire that was later to consume him.

'Here they are!'

The passion in Dhardir's voice and the intensity of his gaze made Mahmud turn his head to see who could command such reverence. Escorted by Ahmed Said, two European-looking men entered the room and joined him at his table. Mahmud, perplexed, turned to Dhardir who answered his unspoken question.

'Russians, here to select students for training.'

The murmur of voices died and all attention was focused on the cell leader.

'Comrades, first the necessity for caution. For some of you, this is your first encounter.' His gaze fell on Mahmud as he spoke. 'For security, we have positioned comrades in the street below. Should a British patrol venture too close, you will be guided out into the street at the back. Do not run.' He paused. 'But for the present we are safe, so now let us get on with the meeting. Tonight we have with us friends of the revolution. Speaking to you tonight is Comrade Ivan Surorov, and I am assured that he has excellent news for us.'

The men looked travel-stained, their Western clothes crumpled and showing signs of wear. Both were sweating profusely even in the relative cool of the Arabian evening, but nevertheless appeared confident and at ease. Colonel Surorov was a Spetsnaz officer attached to the Black Sea Fleet command, ostensibly in charge of special operations for the Middle East. In reality, his task was to select and train young revolutionaries. Those chosen were sent to the Red Army's main revolutionary training centre on the northern edge of the Caucasus mountains and given a twelve-month intensive course in modern warfare.

Surorov stood up. His eyes scanned the room and he appeared satisfied by what he saw.

'Comrades!' he began, 'we are delighted to observe the growth in your movement. Your struggle is a justifiable one. You pursue the basic desire of all men – the right to be masters of your own destiny, masters of your own land. We are here to assist you.'

Mahmud studied the Russian. His Arabic was fluent but he spoke boldly, with a commanding voice and abrupt manner, whereas a native Arabic-speaker would have used more convoluted rhetoric.

'For those of you who presume that we, the Soviet Union, wish merely to replace the British, I say you are wrong. My government has no claim on your soil. We desire only friendship, and to encourage you to throw off the yoke of the imperialist oppressors.' The voice was brusque, but the words clear and poignant.

'The purpose of our visit is to select twenty men for training. They will be taken by ship to the Soviet Union, where they will be the guests of my country. You must understand, however, that the schooling will be severe. The weak will fall by the wayside, but those who survive will be masters of the art of modern guerrilla warfare.'

For weeks there had been discussion among the rebels about the promise of Soviet aid. Everyone wanted to be picked, and in the café murmurs of excitement grew. Revolution is always bright in the hearts of the young, and those gathered there that night were no exception.

Comrade Surorov continued, 'I recognize the fire in your eyes, and I appreciate your motives. But your present tactics will not succeed against the British, and will only serve to bring your movement down. You must force the enemy into the mountains and confront him there, not in the towns and cities. You must first win the people over to your side and gain control of the mountain territory and the fierce tribes who live there. Only then will you be able to progress and expand.'

Continuing to define his ideas, Comrade Surorov outlined the rudiments of a communist revolution. When the Russian paused for breath, Mahmud interrupted and asked in a clear voice, 'Does this revolution expand to Oman?'

Ahmed Said looked up in annoyance, but Mahmud ignored him and stared directly at Surorov.

The Russian returned his look with amused composure and replied, ''*Ma daam jaarak bekhair, inta bekhair* – you are safe as long as your neighbour is safe.' It was an Arabic proverb and it made sense to Mahmud, who nodded in agreement.

Ahmed Said, clearly irritated by this exchange, whispered to Surorov, who merely nodded. With his attention still firmly on Mahmud he enquired, 'You are Omani. Why are you here?'

'I am visiting old school friends,' replied Mahmud, unworried that he had been singled out.

'School friends?' the Russian questioned. 'Why did you not attend school in Oman?'

All heads had turned now towards Mahmud. Seeing the look of antagonism in Ahmed Said's eyes, he hesitated. The memory of that playground fight flooded back to him, and for an instant he felt apprehensive. Dhardir saw the look and placed his hand on Mahmud's arm in a gesture of allegiance. The moment passed and, confident again, Mahmud answered, 'We have no schools.'

With that simple statement of fact the paucity of life in Oman became a reality for Mahmud, and in that instant he knew his purpose in life. The Russian observed Mahmud with new interest.

'Would you like to change that?'

Even as Comrade Surorov asked the question, his hand was already adding Mahmud's name to the list that lay on the table in front of him.

Caucasus Mountains, 1965
The wind wailed and howled through the stunted pine trees that covered the lower slopes of the mountains. As Mahmud lay on the damp earth the night wind chilled him, his only protection the full-length camouflage suit with its hood pulled up tightly about his head. Around his neck hung a 5.45mm AK47 assault rifle, and attached to his waist belt was an automatic pistol housed in a black holster.

Close by lay Dhardir, his camouflaged figure blending into the darkness. Together they worked as a team, as they had done throughout their rigorous training which had begun a year earlier. Three of their comrades had not survived and lay buried beneath foreign soil. Of the rest, only a handful had endured the course to the end, and those few were now engaged in their last exercise.

They had been instructed in the use of an armoury of weapons and trained in the handling of explosives, both in the classroom and in practice. They had mastered the art of self-defence and had learned how to survive in inhospitable terrain. Added to this they had learned to speak English, the language of their enemy.

Now, deep in the dark pine forest, Mahmud and Dhardir waited. This was their final test. Three Spetsnaz insructors were hidden in ambush, ready to trap their trainees. Mahmud and Dhardir must surprise them first.

'There!' Dhardir whispered.

Mahmud followed his gaze and caught the small movement that signalled their instructors' presence beneath two large fir trees. As one, the Arabs inched their way along the ground, their movements no more than the stirring of the wind, lessening the distance between themselves and their mock enemy.

They took no chances, for the Spetsnaz soldiers gave no quarter and, indeed, expected none. Suddenly, as the night wind increased, moaning its song through the trees, Mahmud and Dhardir pounced. Taken by surprise, the Spetsnaz soldiers twisted over in an attempt to deflect the attack. But they were too late, for the shadowy figures were upon them. As Dhardir grappled with one soldier, Mahmud jabbed the butt of his assault rifle against another's head and heard the crack of bone. Even as he heard the man's groan of pain, Mahmud hurled himself towards the third soldier. But the man rolled out of reach and quickly regained his feet. Mahmud dived after him, missed, and grabbed ineffectually at thin air, landing face down on the ground. The soldier aimed his boot hard against Mahmud's head, lacerating the flesh so that the blood ran warm into Mahmud's eye. Blindly he grabbed at the Russian's combat suit, pulling at him, trying to get a better grip. But the Spetsnaz soldier now had the upper hand. Raising his weapon high, he rained blows on Mahmud's large head. With all his remaining strength, Mahmud balled his fist and struck upwards, catching the soldier full force in the scrotum. The blows to Mahmud's head ceased abruptly. The soldier reeled backwards with a cry of agony and in that instant Mahmud was on top of him.

'Let go, let go! You are killing him.' Dhardir's bellowing voice broke through the pain, but still Mahmud kept his hands locked tight around the Russian's windpipe. Frantically, Dhardir tried to lever his comrade's fingers from the man's throat. Finally, with a shudder, Mahmud let go.

The soldier sat up, heaving and gasping, while a few yards away Dhardir started to bind a field dressing around Mahmud's head.

'You almost killed him, my friend!'

Mahmud watched as the Spetsnaz soldier hauled himself painfully to his feet and staggered away to join the others. Despite the pain in his head, Mahmud chuckled to himself.

'He'll be lucky to sire any children!'

Two days later, at the passing out ceremony, Colonel Ivan Surorov congratulated Mahmud as he was awarded the prize for top student. He was just twenty-two years old.

Shropshire, England, November 1944
The pale winter sunshine worked hard, making the day look bright, dissolving the white film of the early morning frost and

giving the day a tranquil appearance. In the chilly air the sweet song of a thrush could be heard. Beside the peaceful country lane stood two small cottages of local red sandstone. In the early sunshine they took on a rosy glow like the embers of a dying fire, while the frost on the lattice windows sparkled with a life of its own.

A young man leaned over the wall which separated the front gardens of the cottages from the narrow lane, down which he peered continually with a concerned expression. On the left shoulder of his British Army tunic was the insignia of the Airborne Division, and above that the words 'GLIDER PILOT'. He had the tough, lean look of a simple countryman, but Sergeant Dan Leathers was anything but simple. He had worked as a farm labourer before the war, but had a quick mind and was fascinated by all things mechanical. This interest had led him to the local airfield at Shawbury, where he tinkered with the engines of light aircraft, and had been taken advantage of when he joined the army.

He was waiting now for the arrival of the district midwife, resting his backside against the wall to ease the twinge in his left leg. It still caused him a great deal of discomfort, but it could have been worse, he thought, casting his mind back.

At 2305 hours on 5 June 1944, the eve of D-Day, he and two other glider pilots had set off on a mission to land D company of the Buckinghamshire Light Infantry as near as possible to the vital Orme bridge. The mighty Halifax bombers had lumbered down the runway before finally roaring into the night sky, towing behind them the troop-filled Horsa gliders. Once over Normandy Sergeant Leathers had released his glider from the Halifax, and to his horror, found that it was vastly overweight. He was forced to trim the glider right back and apply full flaps, but even so his downward speed continued to increase rapidly. In desperation, he shouted at the troop commander to despatch two or three men to the rear of the glider. As their weight was transferred, eventually Dan Leathers regained control. Then, as the glider steadied, he was relieved to make out the unmistakable line of the canal.

Shimmering like a silver thread in the moonlight, it guided the glider to its target.

Suddenly in the distance he saw the bulbous structure of the bridge. 'Brace! Brace!' his voice bellowed above the whooshing sound as the glider winged towards the ground. Behind him the troops sat back in their canvas seats, linked arms and lifted their feet from the floor in anticipation of a rough landing. The bridge was within a few hundred metres as the overweight Horsa smacked the ground, bouncing wildly. Frantically, Leathers fought to control the machine and keep it in a straight line. Sparks flew as the undercarriage ripped away and gradually the glider disintegrated. Then abruptly the nose impacted with the concrete defences around the bridge, and the Horsa's brief life was over.

After a few seconds of stunned silence, the uninjured troops sprang into action. They had the advantage of surprise, and with little resistance or shooting had occupied the bridge in almost total silence. The only sound at that moment came from the pilot, whose left leg was trapped at a painfully distorted angle beneath the controls. It was to leave Sergeant Leathers with a permanent limp.

But now, as he paced the small footpath far away in rural Shropshire, he was more concerned with the pain being endured by his wife. He glanced up at the bedroom window of the modest cottage and smiled, not minding whether it would be a boy or a girl. He loved his family dearly, and when the war was over he planned to acquire a larger home for their expanding numbers. But for the immediate future this cottage was sufficient.

Although small, it was warm and comfortable. The front door led directly into the parlour, which his wife had furnished, according to their means, with second-hand furniture and an old carpet. A black cast-iron stove provided heating, cooking facilities and hot water. A small door at the back of the parlour opened on to a narrow, steep staircase which led up to the two bedrooms. Toilet facilities were confined to an outside privy and a large tin bath placed in front of the fire once a week.

'Morning, Dan.'

Distracted by the voice, Dan looked up to find his neighbour emerging from the adjoining cottage. Miss Sarah Williams had been the local schoolteacher, but now she had been retired for many years, and today she was looking after Dan's two boys.

'Don't fret. She won't be long.' The old lady had seen the worried look on Dan's face, and made to reassure him.

'Are you sure the lads are no trouble?' he asked anxiously.

'None at all – as good as gold. You forget how many children I've had to look after in my life!'

Almost on cue a small figure appeared at the door of her cottage, clutching a jam jar of warm, milky tea.

'Hello, son,' Dan called. 'I hope you and Terry behave well for Miss Williams. Now get back in out of the cold.'

It was strange, he thought: despite all the years Dan had known her, he had never used her first name. More as a mark of respect, it had always been Miss Williams – and probably always would be. His eyes rested on the three-year-old's jam jar and he smiled. Everyone in the close-knit village had their tea in a jam jar when visiting Miss Williams – except the vicar, who was always treated to her best china!

The sound of a bicycle bell made him look up. Seated on an antiquated bicycle was the slim figure of the local midwife, her black-stockinged legs pumping furiously as she rode up the lane at full tilt. The effort of her pedalling had made her cheeks glow in the crisp, sharp winter morning.

She approached the cottage and dismounted with a wobbling movement, resting the bike against the wall. 'Morning Miss Williams, morning Dan.' Unhitching her black bag from the handlebars she handed it to Dan and followed him into the cottage.

'Sorry I'm a bit late, Dan – how's the leg?' the midwife inquired as they entered the parlour. He took her coat and, noticing her trim figure, and felt a twinge of compassion. Not for her the joys of motherhood. She was newly widowed, her husband blown out of the sky during a bombing raid on Berlin some months earlier.

'Fine,' he replied, 'if it wasn't for the broken leg I wouldn't be here.' After the glider crash Dan had been shipped back to England and hospitalized. 'I managed to wangle some compassionate leave, then it's back to duty, I'm afraid.' But the time for small talk was over.

'Well, if you insist on hanging around looking useless,' she said briskly, 'you could at least boil some water – and make me a cup of tea while you're about it. I'm freezing.' With these words she made for the bedroom.

Mary Leathers lay on the bed, covered by a home-made quilt. She smiled with relief as the midwife entered the room; the two women had known each other since childhood. 'Thank heavens you've arrived! I was beginning to panic.'

'How are you, Mary? How fast are the pains coming?'

'Every couple of minutes now.' She let out a gasp, as if to confirm her words.

'Good – we won't have to wait long. Now keep your breathing regular and start tightening your tummy muscles, pushing slowly . . . Now where's that husband of yours with my tea? I'm half frozen from biking here.'

Dan entered the room, clutching a bowl of hot water and dangling a mug of hot tea from one of his fingers. He didn't stay, preferring to wait downstairs. The midwife scrubbed her hands and took a sip of tea.

The short bouts of pain merged into one. 'It's coming!' Mary managed to wheeze as another spasm wracked her perspiring body. Speedily the midwife spread the rubber sheet under Mary's lower body. With practised hands she reached down between her legs, noting that the vagina was stretched agonizingly to its maximum. Filling the open aperture was a tiny head. 'Push! Come on, work at it – almost there.' She spoke with compassion as Dan's young wife strained painfully, the sweat pouring down her contorted face.

Suddenly a shaft of sunlight burst through the window, bathing Mary's face in a radiant light. With a final gasp she felt the baby abandon her body. Carefully the midwife smacked its small bottom, jump-starting the tiny lungs as they sucked in their first gasp of air. Then Mary heard the first cry of her newborn.

'It's a boy – yet another soldier to die for King and country,' said the midwife, ironically but sympathetically. Gently, she leaned forward and laid the small child next to the warmth of his mother. 'What will you call him?'

'Karl,' Mary replied without hesitation, then whispered secretly to the baby: 'And what will this wicked world hold for you, my darling?'

Shropshire, 1962
Karl Leathers was rapidly approaching his eighteenth birthday. Standing in the kitchen, he watched restlessly as his mother prepared the evening meal.

'Go on, Mum. Let me join, please.' He kept his pleading voice deliberately low, careful not to let his two elder brothers overhear him. They were all opposed to Karl joining the army.

After leaving school he had been taken on as an apprentice butcher, a job that dragged him from his bed at four in the morning to work all day in the stink and cold of the old abattoir. It was not that Karl minded the hard work; rather, he had a strong compulsion to escape and discover the world. Daily, as he split the giant sides of beef in two, he day-dreamed. And his mind was always filled with the same dream – to be a soldier . . .

Recently Karl had started to discuss the subject openly at home, only to meet ridicule and resistance from his brothers and silence from his mother, which troubled him.

'No – you've got a steady job at the slaughterhouse and they treat you well. Why do you want to throw it all away?' As always when the matter was brought up, she avoided making direct eye contact with her youngest son.

As if in prayer, Mary Leathers pleaded silently: Don't take him, please. But she knew that in the end he would leave. He was so much like his father: the spirit of adventure, the longing for opportunity, were pitifully plain upon his face. The sudden thoughts of her husband sent waves of emotion through her and her eyes reflected her loneliness; even after all these years she still missed him.

Just short months after Karl was born Dan had flown one of the last glider missions of the war. He had not been so lucky this time, and Mary Leathers had joined the long list of war widows.

'Sorry, Mum.' Karl mistook the tears of memory for those of exasperation. 'I won't mention it again.'

'Height, five foot seven and a half,' the orderly called out, and the army doctor jotted it down.

'The recruiting sergeant told me to tell you, sir, that I'm joining the Welsh Guards,' Karl told him.

'Height, five foot eight.' The doctor 'corrected' the entry. 'Well, you seem to be in good health, young man. When are you joining?'

'Today, sir. After I leave here I'm going directly to the recruiting office to be "sworn in". After that I have to report to the training depot in Pirbright.' Karl's voice rang with excitement.

The decision had not been easy. The previous day he had finished work as usual in the early afternoon, and then walked the short distance to the recruiting office in Shrewsbury. Here he quickly took the entrance test and enquired: 'How soon can I get in?'

'Bit keen!' The recruiting sergeant smiled. 'If you pass the medical tomorrow, report back here for the "swearing in" and you can be on your way.'

At home that evening Karl sat quietly, struggling inwardly as to whether he should tell his mother what he had done. In the end he decided against it. Instead, he kissed her on the cheek. 'Love you, Mum, no matter what.' His conscience momentarily eased, he went up for an early night.

Next morning he got up before dawn, as usual, as if to go to work. But today he put on smart casual clothes and picked up his toothbrush, razor and a few other odds and ends before quietly slipping from the house, safe in the knowledge that the rest of the household always remained asleep long after he had left for work.

By six o'clock that evening, Mary Leathers had become increasingly apprehensive about her son's absence. Finally she put on her coat and went out to check with his employers.

'Sorry, Mrs Leathers, but we thought Karl must be ill – he's not been at work all day.' The slaughterhouse manager seemed sympathetic. 'Perhaps he's had an accident. Would you like me to call the police or check the hospitals?'

'Oh, yes please,' she replied anxiously. 'Would you mind . . . No, wait!' Slowly another possibility began to dawn on her, as she remembered Karl's words the evening before and the kiss on her cheek. 'Do you know where the army recruiting office is?'

'Yes. Go out of here and along Smithfield, towards the Welsh bridge, then turn up Mardol – it's about three shops up on the left.'

When she got there the office was closed, but a light was still on and she banged at the door. At the rear end of the office a door opened and a man in uniform looked at her apprehensively, but then let her in.

'Please could you tell me if my son joined the army today? His name's Karl Leathers. He's been missing, and I'm concerned he may have had an accident or something.' Mary Leathers suddenly wished she'd given her agreement to him joining up.

'He joined yesterday, Mrs Leathers. Had his medical this morning in Copthorne Barracks, and by now should be in the Guards Depot in Pirbright – that's down south, in Surrey.' The major's expression softened as he looked at the sad-faced woman in front of him; he had seen this problem often enough before. 'It's not too late, Mrs Leathers. If you really want him back I'm sure we can arrange it. If you take a seat I'll contact the depot and see if he's arrived.' He moved towards the telephone.

'No – please. As long as he's all right . . . it's what he always wanted. Let him stay . . . as long as I know where he is.' Mary had made the decision long before she said it.

'If you'd like to write or phone I can give you the address. However, in my experience it's best to wait a bit, then drop him a line – let him know you understand. He will be home for his first weekend leave in a month's time. Best sort it all out then.'

Five weeks later Karl returned home, smartly dressed in uniform. The sight of him had brought forth a flood of tears from his mother, who had rushed to embrace him. The two days went quickly, and all too soon Karl had gone again. To Mary Leathers, each time her son arrived back on leave he seemed to have increased in stature, in every sense. Yes, I made the right decision, she thought.

After finishing basic training at the Guards Depot Karl had joined the 1st Battalion Welsh Guards, stationed in Germany, and home leave became less frequent. Then, unexpectedly, Karl informed his mother that the Battalion was to be posted to the trouble spot of Aden for a year. It was to be nine months before she next saw her son, and then only for a brief weekend. That was when Karl proudly told her of his determination to join the Special Air Service. That weekend, as Karl crammed his conversation with the wonders of the last nine months, Mary Leathers observed the subtle changes that had taken place in her son. His body was lean and fit, his eyes clear and his skin glowing. Discreetly, at every opportunity she reached out to touch him proudly. Most of all, she realized that he had matured into a man.

Hereford, 1966
The SAS procedure for recruitment is to run two selection courses a year for volunteers, winter and summer. The basic requirement for admittance to this elite force of fighting men,

based in Hereford but active all over the world, is a minimum of three years' service in the regular armed forces. Volunteers must also be mentally fit, confident and self-reliant, and above all they must possess physical stamina. Karl knew he had all these qualities and more.

The course had started with a three-month build-up, during which the selected students were encouraged to reach their peak of physical fitness before embarking on the gruelling 'Test Week'. This part of the course was designed to stretch each individual to his limit. Daily, a task was set, the already oversized rucksacks were made heavier and the marching distance increased. Rigorous routes were chosen over the Black Mountains and Brecon Beacons – two ranges of rugged Welsh hills that contain no high peaks but are constantly at the mercy of violent weather.

Karl struggled through the final endurance march totally exhausted and in appalling weather conditions. By the time that fourth week was over, the original hundred and more volunteers had been reduced to just sixteen. The survivors were then sent on continuation training, but even here there was no guarantee of passing. Every wrong move, every minor mistake was continually monitored by the hawk-eyed training staff. Yet unbelievably to Karl, five months later he stood proudly before the training major and received the coveted beige beret with its winged dagger emblem. Through hard work and sheer determination he had achieved his ambition and was now entering the ranks of the SAS. A new confidence was born deep inside him – an almost physical warmth that flowed like electricity through his body, waiting its moment until it would send him exploding into action.

Aden 1967
Posted to the Mountain Troop of 'G' Squadron, within weeks Karl was back in Aden. With his SAS beret and those special blue wings on his shoulder he walked ten feet tall; and there were no more tedious duties such as watching road-builders, for all SAS operations were deep up-country stuff.

During the eight months that he had been away in England the situation in Aden became so bad that the British government had decided to pull out. Once this news was announced, the situation became really violent and the rebels started attacking the British with renewed ferocity. One November morning in 1967 the rebels went berserk in the town of Crater, so named because it sat in the base of an extinct volcano. They murdered every white person that they could find, soldiers and civilians alike, brutally mutilating their bodies and throwing them naked into the streets.

At the time of the incident Karl had been sitting in his room at Ballycastle House, the SAS headquarters near Khormaksar Airport. He heard a helicopter landing, and a few seconds later the Squadron Commander stuck his head round the door and shouted, 'Move, move now!' This may have been Karl's first year in the SAS, but he recognized the urgency and sprang into action. Grabbing his equipment and sniper rifle he ran outside where the Squadron Commander made his selection from the small group of men who had rapidly assembled. Taking one look at the L42 rifle in Karl's hand he pointed at him: 'You, on the chopper. All Crater is hostile. Jock's got all the details. Go.'

The helicopter took off and within minutes they were high over Jebel Shamsan, the mountain that looked down over the town of Crater. As the noise of the chopper faded away, the officer told them that their task was to shoot anyone with a weapon or committing a terrorist act. 'That also includes the local Crater police who have sided with the rebels,' said Jock Morrison.

The small SAS patrol consisted of six men, all troopers, three of them armed with sniper rifles. Swiftly they made their way to a good defensive position overlooking the town. Karl, still a novice at the deadly game of no-holds-barred violence and swift retribution, was totally unprepared for what he saw. The bodies of his murdered compatriots had been laid out neatly in the street, deliberately allowing the passing traffic to run over them. With anger surging through their blood the six men took a heavy toll amongst the rebels, firing continually until nothing moved on the streets. Next day, they watched as Lieutenant Colonel Mitchell, known to his men as Mad Mitch, bravely led the Argyll and Sutherland Highlanders into the town of Crater to re-establish law and order.

For Karl it was a terrible baptism of fire, and yet a truthful one. This was the kind of action for which he had half-killed himself on the storm-swept Welsh mountains, and it was just the kind of situation to which the SAS were so superbly equipped to respond. In the years that followed the SAS dealt with many skirmishes like that one in Aden. Karl's kit was always packed and ready to go – to the jungles of South America, to the frozen wastes of northern Norway, and ultimately to the Oman war in the Middle East.

2

Destiny

O *man, January 1975*
When Karl Leathers had last seen Manston Airbase four years earlier it had been nothing more than a desert airstrip – a runway of hard-packed sand and a few tumble-down buildings. It lay immediately north of the mountain massif which formed a huge natural barrier at the edge of the desert. This vast slab of mountain, nine miles deep at its central, widest, part, extended inland from the Salalah plain, running parallel to the coast and stretching for one hundred and fifty miles right down to the borders with Aden. As mountain ranges go it was not a particularly high one, reaching no more than three thousand feet at its highest point. In the extreme east the soil was barren and rocky, with only sparse vegetation and little or no water. But towards the west patches of rich soil and clumps of scrubland grass appeared. In the centre of this region the soil suddenly became deeper, covering the plateau with a carpet of green grass and some stunted trees, while large valleys known locally as wadis ran south to the sea. In some of the larger wadis rivers or streams flowed, and there were occasional natural waterholes in the rock, all of which were capable of supporting life.

Manston Airbase, transformed through the demands of war, now boasted a giant concrete runway and air-conditioned huts. The Shah of Iran, Oman's neighbour across the Gulf, had befriended the new Sultan Qaboos and offered military aid against the rebels. Everywhere could be seen the logistics of war: mountains of fuel and food, tanks of water and crates of defence stores. From this established base the Iranians had been ordered to capture the small coastal town of Rakyut, some seventeen miles south of the base. Once it had been a flourishing fishing village, and not so many years before that it had served as a prominent slave market. But now it lay in ruins, since most of the local population had deserted the area and left it in the hands of the rebels. Now the rebels had declared it the Capital of the Liberated Area.

Militarily, the real objective lay midway between Manston and Rakyut, in the caves of Shershitti wadi. Crossing the desert plain from Manston airbase, this vast wadi opened out so that its steep sides formed great walls. The ancient caves in these walls had been inhabited for over two thousand years, and through the generations had been home to a myriad of peoples. In the mid-1970s they were the stronghold of the Oman rebels, known as the Adoo, a name derived from the Arabic word for 'enemy'. Two days ago a large and impressive battle group of the Shah's elite soldiers had moved south from the direction of Manston in order to attack the Adoo.

The ground approaching the wadi from the north was flat and open until the edge of the wadi itself. Then it appeared as if the floor had fallen out of the desert, leaving behind towering walls of rock on either side. The wadi floor was thickly covered with stunted trees and bushes which extended up the northern lip of the wadi and spilt over on to the plain. Beyond this plain lay the ruins of a once proud village called Defa, and then nothing but empty, open desert between it and the impregnable sanctuary of Manston Airbase.

The Adoo had observed the Iranians coming and allowed them to advance to a spot just beyond the ruins of Defa. In the scrubby bushes along the edge of the wadi the rebels had managed to conceal their excellent firing positions, which covered the wide tract of open desert leading to the ambush. With little or no shelter, the Iranians had been subjected to murderous crossfire, and as the casualties mounted they had been forced to retreat. Despite their superior forces and the support of strike aircraft, they had wilted under the ferocity of the hidden machine gun and mortar fire. Again and again the Iranians counter-attacked, hoping to establish themselves in the thick bushes near the lip of the wadi. But each time they were forced back, unable to cross the exposed ground, retreating to their hastily built fortifications around the ruins of Defa.

At sundown they had advanced once more, protected as before by Strikemaster ground attack aircraft. The jets dived in, released several five hundred pound bombs on to the Adoo positions. But this time the advancing Iranians saw a trail of smoke as a missile streaked up from the wadi, locked on to a jet and exploded in its fuselage. Instantly the aircraft became a ball of flame, visible for many miles. Within minutes that attack was called off and the Iranians retreated before attempting to retrieve their dead and wounded under cover of darkness.

Karl Leathers watched as the bodies of the Iranian soldiers were transferred from the Huey helicopters to the huge belly of the Hercules transport plane. Earlier that morning it had been the same huge aircraft which had roared in through the rising heat and deposited them at Manston. The choppers had been working from first light, shipping the wounded and then returning again and again for bloodstained corpses. From their position at the edge of the runway the small group of SAS men observed the fevered activity, recognizing that events had gone dramatically wrong. Slouched on the edge of the black tarmac, one leaned against his oversized rucksack sleeping; the two others watched, shielding their eyes against the burning desert sun.

Karl, newly promoted to the rank of sergeant, turned his head away from the carnage. He stood up and stretched, relaxing, but with a look of concerned concentration on his face. The soldier beside him broke the silence.

'How about a brew of tea? Nothing's going to happen here

until the Iranians have cleared up this mess.' He spoke with an American accent.

Without waiting for a response, he lit the small camping stove he had produced from his rucksack, carefully balancing a mess-tin of water upon it. Slick Middleton was a professional American soldier. Born Mervin Ames Middleton, but known to all as Slick, he was the only son of a small-town storekeeper from northern Minnesota, and, like Karl, he had run away to join the army. Soldiering came naturally to him, and he had progressed quickly through the ranks of the Special Forces, the American equivalent of the SAS. The US Army, seeing his potential, had selected him to take part in a two-year exchange programme with the SAS, and on arrival at Hereford he had been assigned to Karl's troop. The two men felt an immediate rapport and had become good mates.

'Poor bastards!' Karl continued to watch as the cargo loaders filled the back of the transport plane with more and more body-bags. 'They seem to have lost a hell of a lot of men!'

'A lot more than they are letting on. Those choppers have been going non-stop since dawn. More to the point, are we being despatched to the same place?'

Karl fished a mug from his rucksack and passed it to the American. 'Put plenty of sugar in it, Slick.'

His mate passed him the mug of steaming tea, and they took it in turns to sip the sickly-sweet brew. 'Ha, civilization, the British and their tea!' In less than a year Slick Middleton had become quite anglicized and now preferred tea to coffee. 'Something tells me it's going to get rough around here in the next few days,' he added.

'I hope we get some reinforcements,' Karl muttered, glancing at a group of Arabs sitting nearby. 'Because I, for one, am not going into that hellhole of a wadi with one half-crazed American and forty Firqat. I don't care if they've got the crown jewels hidden in those caves!'

The Firqat were the local town and hill tribesmen who had remained loyal to the new Sultan, and the SAS had taken on the task of organizing them into companies under SAS command.

Although the concepts of discipline and military standards were alien to them, the Firqat were useful go-betweens with the local population. With their assistance, intelligence-gathering had improved dramatically, and, aware of the value of a hearts-and-minds approach, the Sultan had rewarded the tribesmen with a vigorous civil aid programme.

As Karl watched the Firqat, his thoughts ran back over the years. Joining the SAS was the best decision he had ever made. Now, at the age of twenty-nine, he had been involved in several exciting and sometimes dangerous bouts of action – and no doubt, providing he lived, he would take part in many more.

Karl Leathers did not conform to the traditional image of a soldier. He looked like one – upright, muscular and very athletic – but this did not extend to his manner. He could be unpredictable and was very often reckless, but at other times he displayed a gentleness that aroused curiosity, especially among women. His dark, curly hair revealed premature signs of grey at the temples – put there, Karl was convinced, by the quantity of adrenalin that pumped through his body every time he was afraid. Toughened by war, his eyes held the hard edge of challenge, his expression softened only by the lazy smile that came easily to the corners of his mouth.

'The Boss tells me that Matt and his boys are coming down to join us the moment they can get some choppers, so all we have to do is wait,' said Slick, turning the mug upside down and shaking the final drops on to the ground before tossing it back to Karl.

Karl caught it and, stuffing it back into his rucksack, responded, 'I'd better go and find out what's happening. You can count on being stuck here for the night at least. Watch my kit until I get back, and don't strain yourself!'

Slick lay back against his rucksack, an inane grin covering his brawny, sunburnt face, and closed his eyes.

Picking up his Armalite rifle, Karl made his way towards the buildings and searched for the Iranian Operations Room. Given the volume of noise coming from it he could barely have missed it. As he reached the open door he saw that it was crowded with smartly dressed senior officers in a state of great commotion. In the melee Karl caught sight of a dusty British camouflage uniform. Captain Alan Gates recognized Karl and, pushing and shoving, forced his way to the door.

'What the fuck's going on here, Boss? It looks like another revolution!' The officer took hold of Karl's elbow and led him away from the noise and confusion.

'Boss' is the affectionate term used by SAS soldiers for officers in charge, in Karl's case his troop commander. Captain Gates had passed the gruelling selection course just six months earlier and had been presented to Karl's troop one bright spring morning by the Squadron Commander. Despite being just twenty-five years old, Alan Gates had proved to be an excellent officer. Born of a wealthy family, with extensive property holdings in central London, he had followed the family tradition by joining the Brigade of Guards. Later he had requested permission to attempt the SAS selection course, and to his father's joy had passed.

His first appearance in the barrack room was met with mixed feelings. Karl's troop, who had managed without an officer for six months, watched with curiosity to see how this privileged young man would endear himself to a group of professional soldiers. In fact he took the jibes and the mickey-taking in his stride, and slowly they warmed to him. He had spirit and boldness, added to which he both asked for and heeded their opinions. And so, slowly but surely, he came to earn the sobriquet 'Boss'.

'Karl,' he said now in amazement, 'I've never heard such back-stabbing in all my life. Everyone's trying to pass the buck for the massacre in the wadi. I believe there's going to be a court-martial and a firing squad this evening.'

'That sounds about right – if things go wrong the senior officers always feel better if they can pin the blame on some other poor bastard,' Karl remarked cynically.

'Come on, let's leave them to it. Things should have cooled down a bit later on.' Captain Gates led Karl away.

'When you eventually go back, Boss, we'll need all the

intelligence you can get your hands on if we're going to attack those caves ... By the way, how many casualties did they have?'

'They won't say, but it has to be hundreds dead, plus an equal number of wounded. They were caught out in the open with no shelter or protection. It was an absolute bloodbath.' He raised one eyebrow wearily. 'One thing's for sure – they all swear it was an SA7 anti-aircraft rocket that shot the jet down, so I bet their pilots are a bit panicky today! Anyway, there'll be no move until the early hours of tomorrow, so tell the boys to relax – for the next few hours at least. Get them in here for tonight.' He indicated a neat row of tents which they were just passing. 'Leave room for Matt Roberts and his lot – they're reinforcing us and should be arriving before dusk. If you need me, I'll be back in the Operations Room. Let everyone know there'll be a briefing by the tents at eight this evening.'

Karl rejoined Slick and their Firqat and passed on the news. As they struggled with their heavy rucksacks towards the tents, Slick began to protest: 'How long have we been fighting this bloody war?'

'Too long, and as it goes on it gets worse,' Karl stated. 'If this is the Adoo's last stand, they're going out in some style – there can't be many of them left, surely?'

'Tell that to the Iranians,' Slick grunted as he threw his rucksack into the corner of a tent. 'We've beaten the Adoo every step across this bloody inhospitable, God-forsaken country.'

He was right. When they had first arrived the Adoo were in control, but now they were almost beaten. Just four years earlier only the coastal settlements of Salalah, Taqa and Mirbat remained free, and even these had been infiltrated by Adoo forces. The rebels roamed free over the Jebel massif, eating further into the beleaguered areas around Salalah. The British RAF base just north of Salalah was itself virtually under siege, and the Sultan's small defence force was fighting a losing battle. Without outside intervention, the rebels would have seized control of the country and a large portion of the free world's oil would have been at risk.

Although not a military man himself, the old Sultan had decided to send his son Qaboos to Sandhurst, where he had been commissioned into a British regiment. While in Britain the Sultan's heir had also observed the workings of various councils and committees and had familiarized himself with the workings of a modern state. His return home, brimming with new ideas, had not been a joyous one, and his reactionary father had committed him to what can only be termed 'house arrest'. Qaboos could see the plight of his country and argued for change; his father's answer had been to restrict his son's movements even further, and accuse him of becoming a 'Westerner'.

The young Qaboos bided his time, gathering like-minded supporters to his cause. His chance came on 23 July 1970, when, aided by the young Sheik Baraik Bin Hamood, he deposed his father in a bloodless coup. Within weeks the SAS had been sent to provide advice and assistance. The Adoo were about to meet some proper resistance.

Later that day, as promised, more SAS reinforcements were flown in to join Karl and Slick: Matt Roberts, together with two other mates of theirs, Ian and Phil. Now they were all sitting in a circle in the shelter of the tent, leaning their backs against the protective sandbags.

The Boss summarized his plan. 'We counter-attack just before dawn. We will be moving out from here at 0300 hours, travelling by truck southwards on the new road and stopping within two miles of the wadi lip. The Iranian engineers have arranged to clear the road of mines as far as that. They will move out two hours before us with a small cover party. The main attack will be carried out by the Sultan's Jebel Regiment, with the seven of us and our Firqat acting as guides.' He paused there for these instructions to sink in.

'Surprise! surprise!' muttered Matt, echoing all their worried thought. The presence of guides meant that, as always, they would be at the sharp end.

'We will attack in three phases. One, to seize control of the old ruins at Defa.' He pointed with the tip of a bayonet to an area on the outspread map. 'Secondly, we shall advance a distance of approximately one thousand metres, heading for a landmark called the Zakhir Tree.' Because they were so rare, prominent trees in the desert were invariably used as landmarks and meeting-places. 'From the Zakhir Tree head south-west to point 985 and descend to the caves. From there on – if we ever extend that far – we start to clear the caves. Understand?'

They all nodded, and he went on: 'I realize it will be dark when we get there, but in daylight we could only expect the same treatment as the Iranians received. It will be difficult, but we have no choice. At this stage of the war the Adoo must not have a victory – no opportunity to regroup or to gather further support. Taking those caves, at whatever cost, will end the war.

The Boss then turned his attention to weaponry. The British eighty-one millimetre mortar had proved to be one of the most effective weapons of the war so far; coupled with the general-purpose machine gun known colloquially as the gimpy it had done more to preserve the flow of oil to Western shores than any other weapon.

'Phil, I want you to take control of the battalion mortars. Set up your position on the Defa ruins – use the old Iranian positions if you have to – and lay all six mortars ready to fire at my command.'

Phil nodded. 'No chance to bed the base plates in, I suppose?' he asked hopefully.

'Not a dog's chance. Lay all the barrels on the lip.' Again the Boss pointed to the map. 'Make it as accurate as possible in the circumstances, and keep your aim to the left of the Zakhir Tree. We don't want to hit our own men. When the shit hits the fan, start to fire mixed rounds in front of us to clear the way.' The Boss was referring to what was familiarly known as a 'mixed-fruit pudding' – a devastatingly effective combination of high explosive and white phosphorus bombs.

'Phil, when I've completed the briefing go and liaise with B company commander. Each of his men is to carry two mortar bombs for you.'

Phil nodded.

'Now let's go over that again.' The coming night's action was very risky in terms of both personal danger and political objectives, and the Boss was taking no chances. Each man had to understand his role to the last detail if the SAS were to achieve the results that everyone expected of them.

It was cold and dark as they bounced along in the back of the army trucks, but it sure beat the hell out of walking, thought Karl, especially with the weight they needed to carry for this operation. Their bulky rucksacks contained mostly ammunition and water, and until the Shershitti caves were taken it would have to suffice.

At last they came to a halt and the merciless jolting ceased. Karl clambered down from his truck and walked forward to join the small group of men huddled together by the lead truck. The Iranian officer in charge was talking quietly with the Boss.

'Karl, you and Slick take up the point and move out. The Iranian engineers have already been to the Defa ruins and they say it's deserted – but take it steady anyway.' He turned to the Firqat leader and gave him the signal to follow.

'Okay, Slick, time to watch my backside. Let's rock and roll!' With this the two men started off into the darkness.

This was where Karl felt at ease. In the darkness he became alive: his instincts were heightened and he could sense rather than observe the blackness. Most people found darkness distressing, but not Karl – he loved it. It forced primitive instincts from a forgotten past to flood back, sending adrenalin surging into his bloodstream. Acting as lead scout out in front had many advantages. Should you bump into the Adoo, for instance, you could shoot first and ask questions later – there was absolutely no possibility of shooting your own comrades by mistake.

The ground here was flat and open, the hard-packed sand

littered with small pieces of rock. Here and there, the odd plant struggled for survival in the arid conditions. Every fifty metres Karl stopped and took out a small, tube-like object resembling a stunted telescope. The device was no longer than his hand and made a gentle humming sound as he switched the power on. Placing the night vision scope to his eye Karl swept the ground in front of him, searching intensely for any sign of the Adoo. But with no cover for the enemy there was little risk of an ambush, and so they advanced swiftly towards Defa.

Small clumps of stones clearly marked the boundary of the old ruins. Karl stopped and knelt, then motioned for the others to join him. 'It's the ruins, Boss, about twenty metres ahead. The whole place looks deserted from here, but should I do a quick recce?'

'Okay, no point in taking chances. But be as quick as you can,' replied Alan Gates before radioing back to the airbase to give their current position.

Karl made a good sweep with the night scope, observing here and there the discarded defences of the Iranians. Satisfied that there was no sign of the Adoo, Karl and Slick returned to find the Boss and Matt deep in conversation with the Firqat leader.

'He wants to push on now to the Zakhir Tree,' said Matt, the best Arabic speaker among them. 'He reckons that if we wait here until dawn the Adoo will finish us just as they did the Iranians.

The man was right. They were extremely exposed out here, and when daybreak came they would be trapped.

The Boss again radioed through to Manston for approval. Eventually he got permission for them to advance under cover of darkness, but only as far as the Zakhir Tree. He confirmed that B company would provide rear protection and defence for the mortars.

Over the radio the Boss gave his orders quietly. 'Set up as fast as you can, Phil, we're going to push on to the Zakhir Tree.'

Phil acknowledged and, moving swiftly, started positioning

the mortars, knowing that the more his companions advanced the more they would need him.

Karl started forward again, and this time a Firqat guide by the name of Ali Mohd joined up with him. When he had first met this wiry Arab four years ago Ali Mohd had been gripping a Russian AK47 assault rifle. He and three other Arabs had brought a wounded comrade down from the mountains and had walked into the village of Taqa on the southern coast, seeking amnesty and requesting medical assistance. The rebels had been well treated, and not long afterwards all of them had changed sides and joined the Firqat.

Like all of the Firqat Ali Mohd moved rapidly, sure-footed in his own back yard; his swift progress barely allowed Karl time to check what lay ahead of them. Presently the small stumpy bushes became larger, and then the rocky ground was broken up with dwarf trees: all this indicated that they were getting closer to the lip of the wadi.

Suddenly Ali dropped down on one knee and pointed. 'Zakhir Tree,' he whispered.

Karl lifted the night scope and surveyed the ground ahead: there, at the edge of his night vision, he made out the ancient tree. Again Karl signalled for the remainder of the group to close up. 'Zakhir Tree, about one hundred and fifty metres away.' He pointed into the nothingness.

The Boss held the radio close to his mouth and quietly relayed the information back to the others. When he had finished he said, 'Karl, you and Slick take about ten Firqat and move to the base of the tree. The rest of us will move out in an extended line to the left of the tree.' Matt quickly translated to the Firqat leader.

'Phil, are you set up yet?'

'Roger that, ten rounds mixed-fruit pudding. At your command. Over.' Phil was on the ball back at the mortar base.

Putting the small radio inside his camouflage jacket, the Boss eagerly gave the signal to move on to the tree. 'Everybody ready? Then let's do it. Keep well spread out. Good luck!'

The cold, damp atmosphere that signalled the coming day

washed over them as they cautiously advanced once more, covering the final area of exposed ground and shielded only by the darkness. Fear of imminent attack now thickened the air, forcing adrenalin once more into the bloodstream. Aware of the slightest movement or alien sound echoing from the desert, Karl continued to use the night scope. Then, with fifty metres to go before reaching the tree, one of the Firqat stopped. Danger signals filled Karl's brain as he searched the dark emptiness before him. All appeared quiet. But at that moment, just ahead, he saw for the first time the silhouette of a huge rock – the ideal ambush location. Karl knew they were here, and he was afraid. One abrupt instant of pain, and then the eternal blackness of death. He had seen it happen so often before, sometimes to his best friends. But all still seemed well. Moving closer, Karl began to wonder if his instincts were wrong. And then it happened.

From the silence and the darkness came a crashing orchestra of light and sound, and the sky was lit up by a red web of tracer bullets. Men started running or diving for the scant cover, while others, caught in the brutal crossfire, jumped and bounced like rag dolls. Bullets ripped away their clothes and tore into the yielding flesh. *Zip! zip! zip!* came the sound like vicious, angry bees – small copper bees made in the Soviet Union.

Karl had instantly dived to the ground and rolled twice to the right before desperately bringing the automatic rifle into his shoulder. Then his eyes searched for some target to fire at. His immediate fear was now replaced with the instinct for survival: if he had to die here, he would die fighting. Years of training and conditioning took a grip on his system.

Slick was there, rolling beside him and screaming, 'Where are the bastards? I can't see anything!'

'The base of the tree,' Karl shouted as the copper-coated bees returned, their smack and vicious scything sound creeping closer and surrounding them. Blindly, both men fired at the area around the Zakhir Tree.

'This is no place to be. It's time to move, Slick.'

The steadfast sound of a gimpy chattered to their left, while from the rear came a steady plop, plop-plopping sound as Phil despatched the mortars. It was time to do some running.

'Cover me, Slick,' Karl yelled. 'Let's try for the shelter of that large rock.'

Karl was half bent to rise when Slick's arm grabbed the ammunition belt that hung around his neck and dragged him back down. 'You bloody fool! Reload the gun and wait for my covering fire.' Slick lifted the top cover ready to receive the new belt of ammunition, and Karl fed it cleanly into the breach. Without stopping, Slick fired a prolonged burst into the base of the Zakhir Tree. At the same time he screamed at Karl, 'Now! Move now!'

Immediately Karl was up and running hard. For fleeting seconds he flew with the devil, zig-zagging across the open ground. At the same instant a Firqat had also risen and was running with him. Dropping in confusion they fell together, gasping for air, behind the shelter of the large rock.

'Thank God!' Karl cried, but almost immediately the Firqat grabbed his arm and shook wildly.

'Adoo! Adoo!' he shrieked, pointing to their right.

Parallel to them, and in plain view, lay two Adoo. But luckily the enemy's attention appeared to be diverted elsewhere, and so far they had not noticed Karl.

Karl raised his weapon to fire. The hammer fell on an empty chamber. 'Shit,' he muttered, rapidly changing the magazine. With the odds now stacked against him, Karl brought the rifle up to fire once more. But before he could pull the trigger the Firqat had levelled his own rifle and fired at the Adoo, the blast so close that it almost took Karl's head off. The shot missed, but unfortunately it was close enough to attract the Adoo's attention. As they turned, Karl cleared his head and fired. In that same instant came the flash of the enemy's weapon. The Firqat jolted twice and then lay still.

'Bastard!' Karl screamed, firing blindly. 'Die, you bastards!' He squeezed hard on the trigger.

What happened next, Karl was never quite sure. The world

around him suddenly exploded with bright light, and in that split second he felt himself lifted into the air. He hung there for what seemed like a lifetime. Then reality returned and with it savage pain, as his body slammed into the rocky ground with a sledgehammer blow. He felt shards of broken bone in his leg grating together, and his left arm seemed to be on fire. Mercifully, oblivion followed swiftly and for some seconds the pain was blotted out.

Then, through dulled senses, the noise of battle returned and with it the sound his own voice croaking, 'Medic, medic!' Agonizingly he rolled his head to one side and saw the dead Firqat lying next to him. The man's chest had burst wide open, and from the gaping wound blood and bubbles popped and oozed as air escaped from his shattered lungs. The Firqat's unseeing eyes stared up at the fresh dawn sky – a new day he would never see.

Karl's brain grew attuned to the eerie whistling sounds of the mortar bombs as they reached their full trajectory before starting their earthbound fall. Suddenly the whistling was replaced by the ear-shattering thunder of high explosive and the brilliant flash-fire of white phosphorous. They rained non-stop, and the ground beneath Karl's body trembled as if the very earth were alive. Screams punctuated the explosions as the twisted fragments of red-hot metal found human flesh, ripping away limbs and causing pain beyond the brain's capacity to bear.

Yet the hell continued, and the air grew thick with the stench of burning flesh. The white phosphorus splattered on impact – then, on contact with the air the gooey substance burst into flame. Without water to cool it, only death could allay the excruciating pain.

Bewildered, Karl caught sight of a dark face just a few feet away. He had forgotten about the Adoo. Over the short distance the two men stared at each other. As with lovers, only their eyes communicated, transmitting a million messages in the space of a second.

Karl destroyed the spell by glancing sideways to look for his weapon: it lay only inches away, and his hand snatched for it. Too late. His hand closed on the butt – too late, for the Adoo's reaction was a split second faster. Jet-black eyes stared fiercly out of an enormous head. Realizing that Karl was injured, the Adoo smiled triumphantly and aimed the ugly AK47 assault rifle directly at his adversary's head.

With a calm he would never understand, and for a moment when time stood still, Karl watched the Adoo squeeze the trigger, saw a sharp, clear image of a large finger and a dirty, broken nail. He heard a *clunk* as the firing mechanism fell on an empty chamber, and the smile froze on the Adoo's face. Instinctively Karl galvanized himself into action, swinging his own weapon up one-handed, and fired. But the Adoo had disappeared.

'Slick, Slick – over here.' Still shouting, Karl let himself relax and roll backwards. The pain returned. He was lying in a shallow dip in a rock basin, little more than a few inches deep, yet it offered some meagre protection. He felt calmer now. The sounds of battle in front of him were moving away. A heavy machine gun started its steady chatter close by, and the fire from the mortars crept further away as they extended their barrage over the lip of the rock into the wadi below. The patter of small arms fire got steadily louder and Karl knew that his comrades had made it to the lip. They were advancing.

Then Slick was there. He came racing across the open ground, skidding to a halt as he reached Karl, and with a look of concern dropped down beside him. Quickly he began to gather small rocks, piling them up to create more protection around his friend's shallow hiding-place.

'Hold on, Karl, hold on!' Slick was breathless and panting like a dog. 'Medivac choppers are on the way. Now let's have a look, you old bastard. Shit! Phosphorous!' Slick took a knife from his belt and started to scrape away the pieces of burning skin and molten phosphorus from Karl's arm.

'Jesus Christ!' Karl clenched his teeth to arrest the screams. The pain was excruciating.

'Sorry, old buddy, that had to be done. This will make it better.' Slick soaked a dressing in water and tied it tightly around the wound. Ignoring the sudden burst of machine gun fire that passed close by, he continued working on Karl's wounds. 'We have them on the run, Karl. Just hang on, buddy. We'll soon have you back at the field hospital.' Slick spoke reassuringly. He touched Karl's bleeding leg and the pain came like an express train. Vomit exploded from his stomach, covering the body of the dead Firqat with foul-smelling liquid. 'Sorry, buddy.' Karl felt the tiny prick of the morphine syringe, and in the distance he could hear the whirring of the medivac choppers coming in. For the present his war was over.

'Hey, Slick,' Karl said weakly. 'Look over there, about six feet away. Did I get the bastard with the big head?'

'You hit him, but not that bad. He was up and away. I threw a grenade after him. Who knows? Maybe we got lucky.'

'What panicked them into firing so soon?' Karl asked dreamily as the morphine began to take effect.

'I don't know, but Phil did a hell of a job with the mortars – apart from the one that got you!'

Slick and the Boss carried Karl to the medivac helicopter and strapped him on to the stretcher. One of the Firqat who had been hit lay alongside, his face the colour of putty, his left arm missing from the elbow down.

'Get the beers cold for when I get back!' Slick shouted above the roar of the chopper as it lifted off, heading back to the field hospital.

The soldiers had come just before the dawn, as Mahmud knew they would, to avoid being caught in the open without the cover of darkness. Mahmud had anticipated that they would need a starting-point, a landmark, and it had to be the Zakhir Tree.

The cold metal of the Kalashnikov had rested comfortably in the palm of his hand, the trigger already under pressure, as he had lain in wait with his old friend Dhardir; their comrades-in-arms lay concealed all around them. While his freedom fighters waited patiently for their victims to fall into the trap, Mahmud thought back back over the events of the past thirty-six hours. The Iranians had attacked with forces ten times the size of his own, and yet had been beaten back almost to the point of annihilation. His sixty men had fought like fanatics, aided by his clever tactics. All their heavy guns had been trained on the exposed area which the Iranians had had to cross. At first he had ordered his men to use only small arms to cut down the leading soldiers. Those following had dropped to the ground in search of whatever meagre cover they might find. Then he had ordered the mortars to begin their bombardment, and he had the Iranians in a double bind: if they continued to lie down they would be blown to pieces by his mortars, but if they tried to run the crossfire from his machine guns would take its deadly toll.

The Iranians were using strike jets, but Mahmud's men's positions had been so well concealed and fortified that the planes' Swiss-made anti-tank rockets and five hundred pound bombs did little harm. Then a small specialist group of insurgents had concealed themselves lower in the wadi with an SA7 Grail surface-to-air missile. Placing the rocket on his shoulder, one of the group had tracked a target fighter through a simple optic sight and, when he got a 'lock on', had released the rocket. Hungrily the weapon had searched for its target, sensing the heat of its exhaust. Tiny signals had flickered through its electronic brain, changing the path of the missile slightly before it impacted. Both aircraft and pilot had disintegrated in a spectacular explosion that was immensely gratifying to Mahmud, for with this success he had seriously undermined the enemy's air superiority and confidence.

Yet now, waiting in the night-time desert stillness, that exhilaration had dissipated. Mahmud felt he had been fighting this war forever. In the beginning, seven years ago, the rebels had met with little resistance, for the blinkered old Sultan had refused to acknowledge the danger. His poverty-stricken people were being destroyed by their lack of progress and the young men, driven by despair, had joined the rebel bands in the hope of freeing their country from the shackles of a harshly enforced feudalism that Europe had left behind centuries earlier.

But with the arrival of British troops in Oman things had changed. The newcomers had led their native Firqat soldiers up into the Jebel massif and fought the rebels, and there for the first time Mahmud had tasted defeat. Starting in the east, they had pushed his forces westwards, taking the waterholes one by one. Water was gold in this harsh land: without the precious liquid the rebel soldiers could not survive. Then the British had freed the tribesmen who until that point had supplied the rebels with food and shelter, thus denying his men the possibility of future sanctuary. Above all – and this was what Mahmud hated most – the British had not retreated one step since their arrival.

But now, the ambush prepared, he had an opportunity to strike back. He knew the enemy's only advantage was surprise, and at last he could hear their whispering. Staring into the first grey of dawn he saw movement, and vaguely he made out shadowy outlines.

'Now!' Mahmud squeezed the trigger, and the chatter of his weapon was echoed by the rest of his men. The whole area was lit up with flashes of fire as weapons on both sides sent tracer bullets zipping into the darkness, each flicker of light eagerly seeking a body to stop its path.

Suddenly Dhardir shook Mahmud, who was busy changing his magazine. 'Look over there!'

Mahmud peered cautiously over the lip of the rock. In the pale dawn light he could clearly see movement – three of the treacherous Firqat. They were slowly crawling towards his position, unaware of the ambush, completely exposed. Mahmud smiled at Dhardir and instinctively they fired together. Round after round burst into the men, and like grotesque marionettes their bodies danced and twitched, spraying the air with splintering bone, blood and bursting organs.

Quickly Mahmud and Dhardir fitted fresh magazines into

their weapons. Above the noise of battle they heard one of the fallen Firqat screaming away the last few seconds of his life. Dhardir grinned and aimed to fire at the dying man. Then suddenly, before he could squeeze the trigger, his body stiffened. Small flickers of light sparked through his brain as it registered the bullets ripping into his own body. There was nothing more than a warm feeling at first; then his vision retracted, as if he were looking at everything down a long tunnel. One bullet had entered just below Dhardir's armpit, passing through both lungs and exiting via his left kidney. Slowly he crumpled backwards to the ground, and the light at the end of the tunnel went out.

Mahmud swung round, surprised to find the enemy so close. Instinctively he fired a wild burst and saw a man crumple. It was a short victory, for there were others close by and one had already raised his weapon to the firing position. In that split second Mahmud waited for his turn to die, but nothing happened. Mahmud realized that the man was wounded, and then saw that he was white: he had never seen a British soldier so close before. Smiling at his unexpected change of fortune, he lifted his weapon to fire. But for some reason it failed. In desperation he tried to clear the stoppage, and as he did so a hammer-like blow hit him, lifting him violently backwards over the edge of the lip. Dazed and disorientated, he lay still for a moment, not daring to move, conscious of the stiffness in his shoulder. Surprised that he felt so little pain, Mahmud slowly examined his wound; he was pleased to find that the bullet had passed cleanly through the shoulder.

Then the sounds of battle returned, and he realized he must get away. Rolling on to his belly, he started to crawl slowly back down into the wadi. After fifty metres Mahmud stooped to rest, propping himself up by a large rock. He could hear some of his men still firing, but their resistance had diminished. As he rested, the stiffness in his shoulder spread, numbing his right arm totally. He felt sick.

Almost at once he heard the eerie moan of the mortar bombs. The enemy fire was increasing. Mahmud looked up and saw the whole area to the right of the Zakhir Tree burst into bright flame. Through the smoke he saw the fleeing figures of his men. Many were screaming and rolling wildly down the lip of the rock, desperately seeking relief from the raining phosphorus that burned into their bodies.

At long last the ear-shattering bombardment ceased, and Mahmud heard the shouts of the enemy as they moved steadily forward to the edge of the lip. The steady chatter of their machine guns was sending tracer fire after what remained of his retreating men.

In great sorrow he glanced once more at the Zakhir Tree. He did not want to leave Dhardir's body behind – Dhardir, who had been like a brother to him, and without whom he might never have found his mission in life. But now there was only retreat left. With a sadness that hung on him like a physical weight, he gathered himself up. He must go with his men – they would need him. The increasing early morning light allowed him to find his way through the thick bush. From time to time he halted; his arm was aching badly, and the pain seared through his weary brain like a red-hot iron.

To his left he could hear others following his lead. Through the scrub he caught sight of them, carrying a wounded soldier in a blanket. On seeing Mahmud they halted, and laid their burden gently on the ground.

'Take heart, comrades,' he said. 'All is not over yet.' Kneeling down, he looked at the man they were carrying. Mahmud instantly recognized him – another young friend who had fought for years in this violent campaign. His left leg was completely severed just below the knee, and a bloodstained cloth now covered the damaged stump. Thankfully, the man was unconscious. 'Quickly,' Mahmud urged them, 'get him back to the caves where they can attend to him.'

The two men picked up their burden and stumbled slowly on. Meanwhile the mortars had started again, delaying only to adjust their fire and follow Mahmud's retreating men. Slowly he led them deeper into the wadi, where scrub and small bushes offered a little concealment and protection.

It was a ragged group that eventually reached safety. Others had joined Mahmud along the way, and, now, as they approached the caves, those who had been left behind rushed out to assist. The wounded were taken deep inside, where a field hospital had been set up. Here the doctors and other medical staff on loan from the regular army of South Yemen looked in horror at their appalling injuries and mutilations. Luckily, however, their medical supplies were excellent, and swiftly they went to work. In one corner a huge concrete bath had been constructed and filled with water, and those with the worst phosphorus burns were carefully placed in it. Instantly the cool water stopped the burning and reduced the dreadful pain. Then, while the wounded still lay in the water, the doctors delicately scraped away the phosphorus along with the burnt skin. But despite their care, two of the severely wounded had already died since entering the caves.

At the entrance Mahmud conferred with his lieutenants. He was convinced that the enemy would come over the lip and down the base of the wadi: 'We must try to stop them before they reach the caves,' he insisted. 'How many men do we have left?'

'No more than forty — so how can we hope to repel them?'

His dark eyes shining, Mahmud stared at the man who had spoken. 'Never talk of defeat!' He spat the words out. 'We will never give in. We will catch them in the wadi base — our men know the area well and we have the advantage. At the very least we must try and hold them until darkness. One small party is to go and set up the Katushka rockets for launching. We must do everything in our power to hinder their efforts to establish fortifications along the lip.'

As he continued to outline his plans they watched in silence, with dismal faces. 'It is only men we are short of now,' he said finally. 'We still have the weapons and the courage.' While a medical orderly dressed his shoulder, Mahmud watched those men who could still fight hastily re-equip themselves. Then once more he led the ever smaller band of rebels out into the bright morning sunlight.

* * *

Soldiers of the Jebel Regiment were moving forward down the slope into the wadi bed. Higher up on the lip Mahmud could see more men moving around, piling up rocks and making fortifications. He split his remaining force into three smaller groups: some twenty men led by himself would control the centre, while two smaller groups covered the flanks.

Mahmud watched the leading platoon break cover and march confidently into the wadi bed. It had been decided that A company of the Jebel Regiment would clear the area up to the caves, as the Firqat troops had taken something of a beating in the dawn attack. They crossed the small clearing cautiously and were almost into the thick bush again when the small hill in front erupted.

Light and heavy machine gun fire, rocket launchers and mortars created a hideous cacophony as men were scythed down where they stood. Those left standing fled in the direction of some trees to their right, but as they entered this sparse cover they were met by Mahmud's flanking crossfire and were cut down at point-blank range. Within less than a minute more than half of A company lay dead. The remainder halted and quickly gathered around a small knoll concealed by thick brush, where they threw themselves to the ground. But Mahmud's men ran swiftly to the left and, firing rapidly, reduced their enemy's numbers still further.

Within minutes of the battle starting the whole area had become a maelstrom of black smoke, flame and shrapnel. The bodies of the Omani soldiers lay like broken dolls in the dust. Then it was over, with both sides withdrawing, one to lick their wounds and the other to gloat. The fortunes of war had reversed once more.

As the sun rose higher in the brilliant azure sky, a strange calm settled over the wadi. Mahmud had left his scouts to watch the lip, but apart from small parties recovering the dead there was no sign of any further attack. The enemy had grown too confident, and had paid the price. More importantly, this latest skirmish would give Mahmud and his followers more time. He was pleased with himself as he led his small band back to the caves. The enemy would not come again until the following dawn, but by then it would be too late.

'How many men are wounded and cannot walk?' Mahmud asked the doctor who was busy placing a fresh dressing on his shoulder. The enemy bombardment had stopped and Mahmud was sitting on a slab of rock at the mouth of the rocky cave, contemplating his next move.

'There are only three who cannot be moved, and two of them will be dead by the dawn.' The doctor looked for a glimmer of compassion in Mahmud's eyes, but saw none. 'Do you intend to leave soon?' he asked.

'You must say nothing to anyone until I have spoken to the others, but be prepared to move out as soon as it gets dark. Take what you will need to tend the wounded – it will be a long journey. Bring with you only those wounded who can stand the travelling. The others you must leave behind.' Mahmud knew that, the longer they stayed in the caves, the more at risk they became and the poorer were their chances of escape. He knew in his heart that they were finished here; their only hope was to get out with what was left of his battered army and cross the border into South Yemen. There at least he would be able to carry on the struggle.

The Omani soldiers did not attack again, but submitted the whole cave complex to a devastating bombardment. Shortly after midday they started, first with artillery, then with mortars, and finally a jet fighter came screaming in to drop huge five hundred pound bombs with devastating effect.

Courageously, Mahmud and a few of his men braved the bombardment to set up the large Katushka missiles, which they sent crashing down into the enemy defences. Only the low-flying jets posed any real threat to the rebels' position, but even their intrusions were sparse after the earlier SAM7 attack.

For the rest of that terrible day Mahmud sat with his

men in the safety of the caves, his head aching from the continuous barrage. Although they were protected by the tons of rocks above the caves themselves, the vibration and deafening explosions were taking their toll on their already shattered nerves. Shortly before dusk they fired off their last three missiles. Unbeknown to them they hit one of the main munitions dumps near the mortar position, killing six of the mortar crew and wounding a further three. Then the enemy fire, which had decreased over the past hour, finally stopped.

Quietly Mahmud addressed the remaining faithful, who had gathered up their few personal belongings and assembled just inside the entrance to the caves. He told them that they could stay here and fight to the bitter end, but that it would be a wasted sacrifice. No, it was time to leave and continue the fight from over the border. But soon, he promised them, they would be back – and this time it would be the hated enemy who would be leaving. His men half-heartedly cheered, and then prepared to leave. The army doctor caught Mahmud's eye and whispered. 'It is done! We are ready to move with those who can travel.' Mahmud went inside with him and gazed at the peaceful faces of those who would not be making the journey; a lethal injection had ended their suffering.

Then the firing started again. The whole wadi blazed with bright strips of light as tracer bullets from the machine guns wove their patterns like long fingers of fire reaching out, searching relentlessly for victims to punish. Despite the renewed barrage, Mahmud signalled his men to move. Cautiously the small party slipped out of the caves, withdrawing southwards as quickly as they could.

As they passed the last cave Mahmud began to feel angry and frustrated, for he was being forced to abandon all the heavy equipment and supplies which had taken so many years to build up. His emotions were stronger still for his fallen comrades whom he had left behind. As the last man left the cave a fuse was lit, to destroy everything in the caves and send the souls of the dead to Allah in a white-hot blast of high explosive.

They travelled all night, taking care that they were not followed. Every few hundred metres Mahmud halted, looking for signs of pursuit, but there were none. By daybreak the ragged band of survivors was in South Yemen.

Salala Airbase
Karl clung precariously to the door of the open-topped Land Rover as it bounced along the dirt track that ran from the field hospital to the main base camp. It had taken two weeks for his wounds to stabilize and show signs of healing, but now he was on the mend and very soon he would be on his way back to England.

The Land Rover shot through the camp gates and screeched to a halt in front of the HQ building. 'Do you have to drive like a half-crazed maniac? I'm supposed to be wounded!' Karl looked at Graham, the squadron clerk, with severe contempt.

'Don't give me that wounded soldier crap.' The smiling driver made to assist him. 'Come on – I'll give you a hand, Karl. It's just that I've got to get back and collect the mail – the plane's due in at any moment.'

Graham walked round the vehicle to where Karl was struggling to get his bandaged leg on to the ground, 'It's okay, thanks, I can make it. Where are the other lads?' Karl had heard no fresh news since arriving at the field hospital.

'Sleeping it off, most of them. They got back here at dusk last night, raided the cookhouse and they went straight into the bar. I reckon they deserved it after the past few weeks. The Boss is in the Ops Room – he'd like to see you.'

Karl hobbled slowly towards the building, crossing the helicopter pad which also served as a volleyball pitch. He was surprised by the quantity of weapons piled high all around it.

Graham read his mind and told him: 'That's just part of what came out of the Shershitti complex – one cave alone held almost a million rounds of small arms ammo. They'd rigged up a charge to destroy the lot but something must have gone wrong as it didn't blow . . . Just look at those!' He pointed to some neatly stacked green boxes. 'RPGs, hundreds of them, mines and a Katushka missile.' Karl looked at the missile, which must have been almost eight metres long.

As Karl entered the air-conditioned Operations Room he found the cool air welcome after the hot, dusty drive from the hospital. Boss Gates looked up from his desk and exclaimed, 'Hey, the wonder returns.' With the inevitable mug of hot tea in his hand, he jumped to his feet to welcome Karl. 'Glad to see you back – but it's just like you to sod off when the going gets tough!' He grinned and held out his hand. 'You're looking pretty good. How's the leg?'

'Getting better thanks, Boss. Looks like I'll live, and that's more than I can say for Phil when I get hold of him!'

'Don't hold it against him, Karl – he had his orders to lay those mortars that close, and he feels bad enough already about the stray that got you.'

'Don't worry, Boss, I was only joking. He most probably saved my life – that large-headed Adoo was about to waste me.'

'That Adoo, Karl, was none other than Mahmud al Dhuhoori, their young leader.' He pointed to a photograph pinned to the wall. 'After you were hit, we made several abortive attempts to get down to the caves. It wasn't easy, and we lost most of A company. So then we just pounded them into obscurity with everything we had. At the end the Adoo pulled out, but leaving those who were too far gone to travel. They were dead when we arrived – massive overdoses by the look of it. Now how the hell do you fight dedication like that?'

Karl limped over to the wall and looked hard at the face in the photograph. The dark eyes seemed to stare back at him from the huge head, and the black curly hair clustered thickly around the face like a lion's mane. 'Yes – I will remember you, my friend, for the rest of my life.'

Aden, August 1976
Mahmud was sitting in the home of his dead friend and comrade-in-arms Dhardir. He had made his way to the

house in Aden almost a year ago, where he had quietly told Dhardir's father of his son's death. There had been no need to glorify the event – the sad look on Mahmud's face spoke silently of the struggle of the past few years, and of their defeat. Now exiled from his homeland, Mahmud had accepted the hospitality of Dhardir's family and stayed in Aden. But despite their kindness Mahmud had become restless and bitter, for all his efforts to gain support for a renewed struggle in Oman fell upon deaf ears. And so, in the absence of a homeland cause, Mahmud turned his attention to wider issues.

By the end of the Arab-Israeli war in October 1973 the terrorist group known as Black September, who had been responsible for the massacre at the Munich Olympics, had ceased to exist. But their place was taken by more radical organizations, among them the Wadi Haddad group who had broken away from Yasser Arafat's Palestine Liberation Organization. More than any other Palestinian, Haddad continued to mount terrorist attacks on a truly international scale – not just against Israel but against the whole world. Since his split from the PLO Haddad had been condemned to death by the Israelis. But he survived, mainly due to his connections with various Arab governments who implicitly supported his Popular Front for the Liberation of Palestine by offering its members sanctuary. Payment was made by adding the enemies of the host government to Haddad's own hit list.

At his invitation, in August 1976 men from eight different nations, the power barons of the terrorist hierarchy, assembled in Aden. Their assignment was to devise a plan of death and destruction which would breathe new life into international terrorism. Chairing the meeting in the secure setting of the Iraqi embassy was Wadi Haddad himself, assisted by one of his new lieutenants, Mahmud al Dhuhoori. After his loss in Oman, Mahmud's new masters promised greater things. Haddad recognized the potential of this fearless man who was ideally suited and trained for terrorism. Through Mahmud, his masters would achieve the political instability they desired.

DESTINY

At that meeting many pledges were made, designed to show the world that the various revolutionary factions were united in their struggles. The longer the delegates talked, the bolder became their plans. Men's names were spoken and their deaths sanctioned. Aid in the form of weapons and explosives was agreed. Instructors, skilled in the sophisticated art of bomb-making would be exchanged, in turn teaching the new generation. Then the men parted, fired by the inspiration and guidance of Wadi Haddad. That which had been planned would be accomplished, and the world would tremble under this new horror.

3

Too Close to Home

orthern Ireland, October 1976
Karl Leathers and Slick Middleton sat in silence in the back of the vehicle as it cut its way through the darkness. Both were dressed in rough, casual clothing, which they hoped would enable them to pass as members of the local working population. It was almost 2 a.m., but they knew they would not be stopped by security patrols: Karl had taken the precaution of placing the whole town out of bounds to all friendly forces. Anyone else attempting to stop the car would be in for a very unpleasant surprise. The four men appeared calm and relaxed, for they were quite used to working late at night. If all went well they would be back in barracks at Portadown before breakfast.

'Two minutes,' said Tommy, who was acting as navigator in the front passenger seat. No one acknowledged his words, but Karl and Slick took hold of their small backpacks. Merv, the driver, flicked a switch on the dashboard to kill the brake lights temporarily.

'Okay, Slick?' enquired Karl.

'Follow you anywhere, Karl – mostly out of curiosity,' replied Slick with a sardonic smirk.

'Watch it, Yank, don't forget you're only in Northern Ireland under sufferance. If Paddy finds out there's an American Special Forces soldier working in the Province you'll be in deep shit, Middleton,' responded Karl with equally matey sarcasm.

When the American military decided to form a new elite unit to deal with any terrorist activities involving the USA a request had been made to the British government to allow the exchange soldier presently serving with the SAS to observe all theatres of operation, including Northern Ireland. So far Slick Middleton was doing a brilliant job.

The car slowed down and Karl released the door catch in readiness, opening it slightly.

'One hundred metres,' cautioned the navigator. The car came almost to a halt.

'Here we go.' Slick followed Karl out of the door and they dropped quietly to the ground, waiting for a few seconds in the gateway as they watched the car's rear lights disappear into the darkness.

'Over we go, Slick.' Both men climbed the gate and, moving a few yards into the corner of the field, crouched down once more. 'Let's wait here for a moment,' Karl whispered.

'Okay. Shall I give base a comms check?' murmured Slick, remembering the trouble they had been having with communications.

'No. Let's just wait for our night vision to improve.' Silently they knelt in the corner of the field, listening, getting attuned to the darkness, all their senses instinctively scannning their surroundings for possible danger.

Karl Leathers knew the feeling would come. He had been in the SAS for eleven years now and it had never failed him. No matter where he was when danger threatened, that special feeling, that heightened awareness always returned. It guarded his life, sheathing him with an invisible protective skin. Now, as he peered into the darkness, the words of the Maori instructor at the jungle training school returned.

'Yea, though I walk through the valley of the shadow of death I shall feel no evil, or I am the evilest son of a bitch in this valley.'

Karl smiled inwardly, and now, clutching the cold metal of

his automatic weapon, that same philosophy filled him with confidence. Now, as always in such circumstances, his animal instincts came to the fore, pushing deep into the darkness, feeling instead of seeing. Karl could feel Slick close by his side, could faintly hear his breathing . . . He felt the presence of wild creatures in the hedgerow, the damp grass under his feet and the smell of rain that would come before dawn, and absorbed the whispered sounds of the night that echoed about him. All seemed safe.

'Let's go,' he whispered eventually.

Covertly they moved off towards the lights of the town. After cautiously skirting the first houses they headed straight for the silhouette of the church, now visible against the street lighting. It stood facing the main road which divided the town, protected on the road side by ornate iron railings, and elsewhere by a nine-foot wall that encircled the graveyard. On the northern side stood a clump of fir trees which stretched the full length of the east wall, where they met up with a small, two-storey meeting-house tucked neatly into the corner behind the church.

It was to this meeting-house that the two SAS men headed. As they approached the wall, Karl recalled the phone message two days ago and his subsequent visit to Special Branch headquarters in Armagh city.

Chief Superintendent Robert Pardoe was the senior Special Branch officer in South Armagh, assigned to collect and collate every scrap of intelligence, from whatever source, that would help the fight against terrorism. Pardoe's natural gift for piecing together snippets of information into solid intelligence had propelled him swiftly through the ranks. His private list of informants stretched like a spider's web across the Province, and included men and women from both Catholic and Protestant faiths.

Karl had met Pardoe on several previous occasions. Once they had gone, with no back-up, to check out one of Pardoe's tip-offs. They had trudged in the darkness across a wet bog to find a large plastic dustbin, full of arms and ammunition, buried in the side of a drainage ditch. Karl admired the man not just for his skill but for his dedication to duty. Perfectly suited to the complex world of intelligence, he was, above all, a man who could be trusted.

'Hello, Karl. Long time no see. What about you?' Robert Pardoe welcomed him in his soft Irish brogue.

'I'm well, Bob. What is it this time?' He shook the offered hand.

Pardoe sat down and motioned Karl to do likewise. 'Your boys got anything pressing on at the moment?'

'You know damn well we don't. That's the reason I'm here. If you've got any work going, let's have it.' Over the years the SAS and Special Branch had worked in amicable accord. True, there had been times of mistrust, but the SAS had overwhelming respect for any information that Pardoe might impart.

'Do you know Castleford?' he began, taking it for granted that Karl did. 'There's a church there with a meeting-house in a corner of the cemetery. Intelligence suggests that you might find some documents of interest there. I need someone to take a few photos and have a good look round for me.'

'I see no reason why we shouldn't. Any further information about exactly what we'd be looking for?'

'No.'

'That's it? That's what you call a briefing'? Karl said, jokingly.

'What more can I tell you? Just go and have a look. Or would you prefer for me to come and hold your hand?'

Karl ignored the remark. 'Seriously, how good is the information?' he asked, reflecting that Pardoe would not have requested SAS involvement unless the information was delicate.

'To be honest, I don't really know. It's a funny one, this, but as it involves a church I thought a bit of diplomacy and style were needed. So will you do it or not?'

'I'll go and have a look myself. Is tomorrow night soon enough for you?'

'Fine. Just make sure the area is out of bounds, and give me a call if you find anything worth while. But please don't call me in the middle of the night unless it's something really interesting. My wife's becoming suspicious!'

That evening Karl had set up two SAS observation posts close to the church. The main OP lay within the walled churchyard, near the patch of fir trees. Here two men had been so perfectly concealed that, if need be, they would remain there undetected for weeks at a time. Another two men were in a small wood some two hundred metres north of the rear wall. This pair would provide back-up for their colleagues in the churchyard if they were discovered, or in any other tricky situation.

Now, as they neared the north wall, Karl motioned Slick to stop. 'Let's give the boys in the OPs a call now.'

Slick knelt down and lifted the small radio to his mouth. '32 Bravo and 32 Charlie, this is 32 Alpha. Over.'

They waited for a moment, then heard the whispered reply, '32 Alpha, this is Charlie. Where are you? Over.'

'With you in five, Charlie. Bravo, acknowledge. Over.'

'Bravo Roger. Are you coming to our location now or later? Over.'

'Alpha, be with you later. Out to you . . . Charlie, are we clear to come over the wall?'

'Clear. No sign of movement. Over you come.'

Slick tucked the handset inside his jacket. 'Okay, Karl, let's go.'

Karl picked his way carefully through the clumps of nettles that grew unrestrained at the base of the northern wall. He propped his weapon and his small rucksack by his foot, took up position with his back to the wall, and then cupped both hands to give Slick a foothold. Swiftly the American lifted himself to the top of the wall, from where he lowered his own rucksack to the ground and then reached back for Karl's. After taking up Karl's weapon, he disappeared into the churchyard. Karl followed quickly and the two men sat crouched against the wall, pausing for a moment to listen and make sure they had not been spotted.

Karl rapidly surveyed the area. They were about ten metres from the meeting house, which was in complete darkness. The street lighting that could have given them some assistance was blotted out by the huge bulk of the church. Karl motioned Slick to move closer to the building; then, sheltered against one of the massive buttresses, he made out the start of the fir trees.

'Stay here,' he murmured to Slick as he made his way towards the trees. 'Tony?' He waited. But the only response was the noise of the wind playing in the trees. Where the hell were they? 'Tony?' he whispered again.

'Here!' A voice spoke from the darkness under his feet. It made Karl jump and sent the blood rushing through his veins.

'You frightened me to death. Are you okay?'

'Bloody freezing! How come I always get the observation job?'

'Because you're the best. Here, hold this.' Karl knelt and opened his rucksack, then passed down a flask of hot coffee. A hand reached up from the dark earth to take it from him. 'We should be inside for about an hour. If anyone comes, you know what to do!'

'There's a mean-looking padlock on the door,' warned a second voice from the ground.

'Don't worry, Slick can open anything – even Tony's wallet!' Karl baited. Tony's meanness was legendary: he was never to be found when it was his turn to buy a round of drinks.

'Bastard!' Tony spat his good-humoured reply.

Karl left the trees to rejoin Slick, and together they moved silently towards the meeting-house. At the door Karl said, 'It's all yours, my friend.' While Slick worked, he would keep a sharp look-out.

Reaching inside his coat, the American withdrew a small black wallet bearing the initials HPC – the Holden Pick Company of the USA, the finest supplier of lock-picking sets and equipment in the world. With a casual air he selected a tension tool and a rake, both of which showed signs of excessive wear. Gently he inserted the tension tool into the lock in such a way as to leave access to the pins. When the pins had been seated correctly, the tension tool would supply enough pressure to turn the cylinder and so open up the lock. It looked simple, but Karl knew that the technique needed years of practice to perfect: too much pressure on the cylinder and the pins would bind, too little pressure and they would not be seated.

Slick cupped the padlock in his left hand, using his index finger on the tension tool. Then with the raking tool he pushed all the way to the rear of the padlock, cautiously withdrawing it over the pins. The cylinder moved, but only a fraction, and with a swift, composed movement Slick repeated the process. Nothing happened. He released the pressure on the tension tool, listening to the pins quietly popping back on their tiny springs. Slick repeated the manoeuvre once more. This time his index finger relaxed and the tension tool turned the cylinder, releasing the lock. He turned to Karl with a smug grin on his face.

'Flash bastard!' Karl whispered admiringly. Despite the initial failure, Slick had taken no more than forty seconds to break in. 'Right, in you go and take the lock with you.' There would be nothing worse than being locked in should they be discovered.

Cautiously they entered the building and gently closed the door behind them. 'Wait! I'll have a glance with the night scope.' Karl fished the device from his rucksack, brought it up to his right eye and surveyed the room.

'Junk, nothing but junk!' he grumbled.

'Try here.' Slick indicted a corner.

Karl moved cautiously, taking care not to disturb anything. Slick had opened a corner cupboard, but it contained nothing more contentious than hymn books.

'This place looks as if it's only used for storage. There's hardly any room to stand, never mind hold a meeting. Come on, let's look upstairs.'

At the top of the narrow stairs Slick stopped, his progress halted by a door. He opened it and they went in. Compared with the darkness of the floor below, this room was well illuminated by the glow of the street lamps which filtered through the windows. A large wooden table surrounded by chairs dominated the room, and three large cupboards stood against the walls.

'You check out the room – and don't forget the floor. I'll try the cupboards.' Karl crossed to the nearest one. It was empty.

After half an hour of systematic searching they had still found nothing of interest. 'I think this is a dead loss,' Karl said in exasperation. 'Have you found anything?'

'No – but hang on a minute.' Slick pointed to a small loft hatch above them. 'Nearly missed that. Do you want to take a look?'

'Okay. Give me a hand up, will you?' Karl took a thin pencil torch from his pocket and gripped it between his teeth. By standing on a chair which Slick had placed on the table he could just reach the hatch cover. It was hinged, and gingerly he started to lift it open. The possibility of a booby trap crossed his mind, but he could not feel the slight pressure which would have announced the presence of such a device. Gently, Karl felt around the edge of the cover for any pull cord. Finding none, he lifted the cover cleanly and peered inside.

'I'm going to climb up for a better look.' Karl heaved himself up through the opening and, taking the torch from his mouth, shone it around the dark loft space.

Then he froze. His heartbeat quickened as his mind assessed the magnitude of what he was seeing. He felt like some thief who had inadvertently fallen into a vast treasure chest and did not know what to touch first. He forced himself to concentrate, aiming the torch beam first on the stack of rifles – at least ten new AK47s. As he shifted the beam, he saw the boxes of ammo. He was just about to get Slick to join him when the torchlight flickered across a large olive green box tucked away in the corner. It was the sheer size that made him pause, and as comprehension dawned he looked in disbelief. He had seen boxes of just this shape and size piled high at the SAS base camp in Oman after they had captured Adoo's weapons from the Shershitti caves.

Rockets, Soviet RPG7s. These were standard Soviet infantry anti-tank rockets, with a launcher like a piece of metal drainpipe about five feet long. Simple to operate and very effective in the right hands, they had been used with success all over the world. On the streets of Northern Ireland they would cause absolute mayhem.

Karl leaned down through the hole in the loft. 'Slick, pass up the camera. Then get on the radio to all stations. We go live tonight.' It was impossible to keep the excitement out of his voice.

'What's up there?'

'Weapons – a bloody arsenal. Now get me that sodding camera.'

Slick knew better than to waste time asking questions at this stage. He would get to hear the details later.

'Get on to Zero and ask the Boss for more men,' ordered Karl. 'Half a troop at least, and I want them in Portadown by daybreak. And get Zero to phone the Tactical Control Centre in Armagh. I want normal vehicle patrols through the area by tomorrow, but no foot patrols. Got it?'

'Got it.' Slick passed up the Nikon camera.

Systematically Karl started to take pictures, the infra-red filter blanking out the flash to the naked eye as the special film faithfully recorded every detail. As he worked, the temptation to touch was irresistible, but training and discipline over-rode that urge. Karl made one more deliberate pass with the torch. Despite the photographic evidence he must remember it all – especially the RPGs.

When he emerged from the loft Slick was still on the radio. It seemed that the duty operator wanted more information before waking the Boss. Karl took the radio from Slick and spoke curtly into it.

'Zero, this is 32 Alpha. No more air traffic on this subject.

Please relay my instruction for assistance to the Boss. We need troops as soon as possible. The responsibility is now yours. Out.' He passed the handset back to Slick. 'Bloody base wallahs are all the fucking same,' Karl muttered to himself.

Together they checked the room, covering their traces, then they moved quickly downstairs and out into the cool night air. Clipping the padlock back into place, they made their way towards the fir trees and the two mean concealed there. This time the voice in the ground spoke first.

'Why do I get the feeling that we're going to be stuck in this fucking hole for a long time?' Tony's voice had a dismal ring to it.

Karl bent down to impart the news. 'Sorry mate. It looks like a large find – AKs, ammo and at least two RPG7s plus twenty rockets.'

'You're joking!' Tony's voice became serious. 'What if anyone comes tonight?'

'You act only if they start to remove any of the goods, okay? It's late now, so there's little chance that they'll come tonight. By morning we'll have this town locked down tight. I'll replace you in about four days' time, but expect us back tomorrow night.' Karl knew they were good soldiers. Lying huddled for hours on end on the freezing ground required rigorous training and a great deal of patience, but now at least there was something to wait for. 'As soon as I get back to Portadown I'll despatch some more back-up in a van. Until then all you have are the two blokes in the other OP.'

'No problem, Karl. See you tomorrow night.'

Karl and Slick climbed back over the wall and made their way to the second OP. Karl gave them the same briefing, and this time it was their turn to get a flask of hot coffee to ease the misery of staying put.

Back at the gate Slick called for the pick-up car. Ten minutes later it arrived, the rear door open and ready for them to scramble in. Even as they did so the car gathered speed and headed for Portadown. It was 4.30 a.m., and rain had started to fall.

At the barracks Karl saw extra cars, which meant that the additional men requested had already arrived. Pulling out his camera, he said, 'Slick, develop the film. I want wet proofs in half an hour. Tommy, go and inform the cook we need twenty early breakfasts, okay? Any problems, you can find me in the Operations Room.'

Karl heard the familiar buzz of the electronic gate as he entered the security compound and quickly walked into the building. Halfway down the corridor he came across a tall man dressed in casual clothes. 'Hello, Keith. How many men have you brought?' He didn't wait for an answer but went straight into the Operations Room and picked up the telephone.

'What's going on, Karl?' enquired Keith, who had followed him in.

A specialist unit such as the SAS breeds close relationships, Keith Edwards had survived the same selection course as Karl, and they had become friends. Normally the conversation between them was relaxed and easy, but now action was imminent and Keith had picked up the undercurrent of excitement in Karl.

'New arms dump, bigger than I've ever seen before, plus two RPG7s and lots of ammo.' While dialling, Karl repeated what he had seen. Then he spoke down the phone. 'Bob, it's Karl Leathers.'

There was a pause, and Karl realized that the man had probably been woken from a deep sleep.

'Can you get here as soon as possible? . . . Yes, to Portadown . . . No, not over the phone . . . Okay, see you later.' Karl replaced the phone and turned to Keith. 'Where are your boys?'

'Sitting in the briefing room. Come on, mate, the suspense is killing me!'

'Well, it will have to kill you for a few more minutes – I'm not repeating myself. Follow me.' The two of them made their way to the briefing room. Six heads turned as they entered the room, and Karl started to address them.

'Okay, it's a big find – and I mean *big*, so not a word

outside this building.' Briefly he went over what he and Slick had discovered, and explained that they would have to wait for Special Branch before deciding what action should be taken next. 'I suggest we all have breakfast and meet back here at 8 a.m. By the way, no one is to wander off. If we get a fast ball you'll have to move pretty quick, so stay tooled up.'

Karl watched as the men left for the cookhouse, then turned to Keith. 'Come on, mate, let's see how Slick is getting on with those photos and see if we can formulate some sort of a plan.'

'Do you remember the last time we came across boxes like these?' Keith asked, lifting the bromide paper from the wet tray.

'Sure, I remember – Shershitti caves.'

'Did you open the boxes in the loft?' Keith's question was tinged with hope.

'No – I was tempted, though!'

Slick passed over the wet prints. 'Put these in the drier. I'm just about finished here.'

They chatted idly for a few minutes, then Slick turned on the lights and lifted one of the prints from the drier. Karl had seen the find first-hand, but this was the first real assessment for the other two.

'Why do I get the feeling that this stuff is new?' Keith said, throwing out the question to no one in particular.

'Funny, the same question had crossed my mind,' replied Karl. 'It *was* new, come to think of it – still in its packing. I have a strange feeling about all this!'

'What do you mean?' Keith took another photo from the drier.

'Well, for one thing, the size of this find. This isn't a two-man arms cache – it would have taken at least a dozen men to move this lot. It was no mean feat getting that RPG box through that loft hatch. Secondly, when was the last time you saw brand-new weapons in Northern Ireland? The odd one, maybe, but this lot all seems out of place somehow.'

Still speculating uneasily, they went across to get some breakfast.

Back in the briefing room the men sat around in small groups. Two of them were struggling with a large aerial photograph, attempting to pin it to the wall. It showed the centre of Castleford, and once it was secure Slick busied himself sticking coloured pins in it. Most of them, in or around the church, indicated the OP sites and the find itself. Karl was just about to mention the car drop-off points when Robert Pardoe came in. He looked across at Karl and with a jerk of his head indicated that he should join him outside. Picking up the envelope of photographs, Karl led Pardoe into one of the smaller planning rooms and shut the door.

'So what did you find?'

Karl passed him the photographs. 'What do you think of that little lot?'

Pardoe studied them carefully, his trained eye taking in the detail while Karl gave him a running commentary.

'This one shows the rifles. Brand-new AK47s – or, more accurately, their Chinese equivalent.' Karl pointed to the ammunition and what he thought was probably explosives. As Bob took the final photo in his hand, Karl watched his expression change.

'What's this?' he said, pointing at the large box.

'I believe it could hold several RPG7 rocket-launchers and about twenty rounds. Slick and Keith agree – we've seen similar boxes in the Middle East.'

Pardoe stared in surprise. 'What action have you taken so far?' he demanded.

'We still have a two-man OP twenty yards away and a two-man back-up within thirty seconds. In addition I'm sending a van with four boys on board within the hour. The OPs can see all the exits, and if anyone tries to move any of the stuff out in daylight, we'll arrest them.' Pausing, Karl added, 'Or kill them, depending on the situation!' Pardoe did not interrupt, so Karl continued. 'You must understand

71

that until we formulate a plan of action I cannot let a find of this magnitude on to the streets. Keith has come down with an extra six men, but I need to know your intentions before we go further.'

'Who else knows about the find? The army, or just your boys?'

'I told the Boss on the way back and I presume he'll have informed Hereford by now, but basically it's SAS eyes only. Slick, Keith and myself have seen the photos. We'd like to confirm the contents of the boxes and the other stuff tonight.'

'Okay, but do keep this SAS eyes only. I want this kept tight – the fewer people who know, the better. Any chance of keeping it from the Brigade?' Pardoe was not making a request.

'No problem for me, but I can't speak for their people in Tactical Control.'

Security was an age-old problem. To avoid the prospect of troops, covert and overt, banging into each other, a Tactical Control Centre had been established in the Province. Its task was to oversee all operations, collating information and tasking the appropriate organization or unit. But different organizations were represented at TCC, which led to a conflict of loyalties. For example, an Intelligence major might represent his Brigade and thus control all the close observation units at his disposal. He would also assist the Special Branch officers who manned TCC; since most information passed through TCC it was usually discussed openly, but remained safe within the office walls. However, this would place the Intelligence major in an invidious position when pressed for information by his seniors at Brigade. Once the army had information it would go on an operations board, probably placed there by a sergeant or corporal. Shifts changed every eight hours; as a result, more and more people would be briefed and soon information was no longer secret. The SAS had their own man at TCC, but he worked and liaised with a very small group of men, isolated from the contamination of the regular army system.

'Okay, leave Brigade and the TCC to me,' Bob assured him. 'You can put cover on today and check it out again tonight. I need to know exactly what's in those boxes.'

'Do you want to sit in on the briefing?' Karl asked.

'No, but get back to me at TCC the moment you return in the morning. I'll sleep there tonight.'

It took a further two hours to come up with a firm plan of action, each man having had the chance to contribute.

'Okay,' said Karl, firmly but wearily. 'Let's go over the plan one more time. OPs in the churchyard will stay put for the time being, as will the rear back-up OPs. Tommy and Keith will take the van crew into the RUC station as mobile back-up.' Karl turned to the large aerial photograph pinned to the wall and indicated the positions as he talked.

'Action One. If the hall is entered Keith goes mobile, covering the front of the church from the road. This is to be achieved as covertly as possible. Keith, I suggest that you recce the town, probably on foot – I'll leave that decision to you. So all that happens on Action One is that the OPs stay put and we cover the church.

'Action Two. If the weapons are moved – and I want swift action on this – OP One will break cover and challenge, making sure that, before they do so, Keith is in position at the front of the church. Keith, you and your crew will move in around both sides of the church – there are only two men in that OP, so come in hard. OP Two will break cover and go to the rear wall, one to each corner, and that should tie it in tight. The wall should trap them nicely.' Karl turned away from the photographs to face them.

'Okay, the mission is to capture or kill anyone attempting to remove the weapons, and in that order. Avoid any unnecessary shooting. A killing in a Catholic church which contains a large arms cache will do no one any favours. If there's a shooting, let me know immediately. I have a platoon of the Black Watch on standby about fifteen minutes away in Ballykinler.

'If it's all quiet today, Slick and I will go back in tonight and confirm the contents. After that we'll join Keith as back-up in the RUC station.'

As plans go, this one was pretty simple. The position of the weapons and anyone removing them was excellent from Karl's point of view. They would be totally trapped by the high walls on the three sides of the church yard. Once the plan was finalized, and the smallest of details taken care of, they all set about getting ready for the next night's work. For Karl and Slick, sleep was now a priority. Putting his head around the Operations Room door, Karl spoke to the man on duty, 'Trev, I'm going to get my head down, wake me in time for tea please'. With that he walked the few metres to his room and collapsed on the bunk bed. Karl was asleep almost before his head hit the pillow.

'Karl! Karl! Wake up!' As he came out of a deep sleep he felt someone shaking his shoulder. 'It's the phone. Pardoe wants to speak to you urgently.'

'Okay, okay,' Karl muttered, his head still fuzzy. 'Can you make a brew of tea please, Trevor?' he asked the man on duty as he staggered out of bed. Once in the Operations Room he picked up the phone.

'Karl, your plans – could you stand them down for the time being? We have to make different arrangements.'

At first Bob Pardoe's words didn't register. 'It's okay,' Karl replied, 'there'll be no movement from this end before two in the morning. The only thing done so far is to send the back-up vehicle to the RUC station in Castleford.'

'Karl, I don't think you understand me. Withdraw the back-up for the time being. There is to be no movement at all in the area.'

'Are you crazy? No can do!' He was aghast. 'That back-up vehicle stays in the area. If you won't allow them to stay in the RUC station, then they'll have to stay mobile locally. We have OPs in the area, and they're entitled to protection.' Karl stopped himself. Why was he getting upset? Surely he had misunderstood. 'Let me clarify this, Bob,' he said slowly. 'You want me to pull the operation completely – is that correct?'

'Wait by the phone, Karl.'

There was a silence, but he could hear other voices in the background at Pardoe's end. Trevor entered the room a mug of tea in his hand, and Karl snapped at him: 'Get Slick down here *now*. Tell him it's vitally important.' Then someone picked up the phone and Karl was surprised to hear the Boss's voice, requesting Karl to come up to Control immediately. The fact that the Boss was with Pardoe at Control gave Karl cause for concern.

The American rushed in just as Karl put down the receiver. 'Slick, get hold of a set of maps of the area quickly, and a set of my orders.' As he disappeared, Karl called Brigade. It took three calls to pressure them into parting with the duty chopper.

'We need to know the reason. Do you have a fast ball? If so, the brigadier will need to know.'

It's always the bloody same: you want something and they want to know all the ins and outs, Karl thought. 'We are tasking at the moment, but I need a chopper. Can you get me one, or shall I call one from Aldergrove Airport?'

There was a slight pause. 'The pilot will be waiting on the helicopter pad in five minutes. Any time we can help, just ring!'

Slimy bastard, thought Karl, replacing the receiver. He went off to get dressed, and just as he finished Slick returned.

'The new air photos have arrived so I've put them in too. Do you want me to come with you?'

'No thanks, Slick. I managed to get a chopper to take me to Control, but I have a feeling that things are going to change pretty quickly around here. Until I get back in contact everything's the same. Okay?'

Slick nodded.

'Now could you contact the Boss and confirm I'll be with him in twenty minutes?'

'As Keith has gone with the back-up party, does that mean I'm now in charge?' Slick grinned.

'Okay, power-crazy Yank, you're in charge! Just stay near the phone. No matter who calls, the operation still stands. And if Brigade start to sniff around, just play your natural self – dumb, okay?'

'You British are so fucking superior,' Slick replied tartly, but as Karl headed for the door he was already issuing orders to the duty signaller to make him some tea.

Twenty minutes later the chopper touched down slightly on the wet helicopter pad of Lisburn Camp. Through the perspex screen Karl saw the Boss waiting for him, his head bent protectively against the rain and the windy downdraught of the rotor blades.

'Do you want me to wait?' the pilot shouted down above the roar of the engines.

'Yes, I may need to get back to Portadown in a hurry. Can you give me about an hour?'

'No problem. I have to refuel anyway.'

'Come over to Control when you're ready, okay?'

The pilot gave the thumbs up and Karl jumped down, shielding himself from the downpour.

'Hello, Boss, you do look pleased to see me. What's up?' Karl knew by Alan Gates's expression that bad news was coming. They ran quickly towards the shelter of the large building.

'Sorry, Karl, they want to lift you off the job. They want Pardoe and Special Branch out of the way too.'

'They? Who are *they*?' Karl interrupted angrily. 'Don't tell me it's the RUC who are going to take over?' They looked up into the eye of the security camera, and a short buzzing sound told them to go through. After tapping in the security code on the inner door, they entered the SAS main control centre in Northern Ireland.

Karl was surprised to see strangers waiting for them – it was not normal for non-SAS to be in here. The Boss made the introductions: 'George Jackson, this is Karl Leathers.' Both men shook hands and rapidly assessed each other.

Jackson was in his mid-fifties and running to fat. His once-smart suit was shabby and had moulded itself around his body like an ill-fitting skin. He smelled of stale cigarettes and unwashed armpits. Karl was repelled by the man, but masked his revulsion with a stiff smile. Yet despite the image he projected Jackson had a self-assured manner and an air of authority, Karl mused.

His thoughts were interrupted as the Boss introduced a younger man; he too was showing signs of over-indulgence and lack of exercise. His name was Peter Singleton. Robert Pardoe was also there. Karl nodded his head in acknowledgement, and asked the question that had been burning in his head ever since Pardoe's phone call had woken him.

'What seems to be the problem?'

'Let me explain, Karl.' George Jackson took control, as Karl instinctively knew he would. His voice was confident and relaxed. 'According to Chief Superintendent Pardoe, you and your men uncovered a considerable arms cache last night. It may interest you to know that my department lost the weapons you have just found. We have known for some time that they were in Northern Ireland. You see, we have been monitoring the shipment. Unfortunately, due to a slight mishap we lost contact for a while. But now, thanks to you, it has been relocated and we will now re-establish control. I'm sure you understand.' Jackson took it for granted that Karl did understand – he was clearly used to getting his own way.

Karl was confused. His operation had been declared null and void, and he found it hard to comprehend. 'I'm sorry, sir, but could I ask exactly who you are?'

'Shall we say, for the time being, that I represent British Intelligence.' His tone was smooth and dismissive.

Karl, however, was not about to be dismissed. 'Who, sir, may I ask, will be assigned to watch the find? Which unit are you going to be using? Remember, we are already in place.' Karl felt the bitterness rising, but kept his emotions under control. He saw this take-over as a personal attack on the SAS's expertise and reputation. Not only had the SAS found the cache, but this was exactly the type of operation they had been sent to Northern Ireland to carry out.

'Karl, I am fully aware of your professionalism – that goes without question, and we are not trying to undermine your authority. However, at this stage we feel it would be better under our control so we can continue with the operation already started.'

'When you say "we", who do you mean? We're not in England now – this is Northern Ireland. Tell me where in the Province you can find better-trained soldiers than the SAS for this kind of task?' Karl looked over to the Boss for confirmation and support.

'Sorry, Karl, I've been trying for the past half-hour to put across the obvious advantages of keeping you on the job,' Alan Gates sympathized.

'Let me go over this.' Karl brushed his hand across his face with exasperation. He was determined not to give up this operation without a fight, or at least a bloody good explanation. 'We have a tip-off about some documents, which eventually turn out to be an arms cache. This information did not come from you, I presume. Now, as you know, among the find I believe there are two RPG7s. Our role in Northern Ireland is to locate and observe such finds on the chance of catching members of the IRA. More importantly, to ensure that these weapons are never used against the security forces or the civilian population of this Province.' Jackson had been listening patiently while Karl spoke, but now he raised his hand for silence.

'Karl, I fully understand what you are saying and I whole-heartedly agree. I know of no other unit that could carry out this task, or supply the back-up and necessary equipment, as efficiently as yourselves. You must understand, however, that I cannot risk the loss of months of hard Intelligence work, which could lead ultimately to the arrest of several prominent members of the IRA. You must realize that this operation is just a small part of a very large jigsaw, and no way can it be compromised.' Jackson walked over to where his man was standing.

'Peter here is a top surveillance technician. He has enough equipment with him to infiltrate the loft area in the meeting-house, and to monitor any movement or conversation within a hundred yards of the building. I'd like him to accompany you tonight to confirm the find, catalogue it and install his equipment. Once this is achieved you will withdraw your people completely from the immediate area. I shall require you to set up a back-up force at the RUC station, which is about four minutes from the target area but close enough to react in an emergency. Captain Gates has agreed to this.' He looked for confirmation, and the Boss nodded. 'Peter will be on hand in the RUC station to monitor the equipment. Karl, for the moment, until I can bring in my people, you will be required to cover all weapons movements from the loft. We doubt the IRA will move them in a hurry, but the find will need to be checked every now and then. Can you manage this?'

It was only appeasement, and Karl knew it. 'What the hell, we're all fighting the same war – I hope!' He turned to Robert Pardoe. 'Can you fix it for me to have about six men in the RUC station at Newharbour? If one group are out on surveillance I'll need the extra cover.' Then, turning back to Jackson, he said, 'Sir, I will do as requested but with stated limitations. I don't see the advantage of using technical devices instead of men, and your plan is rather sloppy. If they decide to take out the weapons piece by piece we shall have them scattered all over Northern Ireland. This could result in many deaths which could have been averted.'

Jackson gave him a patronizing smile. 'Your point is noted, but once Peter has the devices in place, and we are confident that they are working correctly, we should have no problems.'

'Can I assume that you will take full responsibility for the weapons themselves?'

'I will take full responsibility, rest assured.' Jackson was becoming irritated at Karl's questions, and his silky tone now had a definite edge to it. 'And now I am sure you have work to do, staff sergeant.' Karl was dismissed.

After making various phone calls and confirming the main points of the operation with the Boss, Karl told the chopper pilot he was ready and that there were two more passengers. In addition to Peter, the Boss himself had agreed to come to Portadown to take over the location, releasing Karl to take charge on the ground at Castleford. Just as they were about to leave, Jackson approached. His tone was more conciliatory.

'I would like to give you a clearer picture, Karl, but at the moment I can't. As this operation progresses, maybe I will be able to.'

'Sir, no doubt you have your reasons for taking over this operation, and I am sure they have been well thought out. Bear in mind, however, that this is not Beirut or East Germany. Here the rules are completely different – here we have what's called the "Paddy Factor". That's how you lost the weapons in the first place.' With that Karl turned and walked towards the helicopter pad, leaving Jackson looking puzzled and concerned.

It was 8.30 p.m. as Karl assembled the men in the briefing room. Most had already changed into casual clothes for the night's work ahead.

'This is the latest situation,' he began, 'but before I begin there is something that must be crystal-clear to you all. This operation is under the control of the Security Services in London. It is part of a much larger operation and we are to support it.' He let that sink in.

'So after tonight the present OPs will be replaced by technical listening devies. Once on location, we shall go ahead as planned and do a full sweep of the loft. Keith will supply the back-up from his position in the RUC station. The time required on target is approximately one hour. After drop-off, Delta's crew will take the monitoring equipment into the RUC station and help to set it up. After this briefing Peter here will explain what is required.' Karl's eyes fell momentarily on Peter, who was sitting somewhat apprehensively in this unknown company.

'Once we have set up the technical equipment, myself, Slick and Peter will make our way on foot to the RUC station. The drop-off cars will return on our signal and pick up the two OP groups, who will return to Portadown. Then, after a good night's sleep, they will be responsible for the helicopter surveillance. The drop-off cars will return to the RUC station at Newharbour ready for mobile surveillance. If required, Keith and his crew will also move to the RUC station at Newharbour. The Boss will be in overall control from here – he should be arriving before we leave tonight.'

With Karl's briefing over, he added, 'Sorry, lads, but the truth is we are being replaced by technical devices and these will be monitored from the RCU station. I am informed that no compromise of the weapons will be allowed.'

The murmurs of discontent grew, and Karl sympathized with the men. However, there was a job to be done, and at such a time personal feelings had to be set aside.

When they left Portadown just after 1 a.m. it was still raining. This time as they approached the drop-off point they had Peter with them; so there was no way they could observe the complicated drills for getting in and out of a car without drawing attention, and Karl just hoped for the best.

Shortly before the drop-off, Karl tried to give him a few simple instructions. 'When the car comes to a halt, we will both get out on my side, then move out and over the gate, which will be directly in front of you. Then slip to your right and stop in the corner of the hedgerow. Do you understand?' Peter nodded. Back in Portadown, Karl had been surprised by how little military training Peter had actually received. He knew the basics of weapon handling and little else. To ease matters Slick had taken him to his room and demonstrated the Browning high power pistol, the weapon he was now carrying.

The car slowed to a standstill and swiftly Karl was smoothly out with Peter right behind him. They scrambled over the gate and moved to the corner of the field. 'When we move, stay about three metres behind me, but keep an eye out. If I stop, you stop. If I get down, you drop at the same time. Any shooting needed, leave it to Slick and me. Okay?' Peter nodded his agreement. 'Now we have to wait here for about ten minutes for Slick to arrive. If for any reason we become separated remember this place carefully, as it's the pick-up point. Got it?'

'Yeah, I understand ... I wish this bloody rain would stop.' It was obvious that Peter was not used to working in the wet.

While they waited Karl talked to the OPs, making them aware of his approach. Suddenly a car slowed momentarily, then continued on its way. Seconds later Slick joined them. 'Good weather for ducks! How are you feeling, Peter?' The American was his usual cheeky self.

'I don't think he's too happy, Slick. We'd better get going.' Karl stood up.

He moved off, followed closely by Peter, with Slick bringing up the rear. At the church wall they adopted the same manoeuvre for getting over the wall as the previous night, with Peter going second. 'Kneel there, Peter, and cover us while Slick gets on top of the wall.' Karl cupped his hands and Slick climbed rapidly up. He lay flat on top of the wall while Karl passed up the rucksacks, then Peter was hoisted up. He was clumsy and unfit and Karl almost dropped him, but with a final push and a pull from Slick both men disappeared over the wall, landing on the other side with a deafening thud.

'We've got to get him up into the bloody attic yet!' murmured Slick as Karl dropped down beside them.

'Sorry, Slick,' said Peter, rubbing his shoulder.

'Forget it!' Slick collected his rucksack and headed towards the darkened meeting-house.

As they reached the darkness of the fir trees Tony's voice

whispered, 'What is the point of us lying here in silence, when you lot make a racket like that?'

'Sorry, we got lumbered with a bloody civil servant.' Slick was still annoyed.

Karl quickly explained the change of plan. As he expected, despite the cold and wet of the OP post they did not take kindly to the idea of being relegated to observers from Portadown.

'Sorry, Tony, but a night in bed will make you feel better. When we go into the meeting-house, destroy the OP and make good. Then wait here until we come out again. After, when we make our way to the RUC station, you marry up with the other OP and go for the pick-up.'

Compared to the foul weather outside, the building seemed silent and warm. Karl told Slick to stay on the ground floor and cover the entrance while he and Peter went up to the weapons cache. 'After climbing into the loft we'll close the hatch before using the torches, okay?' he said to Peter.

'I'm not a total novice – I do know my job!'

'OK, sorry.' Karl gently lifted the hatch cover and then scrambled up into the dark loft. It looked just as he had left it the night before. Karl moved aside to give Peter room to follow, took his bag and helped him to climb up.

Karl closed the hatch and swept the room cautiously with his small torch. Peter lifted a much larger lamp from his bag: it was efficient and filtered, its beam aimed carefully in one direction. Then he produced a cordless electric drill and started to search the roof joists. Karl wondered if the drill was going to make an almighty racket, but was relieved to hear just the faintest buzzing sound as Peter started work. He certainly seemed to know what he was doing. Every man to his own trade, thought Karl, looking at Peter with a new-found respect. Leaving him to it, he whispered, 'I'm just going to check the goods.' He made his way gingerly across the roof, clutching the trusses for support.

Karl confirmed the newness of the stashed weapons – shiny Kalashnikovs still in their plastic packing, the date stamp proving they were less than three years old. The ammunition, upon examination, he estimated at close on twenty thousand rounds. The cache of explosives amounted to thirty kilos, together with three hundred detonators. Karl was amazed that the IRA could amass such a store. Where the hell had they originated? The arms black market would have charged a fortune, so it had to be a government or large organization which supported terrorist activity.

At last Karl found himself in front of the large green box. Someone had apparently opened up the box before; all that appeared to hold it down now were two simple twist locks. Slowly, with extreme care, Karl turned both locks and started to lift the lid. He was thinking about how to keep the lid open while he took the necessary photographs when it slipped and dropped down shut with a clatter.

'What the hell was that?' Peter demanded.

'It's okay – no problem.' Karl felt foolish and swore under his breath. Gently he began to lift the lid once more, keeping the torch between his teeth. When he had lifted it to about eight inches he felt some resistance. He checked to see if the rafters were obstructing it, but they were not. So he let the torch beam drop and play inside the lid – instantly he froze. The box was booby-trapped. Sweat started to run down his face as he softly called to Peter, trying the keep the panic from his voice.

'What's the matter?' Peter moved up close to him.

'It's the box lid, I think it's booby-trapped. Could you take very careful hold of the lid and try not to move it, while I look at the device more closely?' Gingerly Peter moved to the side, and Karl felt him take the pressure. 'Don't worry. If it was going to go off, I think it would have done so when I first touched the lid. Just hold it steady.'

Karl shone the torch inside the box – and there it was, as large as life. A thin brass wire was fixed with a large drawing pin to the underside of the wooden lid, while the other end ran down into the box itself, disappearing out of sight between two plastic packets containing the RPG rockets. 'It looks like a quick job – a pull switch, I think. Whoever put it in was nervous – one of the rockets has moved and trapped the wire.'

'Is it safe now?' Peter's voice sounded shaky.

'No, not yet. Very slowly I want you to lower the lid shut.' As Peter did so, Karl watched the wire go slack in the light of his torch. There was a dull thump as the lid closed completely. 'It's okay now, Peter. You can take your hands away.'

The two men looked at each other, exhausted. The nearness of death drains a man of energy. Karl, desperate for some fresh air, asked Peter if he had finished.

'Almost. Just about to test the reception.'

Karl took over from him. 'Hello, 32 Foxtrot, this is 32 Alpha. Over.'

The answer came back almost instantly. 'Roger 32 Alpha, device working perfectly. Everything okay your end?'

'I'll tell you later, let's do it by the book. Confirm reception, wait out.'

Karl and Peter started to count quietly to ten, and as they finished the radio crackled again. '32 Alpha, this is Foxtrot. Reception five by five. Over.'

'Roger that, Foxtrot. Checking alarm, wait out.' Karl turned to Peter and asked him to raise the hatch cover a few inches.

'32 Alpha, this is Foxtrot. We have a count of four. Over.'

'That's a Roger, Foxtrot. Coming out. Over.' Peter went first through the hatch, while Karl made a last sweep of the loft to ensure that everything appeared as normal as possible. Checking where Peter had been working, he half expected to see a pile of wood shavings – but there was nothing. He was a professional.

'We're going to get rusty just sitting here.' Slick was not a happy man; he continued to pace the small room in the police station where he had spent the past three days waiting. Like all police stations in Northern Ireland it was an obvious target for the IRA, and the entire building had been shielded by a wall of concrete and steel. Every angle of attack was covered by security cameras; like malignant eyes they moved and watched every corner and angle of the outside wall and surrounding area. In this small Catholic town the building had been designed for more peaceful times, to accommodate one sergeant and two constables; now it held six policemen permanently on duty. The arrival of the SAS contingent had made further demands on the already cramped conditions.

Karl understood Slick's inactivity and felt concern for the men – it did them no good to be cooped up all the time. One method of alleviating the problem was to set up some form of mobile surveillance exercise, which would also provide them with the opportunity to check out their contingency plans. But in order to avoid suspicion from the locals they would have to wait until 6 a.m. at which time the new police shift came on duty. First he cleared it with the Boss.

'That sounds fine to me, Karl,' said the voice on the other end of the telephone, 'but don't stray too far – you may be needed in a hurry. Tony here has the chopper pilot held captive during daylight hours – Brigade are going mad about keeping the chopper down full time. They can take it up tomorrow and fit in with the exercise.'

'Fine, Boss, but you'd better clear all this with Jackson. If there are any problems, get back to me.'

Karl replaced the receiver and took the mug of steaming tea that Slick was offering. 'Everything's okay. Let's tell the others – that should cheer up their spirits a little. We must tell Peter, too. Can you show him how to use our radio and make sure he has the phone number of the Portadown station in case anything happens while we're out?'

'Leave it to me!' Slick went off to torment Peter.

'Target turning right at junction 40–45. Who's backing?'

'Charlie's backing.'

It was 7.30 a.m., and the Boss had set them up with one of their own cars acting as a target. It had been decided that it would be safer if only two of the three cars from their location were involved plus one from Keith's. This would enable them to deal with any sudden emergency at the meeting-house that might arise during the exercise.

'Still straight 45–50.' The continuous conversation ensured that the target location was always under control, and the speed of the vehicle was also being continuously observed by all monitoring stations.

'All stations, this is Hotel, I am airborne, going over the Banbridge position in figures five.'

'Zero, I Roger that. Echo, give location.'

'Echo, towards Rathfriland, will continue parallel to the target.'

'Target still straight 45–50, Charlie backing. Wait, target indicating left at crossroads, Corbet Milltown. I confirm that the target has gone left. Charlie, can you take?'

'Charlie, that's a Roger.'

'All stations, this is Zero. Target turned left at Corbet Milltown towards Cappagh. Charlie has. Hotel, can you assist?'

'Hotel Roger, now over Banbridge going south. Will intercept Cappagh area.'

'Zero Roger. Echo, stay parallel towards Loughbrickland. Alpha, your position?'

'Alpha, doing a U-turn backing Charlie.'

'Zero, this is Hotel. I have target. Charlie, loosen it up now.'

'Zero, Roger all stations. Hotel has the target. Stay back, give him plenty of room.'

The use of the helicopter made surveillance by day much easier. It enabled the suspect to be followed without committing the ground mobiles in too close, yet they could be guided into shadowing positions to take over if need be.

For another hour the exercise continued before the Boss called it off. 'This is Zero. All cars to return to their original locations.'

'Okay, Slick, get us back to the RUC station. That's the last of your freedom for another few days,' Karl said.

'We should do this more often, Karl – it may come in useful.'

'Yes, but too much exposure and the locals will get suspicious and our cover will be blown. We can't put the operation in – ' Karl stopped in mid-sentence. 'Slow down, Slick. Look!' They were approaching Castleford with the church on their left. Outside was a procession of cars, and a large group of people were leaving the building. 'Looks like a bloody funeral. For Christ's sake slow down, Slick!' But it was too late, and they were past.

'Do you want me to go back for another look?'

'No – forget it, Slick. Get back to the station.'

On their return, Karl asked hopefully, 'Peter have your monitors received anything in the last two hours?'

'Nothing yet. Why?'

'There was a funeral taking place, and I was sure the door to the meeting-house was open when we passed.'

'But nothing has – '

Karl interrupted Peter. 'Slick, Charlie's still out there. Ask them to come back in the same way that we did. One man is to drop off and do a casual walk past – nothing out of the ordinary. There are lots of people about, so it shouldn't look suspicious.'

He picked up the phone as Slick relayed the instruction by radio. 'Hello, it's Karl here, let me speak with the Boss.' He waited for a moment until Alan Gates came on the line. 'There's a funeral taking place at the church – we just passed the position. But nothing's coming through on Jackson's side – only silence.'

'Something must be wrong. You tested all the devices before you left, so what does Peter say?'

Karl turned to Peter. 'What's the sensitivity of those devices? Could you hear if someone was in the upstairs room, for example?'

'If they climbed the stairs we would hear them. All conversation around the table and in the room would be clear.' Peter looked hurt that Karl had questioned his expertise.

Karl spoke into the phone again. 'Boss, if Charlie confirms activity around the meeting-house we'd better take a look tonight. Something *is* wrong, but we'll have to wait until dark.' The Boss confirmed, and Karl hung up.

Slick, still talking to call-sign Charlie, looked up from the handset.

'He's just dropped him off. It's Dave.'

Karl took the handset. 'Dave, this is Karl – don't talk, just click twice if you can hear me.'

There were two distinct clicking sounds.

'Okay, we hear you. It is important that you try to see if the door to the meeting-house is open. But be careful with all those people around – we don't want a compromise.'

Click, click. The message was acknowledged.

They sat and waited. After five minutes Dave's voice came back loud and clear. 'Karl, this is Charlie. The door to the meeting-house is open and I confirm there were people coming out of the building.'

'Shit. Dave, get back in the car and stay mobile. Position yourself just outside of town, on the church side. Out to you, Zero. Do you copy?'

'Roger 32 Alpha. The Boss is here, wait one. Karl, what do you think is happening?'

'We have no reading on either monitor. We either follow the funeral procession or wait until tonight to confirm. Get on to Jackson – this has to be his decision. In the meantime get Hotel airborne again. We'll all go mobile loosely around the town until I hear from you.'

'That's a Roger. Out.'

'All stations, this is 32 Alpha. All vehicles go mobile, wait for further instruction.'

'Let's go, soldiers. We'll stake out the funeral, Slick, and I'll get another car to go northwards – that should give us some cover. Keep it cool, and don't go anywhere near the funeral.'

Karl sat for an hour waiting for the funeral to finish. Then the radio disturbed his thoughts.

'Alpha, this is Zero. What's the situation?'

'Not a lot has changed. We have the town covered on all sides, the funeral seems to be over, and we've taken as many car registrations as possible. Stand by to copy. Over.'

'Roger, send.'

Karl read out the car registrations they had noted down; each would be checked. Northern Ireland has one of the most sophisticated computer systems in the world, giving instant access to records that identify both vehicles and people. It was a long shot, he reckoned, but something might come of it. When he had finished the Boss came back on.

'Jackson has given the go-ahead for an eyeball tonight. He's not too happy about it and requests that the weapons are checked at the same time. Oh, and he said take care, they may have put in another booby trap.'

'How thoughtful of him! Okay, I'll take Slick in with me and two guys for outside cover. If there's any major change you'll be the first to know.'

At 3 a.m. they slipped out of the RUC station and skirted the town to the north, approaching the back of the churchyard as before.

'Cover us from over there,' Karl instructed Tom and Phil as they dropped down over the wall. 'We should be no longer than twenty minutes.'

Once inside the meeting-house Karl swept the night viewing device around the room. 'It all looks the same to me,' he remarked to Slick. 'How about you?'

'I can't see a sodding thing – give me a look with the scope.'

'No, wait. Let's go upstairs and check the devices first, then we can have a good look around down here. You lead the way.'

Slick went slowly up the stairs and into the room, from where Karl climbed into the loft.

'Hello, 32 Charlie, this is Alpha. Can you hear us on the monitor?'

'Roger, Alpha. We hear you loud and clear. What is your position?'

'We're by the table. I'll check out the alarm in about two minutes. Stand by.'

'Hang on to the radio, Slick – see what they can hear when I raise the hatch.' As he slowly raised the hatch, thoughts of the booby trap came flooding back. Karl repeated the exercise several times.

'Anything, Slick?'

Karl heard Slick calling the RUC station.

'Eight, nine, ten. Well, are they receiving?'

'Roger, 32 Alpha. We confirm approximately ten closures. Technical is working perfectly.'

Karl felt a sense of relief. 'Well, at least we know it's working, but since we're here we might as well do a physical check.' He pushed the hatch cover fully back and heaved himself into a sitting position as before. Flicking on the torch, Karl focused on the weapons. A cold chill came over him – the large olive green box was wide open! Quickly he scrambled over and peered inside. It was empty.

'Boss we have a major problem: the RPGs are gone, so have about half the Kalashnikovs and ammo – only the explosive seems to be intact. We've checked both devices, they're working fine, so tell me how the hell did they get them out? 32 Alpha over.'

'Zero, Roger. It had to be the funeral – no matter, can you re-insert the 'OP's from your end tonight?'

'32 Alpha, Roger – we really don't have a choice. Leave this end to me Boss, we'll do the best we can. Inform Jackson, we need a meeting with him first thing in the morning.'

'Zero, Roger – call me if you think I can help.'

Karl handed the radio back to Slick. 'The people who are going to need help are the poor bastards on the receiving end of those RPG7s when they hit the streets.'

Karl left Tom and Phil to move into the old OP under the fir trees. 'Sorry lads, you're going to be a bit spartan for the next twenty four hours. I'll make sure you're changed over with a fresh team tomorrow night. Keith will move back into the RUC station from Newharbour, he'll be here within the hour. We go back to the old plan.'

'What if they try to get the rest out?' Tom asked hopefully.

'No more fucking about – shoot the bastards. Come on Slick, let's get back.'

As Karl entered the Control building in Lisburn he half expected to see hung heads and worried faces after his urgent radio message. Instead they were standing in a small group, chatting amiably in a light-hearted way.

'Ah, Karl!'

The group parted and George Jackson came towards him, his hand outstreched. To avoid offence, Karl shook hands. Then, turning to the Boss, he asked, 'So where do we go from here?'

Jackson was not relinquishing authority yet, and he intercepted the question. 'Do you know what is missing exactly, Karl?'

'Not down to the nearest round, but all the RPGs and at least half the Kalashnikovs, plus a lot of ammunition.'

'What are you doing with the rest of the weapons?' The way Jackson said it made Karl feel it was all his fault.

'We've reinstated the OPs – one of them in the fir trees where they can see the door to the meeting-house, the other about two hundred metres away. The main back-up has moved into the RUC station. Basically the same plan we had before.'

'And their orders?'

'To kill or capture anyone removing any part of the find.' Karl was looking for a challenge. Jackson returned his gaze coolly, then turned away and spoke to Robert Pardoe.

'Bob, tell me what would be the reaction if, say, the weapons were discovered in the churchyard. How would this affect current relations between Protestant and Catholic communities?'

'In general, the Catholic Church does not support the violence in any shape or form. I have in the past received information from the Catholic Church when they have deemed it to be in the interest of human life and their community. But such a find would be a severe embarrassment to them.'

'Of course, of course. Disregarding for the moment what has happened to the missing weapons, our main purpose should now be to discourage the IRA from using them – at least for the present. Would you agree gentlemen?'

Karl saw the 'whitewash' coming. He himself held the belief that problems are best faced up to in an honest manner – they tend to get solved quicker that way.

'Gentlemen, may I say something?' What the hell, Karl was going to anyway! 'No disrespect to your rank sir, but you seem to be glossing over the fact that we have lost a major part of a very large weapons find – weapons that will cause the deaths of many soldiers and policemen. You should have left it alone!' Karl did not intend Jackson to get off the hook quite so easily.

'You are wrong, Karl. I didn't want this outcome, but I would do the same again if need be. There are things you do not understand.'

A silence fell upon the room, and the Boss spoke before it could become an embarrassment. 'What do you have in mind, George?'

Jackson continued to eye Karl as he replied. 'If the IRA were made aware that we knew of the weapons find, what would their reaction be?'

'They would go to ground for a while. But how can we convince them?' The Boss was intrigued.

Jackson walked over to the large aerial photograph of Castleford pinned to the wall. Calmly, as if in permanent thought, he traced his finger across the photo and let it rest on the small meeting-house.

'If Karl and his men were to move what is left of the weapons tonight – say to a new hiding-place, not too far from the church – could you, Bob, pass this information through the normal channels so that the army would carry out a search of the area? Once the weapons were revealed and made public, we would have achieved two things. Firstly, the IRA would know we knew about the weapons in the church, and hopefully delay any attacks with the RPGs. Let's not forget we still have the box, so when our weapons find goes public we can disclose the possibility of RPGs in the Province. Secondly, by taking such action we remove any further risk of the weapons being taken from the loft. Well, what do you think?' It was a brilliant plan, and he knew it.

Even Karl had to admit that Jackson was a cunning bastard. 'But what if they come back before tonight?' he enquired.

'Then you take them. The result is the same, but doing it my way we don't upset the present situation between Protestants and Catholics. The church will not be mentioned or involved – all this will add to the IRA's bewilderment.'

The plan was talked through. Karl was to inform Pardoe first thing in the morning whether the transfer had been successful, and provide him with the new location. Between them, they chose a culvert about five hundred metres from the church. It would be simple enough to make it look like a standard IRA hide. If Karl was honest, it was an excellent idea. However, he still wondered if the first soldier to be on the receiving end of an RPG would think so.

Robert Pardoe set off back to Armagh, and Karl was about to follow when Jackson asked him to stay a moment longer.

'I understand you were wounded in Oman over a year ago, during the attack on the Shershitti caves,' said Jackson.

Karl looked at the Boss as if to say, 'Who's been telling tales out of school?' 'Yes, I was wounded at Shershitti,' he told Jackson, 'but eventually the caves were taken. It's a funny thing, but a lot of the stuff in the loft looked very like the stuff we captured.'

'Alan here tells me the man who shot you was one of their leaders, Mahmud al Dhuhoori – the Arab with the big head.' Jackson smiled.

'Yes, I shot him and at that range I couldn't miss, but one of our own mortar bombs fell between us at the same time, so I was never quite sure. Still, he most probably died in the bombardment that followed – it was a nightmare.'

Jackson studied Karl for a moment, deliberating whether or not to say anything more. 'Mahmud is still alive. You did not kill him – I only wish to God you had.'

Now it was Karl's turn to stare. Jackson put him at ease. 'Alan also informs me that you are fully vetted, and that you are an excellent soldier. What I am about to tell you is highly classified. We have a man working with the IRA – he was at the church. I don't want him killed or compromised.'

Karl was silent for a moment, then said, 'If you'd told me that in the first place, we could have worked something out and avoided all this. Whatever, there's very little chance that the IRA will return for the rest of the weapons tonight, but if they do we'll do our utmost to capture them, and only shoot if really necessary.'

'Thank you. It took a great deal of time and trouble to get him where he is. And you may rest assured that if we get a tip-off about the whereabouts of the missing weapons, you'll be the first to know.'

Three days later the media were full of it. Both newspapers and television gave massive coverage to the huge find of IRA arms in the Castleford area. Meanwhile Karl and the boys returned to Portadown and twiddled their thumbs.

'We have a possible. It's in Belfast, just off the Falls Road. Can you move now?' Robert Pardoe's voice sounded excited.

'Give me the address, Bob.' Karl fumbled for a pen.

'Prospect Street. You have the choice of three houses, numbers 53, 55, or 57. I've checked with the Belfast boys and we do have a possible at number 57 – there's a real bad bastard living there. Goes by the name of Docherty, Jimmy Docherty. As far as we know the other two houses are clean, but I can't give you a guarantee.'

'How good is this information?' Karl enquired.

'There are weapons in one of those three houses.'

He knew Bob was telling the truth. How the hell did he get

his information? Maybe it had come from Jackson. 'Okay, Bob, we'll be moving in ten minutes. That means we should be hitting Prospect Street in about an hour. Will you warn off any local uniformed people who may be in the area, and alert Brigade that we may need some cordon troops if the public get nasty.' Karl did not want the local police thinking they were IRA, or the local Catholic people getting violent.

'Where the hell is the Boss?' he demanded as he burst into Slick's room after his phone call from the Special Branch head.

Slick looked up from the porn magazine he was engrossed in. There was a blank expression on his face.

'The Boss! Slick, where the hell is the Boss? We have a house in Belfast with some of our stolen weapons. Now move! Get the boys together in the briefing room on the double.'

Karl quickly counted heads as they assembled two minutes later in the briefing room. 'Okay, it's a fast ball. Tool up. We have a house in the Falls. I want everyone mobile in ten minutes. You'll get your instructions over the air. No stopping – we go straight in. Now move it.'

One minute an SAS man can be slumped in a chair watching a video, bored to tears with the waiting. But give him just the smell of a job and he explodes into life. Karl led the rush to the main door. But as he passed the duty desk once more he saw Alan Gates putting the telephone down and looking flustered.

'What's up, Boss?'

'I promised George Jackson I'd give him a phone call if we had a tip-off. But it seems he was the one who *gave* the tip-off. He could have saved time by coming to us directly and telling Robert Pardoe later. I don't think I trust that man.'

The drive to Belfast took thirty-five minutes. As Slick drove, the Boss and Karl checked the street map. 'Three cars at the front and one covering the back. Sound good to you, Boss? Any improvements you'd like to make?' Karl watched the young man's face as he studied the map.

'No, keep it simple. The boys have had enough practice.'

It was true. They had practised this manoeuvre, and many more, hundreds of times in the training village at Ballykinler.

'Shall I do the orders, or will you?' Karl queried.

The Boss nodded. 'You do them, Karl. This is your operation.'

Karl settled the map book on his lap and operated the radio. 'All stations, this is Alpha, listen in. The target is 57 Prospect Street. However we will have to cover 55 and 53 until we hit lucky. Okay start points.'

'Bravo, you will move in from the Cannon Hill Street end. Charlie, cover the back. Alpha and Whisky will move in together from the Prospect Street end.' Karl wanted all three cars to arrive in front of the houses at the same time. 'Keep the approach speed down. Let's make it look normal.' He paused to look at his watch. 'Make sure you're all at your start points by three o'clock on the nose. Time now . . . wait, wait . . . two-seventeen. If any car is held up let everybody know, so we can reset the run at the house.'

'Okay, when we stop Bravo de-bus and go straight for 57. Take out the door with the sledgehammer, then remain where you are and cover the street. Roger that?'

'Bravo Roger.'

'Whisky, slow down and tuck in behind Slick as we pass by. Stay behind us and enter the house with Alpha crew. We take the upstairs, you take the downstairs. Roger that?'

'That's a Roger.'

'Charlie, de-bus as close as possible around the back and get up to the rear door. Do not enter the house, but apprehend anyone leaving. Roger that?'

'That's a Roger.'

Soon they were in Belfast, close to the Falls Road area.

'Keep the speed down.'

'Nine, this is Alpha. Are you monitoring our position? Over.'

'Alpha Roger. Pardoe and Jackson are here.'

Karl looked at the Boss in the back. 'They're all waiting for the curtain to go up. Let's hope they enjoy the show!'

'Charlie position?'

'Hanging back, ready to move.'

'Bravo, this is Alpha moving into Prospect Street now. One hundred metres.'

'Bravo, that's a Roger. We see you.'

'All units stand by.'

Smoothly, as they approached the house, Slick let Bravo move in a little ahead of them. 'Do you want to be first up the stairs, Boss, or shall I do the honours?' Karl already had the car door open.

'Hell, I'm the leader round here. Just follow my dust!' the Boss said with confidence.

'Go! Go! Go!' Karl yelled into the radio. Instantly, a large car came directly towards them at high speed. Bravo came straight at them, then braked abruptly and all four doors burst open simultaneously.

The two men nearest the house leaped towards the front door of number 57, their huge sledgehammers already raised. As they thundered down on the fragile wooden door, the other two men adopted covering positions behind the car. While Karl watched this happen, Slick pulled their car to a halt. 'Now!' he shouted, and the three of them baled out.

Karl was on the street, bent low and running full speed for the door, the Boss and Slick half a step in front of him. The door finally swung open under the onslaught of Bravo's sledgehammers. Directly in front of them lay the stairs and a hallway. The Boss dived for the stairs, taking the first four steps in a single bound, with Slick just behind him.

The burst of automatic fire came totally unexpectedly tearing into the wall. Splinters of plaster showered over them and the noise was deafening.

'Up, Up!' Karl screamed at the Boss, who was just standing there. His body seemed to block the whole stairs, and Slick was holding him up. Then Karl watched in horror as the Boss's body fell backwards, his weight pulling him and Slick down together. With a dull thudding sound they came to rest on the floor at the bottom. Instinctively Karl returned the fire, spraying the whole area at the top of the stairs. His arm arched as he threw a black cylindrical object. Immediately the top of the stairs erupted in a crescendo of light and sound, as the Royal Ordnance G60 stun grenade developed its full thirty thousand candlepower.

Through the noise and blinding light Karl raced up the stairs and on to the small landing. Quickly he rolled, crouched into a ball, ready to move again. There were two doors to his right and one at the end of the landing. The noise of the stun grenade was gone, and in the stillness Karl heard crying. It was the sound of a baby.

Slick had dragged himself from under Alan Gates's body and limped upstairs. Now, as he sat hunched on the top step, Karl noticed him for the first time.

'How's the Boss?'

Slick just shook his head.

'What about you? Are you okay, old buddy?' Karl could see that Slick was far from okay, but the American was tough and would see it through.

'What have we got here?' Slick asked. He too could hear the crying sound.

'I'm not sure, but babies don't fire Kalashnikovs. There's someone else in there too ... Are you sure the Boss is dead?'

'He's dead,' Slick said flatly.

'Shit! *Shit!*' First it came out softly, then again in white-hot rage. 'You bastards are going to die!' Karl screamed, pulling the trigger and sending a hail of lead hammering into the door at the end of the landing.

'Stop, stop, please stop! I have a child in here,' came a desperate cry from the first door. It was a woman's voice.

'Stay calm, Karl. Get your act together.' Slick was shaking him.

Slowly Karl responded, and spoke into the radio. 'Whisky, what have you got down there?'

'Alpha, this is Whisky. Clear down here. Two made it out the back, Charlie has them. The Boss is totalled.'

'Okay, we have at least one armed. The problem is he has a woman and child in there. Tom, organize a security cordon around here. This could take some time, and the locals are going to turn nasty.'

'That's a Roger.'

Karl stood up and looked at Slick, then down past him to where the Boss lay upside down and twisted at the bottom of the stairs. His head sat in a pool of dark blood. Karl could not believe that the spark of life had gone for ever out of this young man. He felt like shouting at him, 'Get up, you stupid bastard, you have a lifetime in front of you!' Instead, as the hate boiled within Karl, he turned his attention back to the bedroom door and the immediate problem.

'You have two minutes to send out the woman and child, together with your weapons. You will then come out yourself, backwards and with your hands clasped behind your neck. Do you understand?'

There was a muffled conversation in the room and then the woman called out: 'He says he'll kill us if we move.' She sounded terrified, and the baby started to cry again.

'Don't let this get drawn out, Karl,' Slick murmured cautiously.

'One minute! If he doesn't kill you, we will.' Karl spoke with venom, and then waited . . . 'Time's up. Stun grenades coming in. Get down!'

'No, wait. I'll do as you say.' It was the man's voice this time.

'Be very careful, my friend. Send the woman and child out first.'

There was some more muttering which Karl could only half hear. Then the woman spoke. 'I'm coming out now.'

The door opened and a hand came out, bearing a Kalashnikov assault rifle. The woman looked into Karl's eyes, and threw the weapon away from her as if it was diseased.

'I'm going back to get my child,' she said nervously.

Karl nodded and she disappeared once more. There was more muttering and then once more she stood in the doorway, this time holding a blanket in which she had wrapped the child. She moved to go past Karl.

'Wait. Take the baby out of the blanket. Do it!'

She trembled as her hand reached into the folds of the blanket and produced a pistol. Without saying anything, she let the heavy metal object fall from her shaking grasp. Her eyes looked with sadness and fear at Karl. 'Please, he made me . . . you have no excuse to kill him now, he has no weapon.'

'He's your husband?'

She nodded and moved past Slick, going quickly down the stairs. Karl heard her cry out as she saw the Boss's bloodstained body lying at the foot of the stairs.

'Whisky, one woman and child coming down. Hold.'

'That's a Roger, we have her.'

Karl turned his attention to the man. 'Okay, come out backwards with your hands clasped behind your neck. Do it now!' Slick stood ready, moving to the other side of the door as it opened.

Slowly the man shuffled backwards into the doorway.

'Turn and lie face down on the floor, and spread your legs.'

He quickly complied and the moment he was flat on the floor Karl said gruffly to Slick, 'Plasticuff the bastard.'

He pulled the thin length of plastic from around his waist and made a quick loop. Pulling the man's hands together behind his back, the American slipped the loop over them and locked it tight.

'Check the room, Slick.'

Disappearing inside, he returned almost immediately. 'Bingo! Six AKs and ammo. The floorboards are still up and there's no one else here.'

'Okay, let's get this piece of shit downstairs.' They both got hold of the man and heaved him to his feet, steadying him just at the top of the stairs. Once more Karl looked down at the Boss's body. In anger he took hold of the man's collar and forced him forward, balancing him precariously on the top step.

'Look down there. That's the man you've just killed – he was a good man.' With a mighty shove, Karl pushed him down the stairs. His feet missed the first three steps completely and then he went crashing down the rest, rolling over and over before coming to a sudden, sickening stop at the bottom. With bitter irony his head ended up next to that of the Boss, whose blood stuck to the man's face as he lay there writhing in agony.

Karl turned to Slick. 'Clumsy bastard. I hope he didn't hurt himself.'

Slick bent and picked up the rifle and pistol that the woman had surrendered. 'We should have killed the bastard.' For once he was not smiling.

'I hope you're fucking satisfied! How the hell are you going to explain this one – go on, tell me, you stupid bastard!' The unpredictable side of Karl Leathers was now brimming to the surface and his voice was thick with anger. His fists were balled and he felt like smashing them into Jackson's face.

'Karl, please calm down.' Robert Pardoe spoke pleadingly, trying to play the mediator. 'Go over what happened again.'

'Ask him – he's the one who always seems to have the answers,' he replied contemptuously. 'Secret Service? If you represent the Secret Service – God help us!' Karl spat the words accusingly at Jackson. 'Through your fuck-up you've killed a good man. How many more have to die before you find those weapons?'

Jackson did not respond, but his silence only served to fuel Karl's anger. In a flash he had crossed the few feet between them, grabbed the civil servant by the lapels of his overcoat and propelled him backwards until he slammed hard into the office wall. For the first time in years George Jackson felt frightened.

'No, Karl – leave him.' Robert Pardoe forced himself physically between the two men. 'Let him go, Karl. Let him go.'

Slowly regaining control Karl did so, but his eyes never left Jackson's face. 'Go and find your own fucking weapons, Mr Jackson!' With that he spun on his heel and stormed out of the room.

4

Watching and Waiting

Karl had barely returned to Portadown from Control when the signaller handed him the message. He had shown it to Slick, who had proceeded to read it out loud for everyone's benefit.

' "From OC Hereford Garrison. Priority, Leathers is to RTU immediately. Stop." Short and to the point, old buddy. I think you're in the shit!' he said cheerfully, handing the signal back to Karl.

'Drive me to the airport, Slick. I'll catch the next shuttle.'

Karl arrived back in Hereford at around six that evening. Physically and emotionally exhausted after the events of the past few days, and now unsure of his future, he dumped his bags at home and decided to get drunk.

Home was a small two-bedroom flat about a mile from the centre of Hereford, within easy walking distance of Bradbury Lines, the SAS camp. The flat had one other outstanding feature: it overlooked the River Wye. This was Karl's refuge, his place of peace and quiet after the turmoil of action. Sometimes he had been posted away for more than six months at a time. But every time he returned the flat was clean and warm and there was fresh food in the fridge. This small miracle occurred through the kind efforts of his neighbours.

Recently retired, from the outset the friendly couple had

spoilt Karl. Now, two years on, they were the guardians of his sanctuary. All it took was one telephone call, and even after months away Karl would find the place as if he had left it just a few hours earlier. But apart from reimbursement for food and other essentials, the couple would take nothing. In the end Karl had bought them two holiday tickets to Spain, and the following year he had sent them to Paris; and so the pattern was set.

He had rung this time from Aldergrove, and true to form the flat was immaculate. A note had been pushed under the door: 'Did not expect you back so suddenly. Fresh bread, eggs and bacon in the fridge. If you need anything else, knock on our door.'

What he needed, thought Karl, was a drink. He made straight for the King's Head, a favourite SAS pub close to the city centre. He had just ordered his first pint when a man's voice addressed him. 'What the hell are you doing back here, Karl? Last thing I heard you were on to a good thing over the water.' A small, stocky man was standing next to him at the bar.

'Geordie! Where the hell did you come from?' At the sight of this friendly face Karl snapped out of his mood, glad to have some genial company.

To all appearances, the man who stood before him looked short and insignificant. But Karl knew better. Two years ago Geordie had found out that his wife was having an affair with another SAS soldier, a somewhat larger, tougher character. The affair came to a sudden halt one bright spring morning outside the guardroom. Geordie's squadron were at the nearby armoury drawing weapons for firing practice on the range. Geordie had placed a full magazine into his rifle. Then, with a dramatic crashing sound that attracted everyone's attention, he had cocked his weapon, feeding a live round into the chamber. Calmly he had walked over to where his wife's lover stood talking in a group of other soldiers. They saw him coming, and parted as Geordie pushed the barrel of the weapon into the man's belly.

'If you go near her one more time I'll kill you – do you understand?' The fire in Geordie's eyes showed that he meant every word. For what seemed like a decade the two men stood in silence, with everyone watching but declining to interfere.

'I understand. Sorry, Geordie.' And the incident was over. No one had ever underestimated Geordie Baxter's size again – including his wife, whom he divorced two months later.

By eight o'clock they were well into their third beer and Karl was telling him about the death of the Boss and the bust-up with George Jackson. 'They made a real fuck-up of the whole thing. Why couldn't they just have left the thing to us? We'd have had the bastards by now.' The bitterness surfaced in Karl's voice.

'I really am sorry about the Boss.' Geordie looked at Karl for a moment, then playfully punched him on the shoulder. 'Come on, mate, cheer up. I've got a date with a fantastic girl tonight, and she's bringing a friend – you might get lucky.'

But Karl did not feel lucky as he recollected the problems of the past few days. Then he realized he was letting it all get on top of him, and ordered two more beers. He let the general sense of warmth and enjoyment drift over him and, feeling better, turned to continue the conversation with Geordie. The words never left his mouth. Two stunning young women had walked through the door and were heading straight towards them.

'Hello, ladies, and how are we this evening?' Geordie moved forward to greet them.

Both girls were in their early twenties, and Karl thought he vaguely knew one of them. He seemed to recall that her name was Carol. The other he had never seen before. Carol smiled at Geordie, then turned to Karl.

'Hi there! I'm Carol and this is Gail. You must excuse me, I know your face but I've forgotten your name.'

'It's Karl – Karl Leathers.' He turned his attention to Carol's friend. 'Hello, Gail. Maybe I've been away too long but I don't recall seeing you around these parts before.' Karl felt ill at ease, and he was sure his words sounded corny.

'I've just been posted in,' said Gail.

Her smile was warm and her perfume heady, the combination triggering an odd feeling in the pit of his stomach. 'Posted in'? Then it dawned on him where he had seen Carol before – she was a policewoman. 'So how do you like Hereford?' Karl scratched to make conversation.

'Never mind the chat up. What would you two ladies like to drink?' Geordie broke the spell, and just to let Karl know who was with who he slipped his arm around Carol's waist.

The arrival of the drinks broke the ice and from that point the evening got decidedly better. Both women were high-spirited, lively and full of fun, and after a few more rounds they all moved on for a meal at a local Indian restaurant.

But as they left and headed for the taxi rank, Karl's blues came back. He desperately needed company, so, taking a chance, he pulled Gail to one side. Putting his arms around her slim waist, he looked into her upturned face and gave her his best come-to-bed-with-me smile. For a moment they stared at each other.

'Do you have to go?' Karl asked, his eyes challenging hers. 'We could go back to my place and make lots of little military policemen.' He felt foolish the moment he had suggested it.

For a while Gail just looked at him, studying his face. She slowly shook her head, gently pushing herself free. 'If you play your cards right, you could take me out for a drink again tomorrow night. Do you have a car?'

Although she had freed herself, she still held on to his hand. A sign of hope, thought Karl. 'Sure,' he said, grateful that his neighbours' kindnesses extended to running his car regularly in his absence, to stop the battery going flat. 'What time shall I meet you and where?'

'At the King's Head again, say about seven.' Gail reached up and kissed Karl fully on the mouth. The warmth of her swept over him and his arms enfolded her. Then their lips parted, yet for a second longer they held their embrace.

'Come on, Gail. Time to go.' Carol and Geordie were already in the back of the taxi.

'Don't worry – I'll see you tomorrow,' she whispered. Then, turning quickly, she got into the taxi.

At least one part of his life was showing some promise, thought Karl as he walked home along the river. Tomorrow was another day.

Somewhere in the darkness of his dreams there was a phone persistently ringing. As he awoke the sound continued and, still half asleep, he fumbled for the handset.

'Where the hell have you been? I've been ringing you for ages.' The adjutant sounded annoyed. 'The colonel wants to see you at eleven o'clock.'

'Sorry. I only got back from Northern Ireland last night, and I decided to drown my sorrows.' Karl's mind started to clear as he forced himself to shake off the last vestiges of alcohol-induced sleep.

The adjutant's voice still sounded unsympathetic as he warned him, 'You should know by now not to rock the boat. There are those in Whitehall who just love to see members of the SAS in trouble.'

'I take it I'm really in the shit, then,' said Karl miserably.

'Not too deep, but the colonel's taken a lot of flak on your behalf and he's not a happy man. I suggest you at least try to look apologetic when you see him. After he's finished with you I want to see you in my office. Now get your act together and be in camp for eleven.' Abruptly the line went dead.

Karl put the phone down and looked at his watch – it was almost 9.30. He had plenty of time for a shower and some black coffee before walking the short distance into camp. As he got out of bed the sudden movement set up a mushy singing noise in the back of his head, and he realized that the drink from last night had not completely left his system.

Then he smiled. It had been a good night out, and despite what might happen today at least he would be seeing Gail again tonight. The idea warmed him.

* * *

The headquarters building in the centre of Bradbury Lines was known familiarly as the Kremlin. For security reasons the whole sector was tightly cordoned off by a high wire fence with only one entry/exit point, which was constantly monitored by closed-circuit TV cameras. Karl pushed the button on the security gate and looked up into the eye of the camera. With a loud clicking sound, the gate opened. Into the lions' den, he thought.

Moments later he walked into the large general office. The chief clerk was on the telephone, but looked up as Karl approached. 'He's here now sir, just arrived.' Then, replacing the receiver, he motioned to go through the large door to his right.

Closing the door firmly behind him, Karl marched smartly to the centre of the room. 'Staff Sergeant Leathers, sir.' He stood stiffly to attention, facing the large desk, as a feeling of dread washed over him and gave the lie to his calm, composed exterior.

Seated opposite him was a man whom he admired, Colonel Alex McLean. Standing stiffly next to the colonel stood Regimental Sergeant Major Bill Wilson. Between them they made a formidable pair and both men stared at Karl, their unhappiness clearly written on their faces.

'Have you any idea how much flak I have taken because of you, Leathers?' The colonel paused, his normally smooth manner giving way to an unaccustomed brusquesness. 'You cannot go around telling senior civil servants how to do their job, never mind violently threatening them – do you understand?'

'Yes, sir.' Karl was beginning to think that Jackson was out of line kicking up all this fuss – after all, most of the fuck-ups had been of his doing. But wisely he decided to keep his mouth shut as the colonel continued.

'I don't think you do – not fully, anyway. George Jackson is a very powerful man with a lot of political connections. The only reason he's holding off is that you may just have been correct in your tactical assumption. But certainly not in your actions.' Colonel McLean flipped open a folder on his desk. 'Luckily for you Captain Gates sent me a part report just prior to his death.' The colonel's voice softened a little as he mentioned the Boss. 'Your only saving grace is that he agreed with you.' The hard tone returned. 'However, it does not change the fact that you must obey orders. If you have a problem like this in Ireland, you will sort it out through me. Do I make myself clear?'

'Yes, sir. Sorry, sir. It's just that Jackson got it all wrong from day one – the Boss's death was the final straw.' Karl paused, and then without thinking added, 'Jackson's such a smug bastard, sir.'

That was it, he thought, he'd really messed things up now. But with a sudden nod of his head the colonel's anger dissipated.

'I can understand your feelings, but in this regiment we train men to a standard that makes other people very nervous, and your actions only add fuel to their case. Now take a seat and give me the whole story. Start from when you found the weapons.'

It took Karl twenty minutes to go over the whole affair. Neither the colonel nor the RSM interrupted until he came to the assault on the house in Belfast.

'Tell me again how it happened.' The colonel's head was bent and his chin rested on his fingers as if in prayer.

'We hit the house as planned. The first car arrived just in front of us and their crew took out the door. The Boss was on the near side and entered the house first. He, Slick and I were to clear the upstairs, Tom and Merv were to see to the ground floor. The third car went round the back to protect the rear.' The colonel knew the procedure, but Karl thought it was best to make it clear. 'The Boss and Slick had started up the stairs just as I entered the front door. Next thing there's a burst of automatic fire and both were knocked backwards. I fired blindly up the stairs, but the bastard had gone. It turns out he was in the bedroom with a woman and child – his own wife and kid, we discovered later.' Karl paused to see if either man had any questions, but there were none. 'Well, that's about it, sir. We got the bastard out and Slick cuffed him. While he was doing that, I had time to take a long look at the Boss lying in a pool of blood at the bottom of the stairs. I got mad.'

'So you threw a handcuffed man down the stairs?' The Colonel looked questioningly at Karl. His manner changed again, becoming aggressive.

'Not exactly, sir . . . but I did give him a little push.'

'A little push!' the colonel bellowed. Grabbing a medical form from the open file on the desk before him he waved it at Karl. 'The man has two broken ribs and a three-inch cut on the back of his head.' There was a forbidding silence before he continued. 'I take it you are not admitting to any of this and there are no witnesses?' the colonel enquired.

'No sir. Slick Middleton was with me. The man struggled at the top of the stairs and slipped.'

The colonel did not believe Karl for one moment – but it was the answer he wanted to hear. 'That Yank would swear on a stack of Bibles that black was white if you asked him to. Thank God his tour with us is almost over and we can ship him back to the States! Okay, Staff Sergeant Leathers. The squadron is not due back for another month, and with those RPGs loose on the streets of Northern Ireland they are going to be very busy. You, on the other hand, will remain in the UK. You are to attend a course with the E4 surveillance unit. Interestingly enough, it was George Jackson who recommended you for it – no doubt to impress on the SAS how the professionals work. The adjutant has the details.'

Karl stood up to leave, but the colonel's voice stopped him.

'I had you tipped for better things, Karl, and you've let me down. Don't do it again.' The few words of reprimand stung hard.

'No, colonel.' Karl wanted to say more, to explain himself better somehow, but there was no opportunity. The meeting was over.

The two men watched silently as Karl Leathers closed the door behind him. They had known each other for many years since their early days patrolling the jungles of Borneo and Malaya, and, despite their difference in rank, they were closer than many brothers. Now, with Karl gone, they were alone and all rank was forgotten. The colonel looked up at the big man who was now sitting casually on the edge of his desk. 'What do you think, Bill? I seem to remember you being a bit of a rebel in your day. Did I do right keeping Leathers in the regiment?'

'If it had been you and me in the same situation, Alex, how would we have reacted? It's a pity he didn't kill the bastard. Karl Leathers is a good SAS soldier – too good to throw away.'

The colonel nodded, putting the matter behind him. 'Let's just hope we manage to find those RPG rockets before the IRA start using them again.'

As Karl walked through the general office that controlled the very heart of the SAS, a door marked 'Adjutant' opened and a tall, lean figure stood in the doorway beckoning him over.

'Bad as that, was it? Good! Serves you right.' The adjutant adopted a holier-than-thou look. 'Come on in, I have a job for you.'

Karl pushed past him and took the offered seat. As long as you didn't step too far out of line, the adjutant was a decent guy.

'So tell me all about it!' he said. 'Did the old man lay into you? Quite right too – you got him a hell of a ticking-off from some high-powered sod in Whitehall.' He scrutinized Karl's face, on which a look of embarrassment still lingered.

Karl explained about George Jackson and the Security Services taking over the operation. 'It has to be said that that arsehole, Jackson – if that's his real name – is responsible for Boss Gates's death. What should I have done?' Karl enquired. 'Given in gracefully? Besides, we haven't heard the last of it yet.'

'I'm sorry about Alan – hell of a way to go. My wife went round to sit with Susan Gates when the Padre broke the news.

113

She took it hard – only been married five months . . . Anyway,' he went on, changing the subject, 'now to you.'

'The colonel said something about working with E4 surveillance.'

'Correct. We've received a request for your services on a training course with E4 surveillance section in London. I think it's Mr Jackson's way of showing you that his department are not as bad as you think. On the other hand, it's also a way of saying that they are in charge. But look on the bright side – it could do you some good, I hear that E4 is quite excellent, so you may learn something.'

'How long is the course and where do I report?' Karl was by now resigned to the fact that he was not going back to join the boys in Northern Ireland.

'Be outside Euston Square tube station, the Gower Place entrance, on Monday morning at nine-thirty. You will be met.' Smiling, he handed Karl a small envelope. 'The pay office knows about it, and lucky old you will get local lodging allowance. Okay?'

'No problems. Am I free until Monday?' Karl asked, a touch of hope in his voice.

'Sure, the less we see of you around here for a while the better. By the way, Alan's funeral is on Friday, ten o'clock at St Martin's church. Buffet and drinks in the Paladrine Club after.'

'Yes, I know. I'll be there. I also intend to see Susan Gates later today. Is that okay?'

'Just be careful what you tell her.' The smile had gone completely from the adjutant's face.

It was not a visit that Karl relished. Between returning from Oman and being posted to Northern Ireland Captain Alan Gates had married Susan Howard, the only daughter of a wealthy Norfolk landowner. It had been a society wedding at the church in the grounds of her family estate and the boys from Captain Gates's troop had not been invited, despite several pointed hints.

But Karl had secretly negotiated with Alan Gates's father, and the entire Mountain Troop had driven over to Norfolk. As the ceremony ended and the bells rang out, the Boss and his new bride stepped out of the church to find fourteen men in the smart dark blue SAS mess dress uniform, forming a guard of honour with white snow skis. It marked the final acceptance of Alan Gates by the men of his troop, and was an intensely proud moment for him.

After their honeymoon Alan and Susan had returned to Hereford, to officers' married quarters. Two weeks later the troop had been invited to a house-warming party, and had bought Susan Gates a King Charles spaniel puppy as a present. The gift had made her cry, and from that moment she took the boys to her heart.

'Yes, can I help you?' The lady who now stood in the doorway seemed very annoyed at being disturbed.

'My name is Staff Sergeant Karl Leathers. May I see Susan for a moment, please?' Then, to allay any further questions, he added, 'Her husband was my troop officer . . . I was with him at the time.'

The stern look faded and was replaced with one of understanding and recognition. 'I'm Susan's mother – we met briefly at the wedding. Please do come in.'

Karl followed her into the sitting room. Susan Gates was sitting on the sofa, the dog curled up beside her, but as Karl entered she stood up and ran into his arms, laying her head on his chest and letting the tears roll down her face. Karl could feel the grief racking her body as she clung despairingly to him.

'Tell me he's not dead, Karl . . . Please tell me he's coming through the door in a few moments . . . I loved him – I really loved him so much.' The words were sobbed out, and it was all Karl could do to hold back his own tears. Gently, he lifted Susan away from him and sat her back down on the sofa, moving the dog and sitting beside her.

'No matter what we say, or what we do, Alan will always be with us. A spirit that strong cannot die.' Karl held Susan's hand as he spoke.

'I know he'll never leave *me*, Karl – I'm pregnant.' With a quiet assurance she looked up at him. 'Now I'll always have him with me.'

Alan smiled at the news. 'Then part of Alan lives on – he would have liked that.'

By seven that evening he had met Gail in the King's Head. After one swift drink there Karl had suggested that they drive out to a small country pub he knew. The evening was chilly, and the Tram Inn at Eardisley had a large log fire burning.

The two of them sat close together on a deep settee and relaxed in the warmth. Gail talked about her career as a policewoman, and in turn Karl dispelled the myths which surrounded the SAS. At closing time he had shown a little more tact than on the previous evening.

'Fancy a nightcap at my place? We can sit and watch the river by night.'

Karl was genuinely surprised at Gail's answer: 'I have no objection!' Her big brown eyes looked straight at him, then she laid her head on his shoulder and continued, 'Please don't get me wrong – I don't make a habit of going home with everyone I meet. Geordie told me a lot about you on the way home last night. He sang your praises. Said you were a genuine guy and didn't mess around. I don't want to be forward, but since coming to Hereford I've been more than a little bit lonely.'

Karl was taken aback, and struggled to find the right words. 'Gail, I don't fall in love after two nights, and I doubt if you do either . . . but I do feel a special warmth towards you.' Suddenly it all seemed to be too serious, so he laughed and said, 'Apart from all that, you shouldn't believe everything people tell you. I've been away in bloody Northern Ireland for three months – are you sure you're quite ready for this?'

'Then take me home, soldier, and I'll kiss it better.' Small shivers starting going down Karl's spine.

Back at the flat he took her into the lounge and, without switching on the lights, guided her to the big picture window. They stood side by side looking down at the river and over to the playing fields beyond. The water sparkled in the moonlight, throwing up a million tiny reflections that danced across its surface. On the far bank a bird dipped its beak into the dark waters before silently slipping away into the nearby reeds.

'It's wonderful!' Gail was completely absorbed by the setting. 'How on earth did you find this place?'

'It wasn't easy. Sometimes I spend hours just sitting by this window. But in truth, very few people come here.' Karl changed the subject. 'Drink? I've got a couple of bottles of champagne chilling in the fridge.'

'I'm impressed. Do you always treat your ladies to champagne?' Gail enquired, sounding out the competition.

As Karl went into the kitchen he replied, 'I've just told you, very few people come up here. Now put some music on, please.' Carefully he removed the wire from the bottle, pulling out the cork with a small popping sound. As he did so, the gentle deep rhythm of the Platters singing 'Smoke Gets in Your Eyes' started to drift in from the lounge.

Karl handed Gail a glass of champagne and made a toast: 'Here's to absent friends and the beginning of new life.'

'That's a funny thing to say.' Gail was puzzled.

'It's private – I'll tell you about it another time. Right now I'm going to take you and this bottle to bed.'

'Would you give me a moment, please. And point me in the right direction?' Gail asked, kicking off her shoes and kissing Karl lightly on the lips.

'Bedroom's at the end of the passage. You've got two minutes, then I'm coming to get you.' Karl continued to sip his drink as Gail slipped out of the room.

When Karl entered the bedroom he found it in darkness. She was standing by the open window in the moonlight, her fine-spun, dusky hair moving slightly as the breeze blew it against her bold, vital face. She had removed most of her clothes, revealing her lithe, shapely body. She pointed down at the river and whispered, 'I have never seen such beauty.'

'Neither have I,' said Karl, his eyes firmly fixed on the vision before him. 'Neither have I.' He reached out and wrapped his arms around her waist. 'Having second thoughts?' he enquired.

'No. But it's so peaceful here – just hold me a while.'

They stayed locked together, gazing out over the river. Then slowly Karl turned her round and her head tilted to one side, bringing her mouth up to meet his kiss. Their lips touched, and Gail's tongue flicked over Karl's with the lightness of a butterfly's wing. For what seemed like a lifetime they melted together, and then Gail's voice murmured softly in his ear, 'Make love to me, Karl. Very, very slowly.'

Swiftly he undressed, dropping his clothes to the floor. When he turned round she was already lying on the bed. His heart pounded as he saw her perfect naked body stretched invitingly before him. Karl leaned over the bed and gently kissed her, then lay down beside her.

Softly, as her dark hair fanned out on the white pillow, Karl began to kiss her face. Starting at her eyes, and then moving to the tip of her nose, his lips tenderly brushed all her exquisite features. As he reached Gail's neck his tongue flicked out, tasting her flesh. Gradually Karl progressed downwards, coursing over her firm round breasts, across her flat belly, until finally dipping down to the small triangle of black silky hair. By now Gail was fast approaching ecstasy, relishing the smooth, sensitive movements. 'Love me now Karl, quickly.' Her voice was soft and deep.

Gently he rose to cover Gail's body with his own. As he did so her legs parted and she willingly bent her knees, bringing them almost to her chest to expose her dark, secret depths. And then they were one, meshed together as their bodies moved in rhythm. Outside the window the dark waters of the river flowed endlessly on, its shadowy surface still shimmering vividly.

Afterwards, they lay silent on the bed. Neither of them spoke, fearful of breaking the magic that still bound them. Finally Karl reached for his glass and took a mouthful of champagne. Rolling back towards Gail, he placed his lips on hers and delicately dribbled the liquid into her mouth. When he had finished he put his cheek next to hers and said, 'Let me know when you're ready to do that again.'

She turned to him, her eyes twinkling. 'Any time you like. Don't ever stop loving me – not ever.'

The traffic roared continually down Euston Road like some great noisy metal reptile. God, I hate the city, thought Karl, trying to ignore the grimy pavements and fume-laden air. He had been waiting for over ten minutes, standing against the railings that prevented the herds of commuters from spilling out of the Tube on to the busy road. Despite his thick sheepskin jacket Karl was getting cold. It was now 9.35, and whoever was supposed to be meeting him was late. Picking up his suitcase, he decided to do one more circuit of the other exits from the station. His path took him past a little café which looked warm and inviting inside. Sod it! he thought: let's have a cup of coffee.

Karl was halfway through the door when a hand fell on his shoulder. His head snapped round in response to the sudden shock of physical contact, his body tense and ready for swift action. Then he relaxed and smiled as he recognized the man standing before him.

'Sorry I'm late, Karl. How are you, you old bastard?'

'Tony Kelly! – What the hell are you doing here? It's ages since I last saw you.' Karl dropped his suitcase and took hold of Tony's outstretched hand, pumping it enthusiastically.

They had first worked together shortly after Karl had joined the SAS. For sixteen weeks they had sat side by side in the same classroom learning Morse code. At times the intensity of the course and the constant *dit-dit, dar-dar* sounds had brought on temporary derangement, relieved only by taking the afternoon off and going to the pub. Then quite abruptly, some eight years back, Tony had disappeared without explanation. Karl had missed him: he had been a real rebel and one hell of a womanizer.

'I couldn't believe it when they told me some SAS guy by the name of Karl Leathers was coming. They also said you'd been a naughty boy just lately, going for our poor Mr Jackson like that!' Tony grinned. 'Come on, we're late already,' he said, grabbing Karl's suitcase. 'It's not far.

'Hang on. Are you trying to tell me that the great Tony Kelly works for British Intelligence? I just don't imagine you as a surveillance operator – I had no idea that things had got so bad!' Happy with the returned verbal slap, Karl fell in step beside Tony.

As they walked along, he enlightened Karl about his hurried departure from the SAS. Unbeknown to his mates at the time Tony had managed to get a lady in Hereford pregnant; unfortunately she was married to a local councillor. To avoid any further recriminations or embarrassment to the regiment he had decided to resign and seek his fortune in London. Things had not gone very well for him and he had found himself on the dole, living in a cheap bedsit. Some five weeks had passed before two men had appeared at his door and offered him a job.

'Would you credit it?' Tony made a wild gesture to emphasize the point. 'In they marched, bold as brass, and asked if I'd like a job working for the government. When I asked what doing, they simply informed me about all the checking-up they had done on me, and what a patriotic person I was. The job, they said, involved security work. Well, to cut a long story short it beat the hell out of being on the dole, so I took it. Now you see before you one happily married civil servant.'

'You're married? *You?*' Karl looked in amazement at his old friend.

'Married with two kids. Comes to us all, you know. How about you?'

'Not yet, no time – but I've met a really nice girl recently and she's keeping me sane.' The memories of the past few days returned vividly to Karl and he realized that he was missing Gail already.

'Christ, your suitcase is bloody heavy!' complained Tony. 'What the hell have you got in here?' He stopped at a set of traffic lights and, while they waited to cross the busy street, pointed at a large tower block opposite. 'There, my friend is where we are going.' As Karl looked up, he continued. 'This should be a good couple of weeks. By the way, I told them not to book you any accommodation – you're staying at my place. Just think how much lodging allowance you'll save.'

'Tony, things are getting better by the minute.'

The principal function of the three-week course was to assess and train new recruits for the British Security Services surveillance division, known as E4. As Tony and Karl entered the classroom on that first morning they saw that the seven other candidates, five men and three women, were already assembled. What surprised Karl was their age range, from about twenty-five to forty. Taking a place at the back of the room, Karl studied his fellow course members. It was evident that the last thing a good surveillance operator needed was any outstanding feature; here, greyness and ordinariness were assets.

For most of that day they remained in the classroom, where the various techniques currently in use were explained and backed up with videos and slides. By the time they left, Karl's respect for British government surveillance operations had increased greatly.

He and Tony then joined the mass exodus from central London and took the Tube north to Mill Hill. After a short walk Tony turned down a pathway towards a small semi-detached house, and as they approached the door it was opened by a woman who had clearly been keeping an eye out for them. She looked much taller than Tony, with long blonde hair, and Karl could not help noticing the sensual figure beneath the simple blue dress.

'Get your eyes off, Leathers! This one is spoken for,' said Tony jokingly, and to emphasize the point he placed a noisy kiss on the woman's lips. 'Mrs Ingrid Miller – meet Karl Leathers.'

Karl took the outstretched hand and was about to shake it when Ingrid's head shot forward and she kissed him on both cheeks in the continental fashion. 'Hello, Karl, welcome to our home. Tony has told me all about you. Please come in.' Her voice was deep and she spoke with a foreign accent.

The two men went into the small sitting room, and a few moments later Ingrid reappeared balancing a tray containing several beers and two glasses. No sooner had she put it down than she disappeared again.

'Does she normally run around after you like this, Tony, or is this just for my benefit?'

'Let me tell you, Karl, if you ever contemplate marriage make sure it's to a German girl. They keep the house immaculate, cook food fit for a king, and are more fun in bed than any woman I have ever known!'

Karl smiled and took a sip from his beer. 'You just like being waited on . . . So what are we doing tonight?'

'Ingrid has cooked us a meal. After that you and I can go down to the local. It's nice round here – you'll like it.'

'I'm sure I will,' came the sincere response.

For the rest of that first week they concentrated on foot work, operating in teams of three. Every day they would pick on an unsuspecting member of the public and just follow him or her. In the second week they were introduced to vehicle surveillance. Small family cars were used, but with one difference; the engines had been ripped out and replaced with the most powerful unit the engineers could cram beneath the bonnet. The cars were kept deliberately dirty and the number plates changed to those of earlier years, in order to make the cars seem older than they were. Vehicle surveillance was an area of which Karl had a real understanding, for unlike the other recruits he had done plenty of this kind of work in Northern Ireland.

Finally they had broken down into four teams of three, each consisting of two new recruits and an instructor. Karl had finished up alongside Harry, the oldest guy on the course, with Tony as their instructor. Every course has a rebel faction, and they were it. Harry Logan could consume beer all day and still preserve a sober appearance. Tony and Karl had made several attempts to outdo him, but to no avail. To Harry's immense satisfaction their surveillance sorties were mostly centred on the beautiful countryside of West Sussex, with all cars meeting up at a pub for lunch. Then it was back to the dusty, windswept London streets once more.

'Okay, ladies and gentlemen, week three,' the chief instructor addressed the class. 'Now this week we will be splitting you up into the same groups, and setting each group a task. Basically you will be allocated a soft, low-grade target. It will be your task to locate, identify and report on all target movements. At the end of the week you will be required to present a full written brief.'

The chief instructor looked at them all and his manner became deliberately serious. 'The targets we have chosen are all real players – minor, I admit, but nevertheless players in a very dangerous game.' He let this sink in before continuing. 'If you think you've been compromised in any way, pull off and consult the group instructor, whose advice you will heed at all times. You will remain in radio contact both with your group and with this office during all operations. Is this understood? Now use what you have been taught, and good luck!'

'Who've we got, Tony?' Harry was trying to take the photograph from him but Tony pulled it away.

'Hang on – I'm the instructor around here! Okay, here we go.' Tony held up the photograph for Harry and Karl to see while he read out the label stuck to the back. 'John Arthur Barkley, born 15 March 1946, Detroit, USA. An official British member of Noraid.' He removed some cards from the envelope in his hand and continued. 'Now for the truth. Believed to be some kind of British IRA quartermaster responsible, it is thought, for supplying weapons from America and Europe directly into Northern Ireland. He has no previous convictions and his direct connection with the IRA is not wholly established. Present whereabouts unknown, but believed to be London. Several reported sightings . . . some at Heathrow, and two at the Cat and Moon public house in the City. That's your lot.'

'I know the Cat and Moon,' confirmed Harry, looking hopefully at the others.

'Let's make a plan first. Then we can go to the pub.' Karl picked up the photo and studied it. 'We could take a quick look round the area tonight – who's for a swift half at about six o'clock? In the meantime, Harry, you check out the phone book and DHSS files. Tony and I will have a chat with the local Special Branch IRA collator to see if we can find where the local boyos are performing at the moment. Let's say we all meet back here around four, before we go to the pub.'

Tony nodded his head. 'Well done, Karl, that sounds good enough to me. But don't forget we need to establish a starting-point. The only thing we can be sure of is what he looks like – he may not be using his real name.'

They split up to go about their tasks. It took Tony and Karl almost half an hour to weave their way through the busy traffic to Cock Lane police station among the banks and tower blocks of the city. It then took another half-hour to locate the Special Branch sergeant who operated from the station. But the good news was that he knew he he his territory really well. And although his information on Barkley was somewhat thin he padded it out well with general background knowledge on the local Irish community.

'Most of the Irish in the area are pleasant enough. They've been away from the Troubles for so long that they only remember the 'Cause' when they've had one drink too many on a Saturday night. To be fair, if the majority of the population were as well behaved as the Irish we wouldn't have half the problems. I can tell you that the Cat and Moon is clean – never any trouble there. The best I can do for you is to keep a look-out for Barkley and ask around discreetly. Where would you like the information sent?'

Tony took out a pen and a scrap of paper. 'This telephone number is good for one week only.'

They were about to leave when the sergeant added, 'There

was a rumour some time ago that John Barkley was seeing a nurse at Bart's – St Bartholomew's Hospital. But nothing was ever confirmed. I can't recall her name – Mary something-or-other.'

'Thanks, we'll check it out.'

'Where to next, Tony?' enquired Karl as they left the building.

'What say we check out passport control at Heathrow? They might give us a lead.' Tony sounded optimistic.

Out at the airport an hour or so later, Tony led Karl swiftly through the crowded transit halls and up a flight of stairs to the first-floor administration level. He stopped at an office marked 'Immigration, Strictly Out Of Bounds' and walked confidently in. Unlike the hustle and bustle of the terminal downstairs, this office was quiet and had an air of neat efficiency. There were several desks in the room, and in one corner, partitioned off by a glass screen, a small alcove which Tony headed for.

A middle-aged woman looked up from a mountain of paperwork as the two men approached. 'Here comes trouble. What can I do for you, Tony?' She smiled a welcome.

'Cathy, may I introduce a new man to you? Karl Leathers.'

The hand was firm and she had the grip of a man, Karl noted.

'Now I'm a busy lady, Kelly, so what do you want?' The tone had become less social and more business-like.

Tony hadn't noticed the signals and said conversationally, 'Karl, if you ever need any information in connection with people's comings and goings, ask this lady.' At last he saw the look on Cathy's face and decided to cut the crap. 'Barkley, John Arthur,' he said hurriedly, adding the few details that he had been given.

'When do you want it by?' enquired Cathy, writing down the name.

'As soon as possible, please. You know the number.'

She smiled once more, this time to indicate a firm but pleasant dismissal, and the two men took their leave.

Back at the office, Harry's hound-dog face greeted them.
'Find anything?' he enquired hopefully.

'Not much – how about you?'

'Nothing. I've drawn a blank at the DHSS – there are two
John Arthur Barkleys listed in this area, both on the dole, but
neither is our man.' Harry sounded dejected.

'Call for you, Tony,' shouted a man a couple of desks
away.

While Tony was talking, Karl told Harry what they had
gleaned from the Special Branch sergeant. 'Not a lot to go on
– the man has good local knowledge, but the best he could
come up with is this possible girlfriend called Mary. She may
be a nurse at St Bartholomew's Hospital.'

Harry groaned. 'There must be hundreds of Irish nurses in
London, and at least half of them will be called Mary!'

Tony rejoined them, rubbing his hands in satisfaction. 'John
Barkley is still using the same name. So far this year he's made
several journeys to Northern Ireland – the last time was less
than a month ago. On that occasion he was accompanied
by a woman with a passport in the name of Mary Langley,
occupation nurse. Bingo!'

'I'm impressed. Where did you dig this up from?' Karl was
genuinely surprised.

'Compliments of our Cathy at airport security – and we have
an address for both of them in Holborn. Harry, get your arse
round to Bart's and find out if they still have a nurse there by
the name of Mary Langley. If so, see what shift she's on.'

'You think Barkley's still seeing her?' Karl asked hopefully.

'I'll bet you ten to one,' said Tony with an air of
confidence.

Karl felt the first sudden rush of excitement at the start of
the chase. Surveillance, he had discovered, was a great game.
Forgetting that Tony had spent his last eight years playing this
game, Karl was impressed by the logical deductions he was
making. He listened intently as his friend continued, 'All the
normal indicators to his whereabouts in our files are either
out-of-date or false – and something tells me this man is up to

no good. So our best start is to pin him down. We'll concentrate on the Holborn area and find Mary Langley.'

Almost two hours later, as Karl and Tony were studying a large street map of London and trying to work out a sensible approach to the problem, Harry returned from the hospital beaming.

'Sister Mary Langley lives in a bedsit in Philip Street – same address she gave to airport security. It's not far from the Hospital and the pub lies in between. The Cat and Moon, it would seem, is a regular hang-out for nurses coming off duty.'

'Well done,' said Tony. 'Did you find out what shift she's on?'

'She'll be off duty at eight this evening,' boasted Harry, who had pulled off a stroke of genius. He had bought a large bunch of flowers and, posing as a delivery man for a local florist, had addressed a card to Sister Mary Langley and personally delivered the flowers to her. She had been delighted. The card carried no sender's name, but it was not uncommon for ex-patients to say thank you with chocolates or flowers in this way. During their brief conversation Harry had been sympathetic about nurses' long hours and low pay. She had opened up to him and told Harry that she finished at 8 p.m.

'Okay, lads it looks as if it's time for that swift drink in the Cat and Moon. After that we'll walk to the hospital and take a look at Mary Langley when she comes off duty.'

It was dark by the time they reached the hospital, and a cold wind had sprung up. All three of them stood on the opposite side of the road, out of sight but close enough to observe the main entrance. It was close to 8.15 before they saw the first group of nurses leave the hospital. Harry scrutinized them going by, but shook his head. Two minutes later a lone nurse appeared in the doorway carrying a bunch of flowers. With Tony just in front of her on the opposite side of the road, they shadowed the nurse as she walked through the lamp-lit streets. As she approached the Cat and Moon she crossed the road and headed for the door.

Karl pressed the small button in his coat pocket and whispered into his radio, 'Tony, it looks like she's going into the pub. You go in first, we'll follow.'

There was a *click-click* in Karl's earpiece, indicating that Tony had heard and understood. Ahead of him he saw Tony open the pub door and enter, some thirty metres in front of Mary Langley.

'Harry, she may recognize you, so stay outside and keep watch. I'll join Tony.' Karl expected a disgruntled reply from his ever-thirsty companion, but all he received was *click-click* of acknowledgement.

Karl saw that Tony had already pushed his way to the bar. Leaving him to buy the drinks, he found a quiet corner from where they could best watch Mary Langley. She had seated herself with a group of people, most of them in nurses' uniform.

A couple with their backs to Karl parted suddenly as Tony did his reversing act through the crowd, trying hard not to spill the beer. Karl reached out to assist. Tony took a mouthful of beer and discreetly indicated two men who had just walked in and were now chattering happily with the nurses – but neither was John Barkley.

Mary stayed at the pub for about an hour, after which they followed her back to her bedsit. It looked a busy house, and it was clear that Mary Langley was not the only nurse living there. They waited a few minutes, but no lights came on to indicate which was Mary's room.

'So what do you want to do?' Tony questioned Harry and Karl as they walked back towards the pub.

'There seems little use in watching the house all night,' said Karl. 'However I wouldn't mind coming back early in the morning – say around six – to see who comes out,' said Karl.

Neither Tony nor Harry made any comment. Karl guessed that surveillance did not start until rather later in Britain, unless it was absolutely necessary!

'We could check out a few more pubs,' Harry butted in. 'It's still only quarter to ten!'

Karl looked at him. 'It's pathetic . . . well, Tony, it's up to you. What will Ingrid say? Shall we treat this old dwarf to one more?'

As they reached the Cat and Moon again Harry disappeared eagerly through the door. Karl and Tony joined him for just one more pint before saying goodnight.

'Just make sure you leave at least one brain cell still functioning for tomorrow, Harry,' Tony shouted as he headed for the doorway. Karl was holding the door open for his friend, but stood aside as two men entered.

Now you can pass a million people in the street and a second later they are forgotten, but some people have features that make you look twice. Sometimes they remind you of a friend or a member of your family, or maybe they resemble someone famous; and some people have unusual looks or are disfigured in some way. All these stick in your mind a little longer.

One such man had just pushed his way past Karl. It was the size of the man's head which triggered the response. Thick black curly hair surrounded his face like a halo or a lion's mane.

As Karl passed through the pub doors and out on to the pavement his mind reeled and he felt he must be seeing things. But in his heart he knew he was not. Tony stared at him and exclaimed, 'What the hell's wrong with you? You look as if you've seen a ghost.'

'Tony, that man we just passed, the one going in as we came out – I know him!'

'Who? Where?' Tony seemed confused.

'The two men that we just passed in the doorway. One of them was an Arab.'

Before Tony could reply Harry came rushing out of the pub, almost banging into them. 'I was hoping I'd catch you two before you got to the Tube,' he said excitedly. 'Barkley's in the pub – actually came up and stood by me at the bar. He's with an Indian or Pakistani or something.'

'He's not Indian or Pakistani,' Karl broke in. 'He's an Arab – an Arab terrorist. His name is Mahmud al Dhuhoori, and the last time I saw him was over the top of my rifle in the Oman desert. So what the hell is he doing here?'

It was still dark and very chilly when they arrived next morning at Philip Street. After the shock of the encounter in the pub doorway Karl and his companions had concealed themselves outside until time. Then they had followed Barkley home to Mary Langley's bedsit, and now they were back to watch his movements again. Tony and Karl found Harry already parked a little way along the street, from where he had a clear view of the house. Karl went to join him. One problem they faced was communication. Since they were driving their own cars, all they had were their covert body radios, and although these were excellent for foot work they would soon become useless if they got too spread out in traffic.

'Let's hope he takes the Tube to wherever he's going,' said Harry, settling back in the driver's seat.

'Bloody hell, it's cold in here!' Karl pulled his light coat tightly around him, wishing he had thought to bring something a little warmer.

Although several people left the house, there was no sign of John Barkley or Mary Langley. Then, at twenty past eight, Barkley emerged. He was smartly dressed and walked briskly down the road. As he passed Harry and Karl, they saw that he had a small green holdall in his hand. They watched him as far as the junction, where he turned left.

'Looks as if he's on foot or going for the Tube.' Tony's voice came clearly through the small hearing aid stuck in Karl's ear.

Karl pressed the clicker twice in acknowledgement, got out of the car and moved fast to follow their quarry.

'Karl, if he's aiming for Farringdon, turn right down Wharfdale Street and go round the block to see if you can get in front of him. Harry, stay behind me on the other side of the road.'

Just as Tony had predicted, Barkley turned right and took

the slightly shorter route to the Tube. Karl ran at a steady pace, then slowed to a walk and quickly crossed the road to the station, going directly to the ticket machine. He purchased three tickets and waited, pretending to study the Underground map on the wall. About thirty seconds later Barkley walked in, bought a ticket and went through the turnstile. He was closely followed by Tony and Harry.

'Harry, you stay with him. Karl, you take the carriage in front. I'll take the one to the rear. Come on, we don't want to lose him.'

The morning rush of commuters provided them with plenty of cover as they followed Barkley on to the westbound Metropolitan and Circle Line platform.

Six stops later Harry's voice whispered on the radio, 'He's getting off at Paddington.' Karl and Tony got out and watched as Harry followed Barkley up the escalator towards the main line station. But in the morning gridlock at the ticket turnstiles he lost contact. 'Sorry guys,' he apologized. 'One moment he was there, next he was gone. Too many people packing the place this time of the morning. There's one thing, though – when he got off the train he wasn't carrying the holdall.'

Leaving a reluctant Harry at the office to write up their report, Tony told Karl to come with him. When Karl enquired where they going, Tony replied secretively, 'Shut up and don't be so impatient – it's a surprise.'

It was indeed a surprise when Tony led him into the offices of a well-known television station. After showing their passes they got into the lift, and here at last Tony was prepared to give Karl a clue.

'Let's just say we've come to check on an old acquaintance of yours – one who's been very much in your mind for the past twenty-four hours.'

Several floors down, the lift door opened to reveal a wide corridor. Fascinated, Karl followed Tony as he disappeared into a large, well-lit room containing row upon row of grey steel filing cabinets. 'Nice place you have,' he remarked facetiously. 'I've often wondered how far the files of British security were scattered over London.'

Tony ignored the remark, but volunteered a further snippet of information: 'There are some great women working down here!' He gave Karl a knowing look.

He was right. As they approached the reception desk, they came face to face with a security guard. He was talking to a slim, long-legged woman of about thirty – a real stunner, Karl thought. Tony put his arms around her and rebuked the guard: 'I'll tell your wife about you!'

'Tony! To what do we owe the honour?'

'Stephanie, say hello to a very old friend of mine – Karl Leathers. Karl would like to see some of your dirty pictures.'

'Not before you two sign in,' the guard protested, put out by the transference of Stephanie's attentions.

'Okay, Karl,' she said, when they had sat down and tea had been produced. 'From what Tony's told me on the phone I've selected a few albums for you to look at. Each photograph has a number after it and the rough date it was taken. Look through the books and write down any numbers that look like your Arab.'

'Why not just put the name down?' Karl asked her.

'We want an impression of who you saw, and not who you think you saw. If I give you the name it would influence you.' She left him to his task.

It didn't take long to flick through the pages, and he was over halfway through the second book when a face in one of the photographs jumped out of the page at him. It was a young Arab in his early twenties, and the youthfulness of the face did not show the eyes as they were now. But there was no mistaking the head and those black curls. He wrote down the number. Two pages further on, there he was again. This was more like the man they had seen last night. He was now several years older, and the head seemed not to be quite so large – perhaps because the frame of his shoulders had broadened. The jet-black curly hair was still the same, but now the eyes were filled with fire and hatred.

There was nothing else in the book. Karl closed it and sat there thinking.

'You found something, then,' said Stephanie, who had returned and seen the numbers Karl had jotted down on the pad.

She returned with a single file and handed it to him. 'You were right, Karl. Both photographs were of the same man.' She stood watching as he opened it. At the bottom of the first page was the name Mahmud al Dhuhoori. Karl turned over, and there was a copy of the first photograph, showing Mahmud as a young man. He read the accompanying text: 'Taken in the Caucasus mountains at the Stavropol training camp 1966. Subject passed out top student of his class, believed to have been returned to South Yemen, from where he joined rebels fighting in southern Oman.'

Karl turned over yet again, to find a group photograph of several men sitting round a table. Below it was a list of names: 'Photograph taken Aden 1976. Left to right: Peter Stoll (Baader-Meinhof), Paolo Cinelli (Italian Red Brigades), Wadi Haddad (PFLP), Mahmud al Dhuhoori (PFLP), Sean MacNally (IRA), sixth person unknown.' By this someone had written in pencil 'John Barkley'.

Finally there was a single sheet of paper which read: 'No further access to extended file details without prior approval. Contact ref: 2746/GJ.'

'What does that mean, Stephanie?' Karl was intrigued.

'It means that's all you get to see without further authorization.'

'Why?'

Stephanie hunched her shoulders in a gesture of 'who knows?' 'Normally it's because there's an operation in progress, involving those personalities.'

There was little else in the file and Karl closed it, handing it to Stephanie. Then suddenly he snatched it back. 'Stephanie, do you record all the dates of access to the file, and by whom?'

'Yes. Just a moment.' She walked over to the desk and returned with a well-thumbed book. Flicking through the pages in reverse order, she stopped. 'Here you go – that file has been taken out several times in the past month, mostly by the same man. Your boss, George Jackson.'

'Well, at least it proves a connection between the IRA and Mahmud. What do we do now, Tony?' he said excitedly.

'I would say it's about time we told someone about this. Let's go, Karl.'

Back at the office, Tony left Karl to brief Harry on the latest developments while he went to report the sighting of Mahmud. Thirty minutes later Tony returned, looking chastised.

'What did they say? Are they going to take any action on it?' asked Karl eagerly.

'No, we're to finish writing our report and that's the end of the matter.' Tony's face looked as if it was carved from stone. Someone had obviously torn him off a strip.

'Pass that by me again!' Both Karl and Harry stared at Tony.

'We drop it. All we do is write up the report on John Barkley, with no mention of Mahmud, and we can all sod off home. Come on, Karl, I need a drink. I'm buying. Sorry, Harry, but you'll have to sit this one out – I need a private word with Karl.'

Five minutes later they were seated in a pub bar, drinks in hand, and Tony came out with it. 'At first the section boss was all excited, thinking we had stumbled on to something important. Then George Jackson was told. He was not a happy man – don't ask me why – but he put the blocks on all of it. When he heard your name mentioned he just said, "Close it down and send Leathers back to Hereford." '

'But why? It doesn't make any sense. What the hell is going on?' Karl was both baffled and dismayed.

'I just don't know. But Jackson did say to give you a good report,' Tony added, equally nonplussed. 'That's it, Karl my old mate. The party's over.'

Mahmud felt the cold night air bite into him, cutting through his clothes and sticking to his body like ice. How could anyone live in a country like this? They had told him it would be cold, but for him, as for most Arabs, there was cold and there was England in the grip of early winter. He crossed the street and made his way to the rooming house, fumbling for his pass key. Quickly opening the door, he felt the sudden rush of welcome warm air wash over him. Mahmud had made it a rule never to go out or return when the house was busy. This meant that he could avoid the other inhabitants, mostly Irish labourers employed on construction sites in London. They would leave early in the morning and return late at night, many of them the worse for drink. He knew of other Arabs who were visiting London at present, but contacted no one except John Barkley and then only when he wanted something.

Taking from his pocket a street map of inner London, Mahmud spread it out on the bed. For the past two days he had taken the Underground to Paddington. From there he had walked through the streets towards the junction of Sussex Gardens and Westbourne Street. Each morning he had arrived before 10.30 and waited. At eleven o'clock on both occasions a dark blue Mercedes had positioned itself close to the hotel steps. Within a few minutes two men, Arabs dressed in European suits, had emerged and got into the car. Today Mahmud had noticed that when the car pulled up a curtain on the third floor had parted slightly. Once the car had gone Mahmud had paced the distance from the spot he had chosen to where it had parked. Walking slowly, it had taken him less than twenty seconds.

For the rest of the day he had slept, waking around 8.30 in time to leave for his meeting with John Barkley in the City. Mahmud found the way and pace of life in London fascinating, especially the pubs. They walked into the Cat and Moon a little after ten, when it was packed with people. He had been amazed by the number of girls and women who stood together, talking with men of all nationalities.

'Brandy, is it, Mahmud?' Barkley had asked, remembering the drinking bout that had finished off the meeting in Aden.

Most of the Arabs he knew did not touch alcohol, but Mahmud could drink any Irishman under the table.

'A big one.' Mahmud's large hand indicated the size.

Barkley had moved along the crowded counter to catch the barman's eye. When he returned a little later with two double brandies and tipped one into the other Mahmud looked at him questioningly.

'You can ask for a double in one glass,' explained the Irishman, 'but people will get suspicious if you ask for anything larger. Your health, and good luck.' He held his own pint up in a gesture of salute but both words and action were wasted on Mahmud who had downed the fiery spirit in one gulp and banged the glass down on the counter.

The barman heard the noise and came down to where the two men stood.

'Two big brandies – in the same glass.' The Arab held the glass and a ten pound note out together.

It was the expression in Mahmud's eyes that had stopped any questions, and he got his drink as ordered.

As Mahmud pocketed his change he looked at his companion challengingly. 'Luck has nothing to do with it. Here's to co-operation!'

I'm glad he's on my side, the Irishman had thought to himself. This was not a man to have as your enemy. 'The weapon with one full magazine of thirty rounds will be delivered to you late tomorrow night,' he told Mahmud quietly. 'The delivery will be made by a girl. She will come to your room with everything you need. After the job is done I'll be there to collect you as arranged, and take you directly to the airport. After that we will not see each again for some time. I hope all goes well for you.'

'I thank you for your support. There will be no problems – no one else knows I have been in London. Let us keep it that way.'

John nodded as he finished his beer. 'We too are very grateful for your support. You will thank Haddad, on behalf of the Movement. I wish you safe return.'

The two men had sat talking for a short while longer, then went their separate ways. Mahmud had found his way back to the Tube and eventually to the privacy of his rooming house.

Thump, thump. He waited a few seconds and then opened the door, his body balanced and ready for any trouble. The girl who had been knocking was taken by surprise. In front of her stood a tall, brown-skinned man with a huge head, crowned with a mass of jet-black hair.

'John sent me.' The words came out in a half-whisper.

Mahmud looked past her and down the stairs. There was no one else. He turned his attention back to the girl and saw the fear written on her face. As he motioned her to come in she slid around the door frame and into the door, her eyes never leaving his. Now, as he closed the door behind her, she knew how a mouse must feel when cornered by a cat.

'I will not harm you. Do not be afraid. But I must be careful, you understand?' Mahmud tried to calm her by moving away from her a little, and as he did so he spotted the small holdall slung over her shoulder. 'Give it to me.'

The girl dropped the bag on to the bed. Still she did not speak, but her gaze followed his every move.

Mahmud unzipped the bag, reaching inside for the small black machine gun. Good, he thought. It was an Israeli Uzi, which would help throw the police off the track for a little while. He pulled the working parts several times, checking the action of the weapon. When he was satisfied, he clipped in the full magazine. With a slight crashing sound he cocked the weapon. He was ready.

'Do you want anything else?'

Engrossed in his work, Mahmud had almost forgotten about the girl. She still stood in the same spot as if transfixed. 'Are you a freedom fighter?' Even as he said it he knew she was not – there was nothing more than a dull look in her eyes.

'I believe in the freedom of Ireland.' Her voice became a little bolder and she raised her chin a little.

'Do you know who I am and what I do?' Mahmud's gaze crushed her.

'No, I was just told to bring you this.' She paused and cast her eyes to the floor. 'I was told to ask you if you wanted anything else.' Her heart pounded as she spoke. If he demanded her body she would have to give it, and it was her body she was offering.

Mahmud eyed the girl. She was about twenty, and her face was pretty with a soft roundness to it, but the effect was spoilt by the unkempt hair and dirty clothes. A strange sexual emotion gripped him and fused with the anticipation of tomorrow. He felt powerful. Yes, he would take this girl. He moved to the door, cutting off her escape. 'Take off your clothes and get on the bed.'

Her knees went weak, and she pressed her hands flat against the wall for support. The harshness of his words filled her with dread, but she closed her eyes and, starting to undo her coat, moved towards the bed.

It was several hours later when he awoke. A little before seven, he guessed: he could hear movement in the rooms below him. His thoughts toyed with the pleasures he had felt before the girl left and he had fallen asleep. At first she had been stiff and fear had made her act like a robot. Mahmud had treated her roughly, like some animal, turning her body into different positions to satisfy his needs. But curiously she had offered little resistance. The next time he was calmer and she seemed to relax a little. As he was about to penetrate her, she spoke.

'I need a fix. It will be better for you if you let me have it first.' She looked pleadingly at him.

He did not understand at first, then realized she was a drug addict. It all fell into place – why John Barkley could control her, why she was so tense. He rolled away from her and nodded.

In a flash she was off the bed and, grabbing her coat, fumbling through the pocket until she found a small bag. With hands that had started to shake she emptied the bag and prepared the injection. Slowly she pushed the needle into her arm. Mahmud was fascinated: he himself had taken soft drugs, but nothing like this. She was totally under its control. He watched as she put the hypodermic back into the bag and slowly lay back beside him. This time a small smile played around on her mouth.

The cold morning wind rushed up the small side street. If Mahmud noticed, he did not show it. He sat huddled with his back to the door and looked across to the hotel. No one took any notice of him: to the casual passer-by he was just one more homeless down-and-out. But despite his appearance he was very much alert, and the dirty old overcoat was just camouflage. Underneath it he wore a smart dark grey suit in which he would escape. Only the freshly polished shoes threatened to betray his disguise.

Not much longer now, he thought, as he watched the window on the third floor. The first part would be easy and he knew it would work. Using a French passport he had booked a flight to Rome leaving Heathrow at ten minutes to one. If he could make the airport without any real delay, in six hours' time he would be in Baghdad.

Suddenly the car was there. As usual the driver had doubled parked the Mercedes as close as possible to the hotel entrance. Mahmud waited . . . he wanted to move, but any sudden movement now might tip them off. The curtain parted. The face at the window glanced down at the car, then up and down the street, but he did not look in Mahmud's direction. Then the face was gone.

'Now!' Mahmud whispered to himself as he stood up in the doorway. Still watching the hotel entrance, he unbuttoned the front of the old overcoat and felt inside it for the big pocket that held the Uzi. Firmly he gripped the pistol while his other hand held the coat closed around his body, Mahmud started forward, keeping his head bent low as if protecting it against the wind, gradually making his way towards the rear of the car.

Mahmud was twenty metres from the vehicle when he saw the

family come out of the hotel and down the steps towards the Mercedes. They were moving quickly, eager to be out of the cold wind, and did not even notice the old tramp approaching them. The tall man was last, smiling and saying something to one of the two children. Mahmud's coat fell open, and in one swift movement the small but deadly weapon was clear of the hidden pocket. Calmly he pulled the trigger.

The squat gun spat four bullets with deadly accuracy into the man's head. It burst like a ripe melon, the skull shattering into fragments. For a moment the decapitated body stood rigid, then finally collapsed. Screams and bewilderment and terror pierced the air.

In a bound Mahmud had reached the car. The back door was still wide open and he bent down to look inside. The startled driver was looking back over his shoulder; Mahmud killed him with a single bullet. Then, without moving his body and still crouched by the back door, he fired a long burst into the small huddle of humanity on the back seat. The screams stopped.

It had taken no more than six seconds from firing the first burst to the last. Casually Mahmud dropped the gun on to the car seat and, keeping his head low, dashed across the street and disappeared.

After the abrupt end to his E4 surveillance course Karl had caught a train back to Hereford and spent that night and most of the following day with Gail. When she had to leave for her 6 p.m. shift at the police station Karl reluctantly turned to matters in the wider world and switched on the television to watch the early evening news. The lead story concerned the assassination in London that morning of the former Prime Minister of North Yemen, his wife and one of the country's diplomats. It was only when a photofit picture of the gunman was flashed up on the screen that a shocked Karl realized the implications: the description fitted Mahmud al Dhuhoori perfectly.

Instantly he was on his feet, grabbing the telephone and dialling Tony's number.

'What the hell's going on?' he yelled as soon as he heard his friend's voice on the line. 'George Jackson knew Mahmud was in London, and we tailed Barkley to Paddington yesterday morning. Those Yemenis were killed just round the corner from there. And what about the holdall that we saw Barkley carrying? The weapon was probably inside it!'

'Don't say any more, Karl,' said Tony in a strained voice. 'I only found out myself this afternoon. Take some advice and just drop it – forget it ever took place . . . And Karl, I give you my word I don't know what's happening. To be frank, I don't want to. Just take care of yourself, my friend.'

5

Immediate Action

L inate Airport, Milan, 1977
     Even in October the midday sun was strong enough
to make the place unbearable. Small groups of people
sat or wandered about with the mechanical look of those
condemned to airport delays. The terminal itself had been
designed with typical Italian flair; unfortunately it had also
been built with typical Italian concrete and glass.

The dramatic entrance of a party of Italian beauty queens
momentarily lifted the stifling monotony. A small pack of press
photographers accompanied them, dancing about like wolves
around their quarry. The spectacle offered a welcome diversion
to the young women's forty-seven fellow passengers patiently
waiting for connecting flight BA120 from Lod in Israel to
London Heathrow.

With such distractions, no one paid any attention to the two
couples with dark-skinned faces who sat drinking cokes in the
airport café. Such is the cosmopolitan nature of humanity at
airports these days that the casually dressed group passed for
holidaymakers. Mahmud put down his glass: the drink had
warmed in the stuffy atmosphere, causing its stickiness to hang
in the back of his throat. The others carefully watched him. He
was their leader and inspiration, a hardened freedom fighter.
Stories of his exploits were legend: all three absorbed his every
word and movement, and on his command would willingly die

should it prove necessary. Mahmud was agreeably surprised to see how calm his three companions were. This was their first action, but they had been well chosen.

Arriving in Milan two days ago, the four had booked into a small tourist hotel and, like most tourists, had spent their time wandering the streets and seeing the sights. So as not to arouse suspicion they had posed as two married couples, Mahmud sharing his room with Selina and Hassan with Leila. Free from the ever-watching eyes in the training camp, Selina had thrown herself whole-heartedly into two nights of lovemaking with Mahmud. For a while all four had relaxed, but now the time had come to set in motion the operation for which they had meticulously trained in the hot deserts of Iraq.

The guerrilla training camp was the best the PFLP had. From here most of the major terrorist incidents of the past few years had been successfully launched. Of necessity it was also their most secret camp, in the middle of a hostile landscape and surrounded by high mountains. It was a simple set-up, with several flat-roofed buildings which accommodated the Russian instructors and the camp commandant, while neat rows of tents had been erected for the trainee freedom fighters. In the centre of the tents stood a simple cookhouse arrangement which also served as a general meeting and lecture area. About a mile to the south, a shooting range had been constructed. Although the camp was not fenced, and did not bear any resemblance to a Western military barracks, those who trained there did so with the utmost dedication. Here there was only one criterion, the transmission of knowledge – knowledge of high explosives, weaponry, hijacking and all the military arts that cause death and destruction.

Mahmud had spent two months watching and assessing the trainees, and in their final weeks had made his selection. He had chosen two women, both in their early twenties, and a man who was a little older; all three could speak reasonable English. They were separated from the other recruits and kept in isolation for a while, and then the rigorous training for their operation had started in earnest.

In the final days before leaving they were told of their assignment: to hijack a British airliner. As they learned of their mission, Mahmud had handed each of them a false British passport. The excitement and enthusiasm grew, and with it their dedication to their task. In a covered tent they practised the manoeuvres and deceptions required to get past airport security undetected. Milan's Linate Airport had been chosen for this very reason: security there was incredibly slack, Mahmud assured them as they went through their routine time after time.

The three new recruits also wanted to know how they would obtain the necessary weapons. Bluntly Mahmud had told them that that was his responsibility, but gave them some brief details so as to keep up their sense of involvement.

'Two travel bags were purchased in Italy six weeks ago, at the same time as the seats were booked.' Mahmud held up a black bag for them all to see. 'The brother of this bag remains in Italy. It contains two percussion grenades, four pistols and a specially prepared explosive device to blow up the aircraft. Once we have cleared security and entered the final loading bay, this bag will be exchanged for the one containing the weapons.'

He watched their faces. The three recruits were clearly impressed by the amount of planning that had gone into the preparations for the hijack.

'We will now go over the details of the aircraft layout,' Mahmud continued. Relentlessly he talked them through the sequence of events, going over details time and again so that any weakness in the plan would be exposed.

In the end he was satisfied, sure in his mind that he had selected the best available fighters to support him on this daring mission. Nevertheless one final test awaited them.

'We have captured a Zionist spy who has infiltrated the camp, but we are confident from our interrogation that he has no knowledge of our mission.' Mahmud looked at all three, then addressed Selina: 'Come, I have a small task for you. The others can watch.'

*   *   *

Despite the Palestinians' rigid security, the secret location had been discovered by Israeli Intelligence – Mossad. For three months a young Israeli called Peter Allon had been working undercover in Baghdad, spending hours in back street cafés and joining gangs of young thugs. Eventually he achieved his aim and, together with a small group of Palestinians, passed the initial security screening. Soon he would be on his way to the camp with the new intake of trainees. There was no reason why Allon should be detected – he looked like an Arab and spoke like an Arab.

The Israeli worked hard at the training camp and fitted in well, impressing the Russian instructors with his quick, intelligent mind. After a few weeks he felt sure that something important was about to happen. The whole camp was alive with rumours of some impending attack. Unfortunately, ill fate then touched him. During the final week of training the primitive water supply infected him with a stomach bug which developed into a severe fever. In the camp's medical tent he became delirious – and all his rambling were in Hebrew.

The pain that followed continued for two days, as crude techniques of torture were used to elicit the last vestige of information from the agent. In the end Peter Allon was incapable of answering, his vocal cords long since ruptured by his screams of agony. Yet still his torturers continued to inflict atrocities on his shattered body, forcing his bare feet into one of the camp fires. Finally, as they dragged the blackened stumps out of the embers, they wearied of him.

Then, as if in compassion, a beautiful young woman had knelt next to the young Israeli and pressed a pistol against the side of his head. Abruptly all the pain departed, buried in eternal darkness, as the bullet penetrated his brain.

'This is the first call for passengers on flight BA120 to London Heathrow. Would passengers please extinguish all cigarettes and proceed to Gate 5.' The tinny voice echoed around the terminal at Linate. With relief small groups of people stood up, collecting their bags of souvenirs, and to the clatter of duty-free bottles straggled towards Gate 5. Selina rose to follow them, but Mahmud's hand shot out to stop her.

'Wait! We must wait until the very last moment. Only then will we rush through the security gates. Remember what we planned.' Mahmud's eyes displayed no sign of annoyance, but Selina was aware of her mistake and knew that it would register with him. She looked back at Mahmud. He still had has hand on her wrist and he was smiling at her.

From the first moment she had seen Mahmud she had tried so hard to put everything she had into her training, conscious that he was watching. When Selina was finally chosen for the hijack mission it was to her that Mahmud had handed the pistol, and without hesitation she had placed it against the head of the Israeli spy and pulled the trigger.

That night she had gone to Mahmud's tent and offered herself to him as he lay on his camp bed. Like a slave she had stood blushing in front of him, and in the soft glow of the lamplight she had opened her combat shirt to reveal the firm beauty of her breasts. Mahmud had raised himself on one elbow and appraised her. In a quiet voice he had asked if she would let him see all her body, and with only a moment's hesitation she agreed. With shaking hands Selina unclipped her belt and removed the rest of her clothing. Mahmud's dark eyes gleamed in the lamplight as his gaze fell on the tiny triangle of silky black hair. His hand reached out to touch her inner thigh with the delicacy of a butterfly alighting on a flower.

'Would you do anything for me?' There was a thickness in his voice.

Selina began to tremble. She had no excuse for coming to his tent. As an Arab girl she had already shamed herself.

'I will do anything!' She dropped to her knees beside the camp bed and her arms stretched up to grasp the great head, her delicate fingers locking themselves into the tight curly hair. For a moment she faltered; then, thrusting her breasts forward, she drew Mahmud's head between them.

For over an hour his body pinned her to the small camp

bed as he thrust into her. Oblivious to the pain, Selina pushed upward to match his passion. At last his body stiffened and then slumped, and it was over. Gently he rested himself on her soft form. Then Selina felt her own passionate warmth spill within her and, despite his size and weight, she clung desperately to him. At that moment Mahmud became her god.

'This is the last call for BA120 to London, boarding at Gate 5.' Mahmud stood up and the others followed him.

'Now we must go. Remember to hold each other's hands – we're on holiday. We've arrived just in time to catch our flight. And speak only in English.'

Together they started the pretence aimed at getting them through the security check undetected. As they ran the men playfully pulled the girls along until, laughing, they slithered to a standstill at passport control.

'Flight BA120 – we can just make it. Hurry, please!' Panting as if out of breath, with a flourish Mahmud slapped down the four British passports on the desk in front of the official. Selina and Leila shoved past Mahmud, then turned back towards him.

'Quickly, we will miss it!' they cried. Selina reached out for Mahmud's arm and tugged at him. With a casual glance the official handed the passports back to Mahmud.

'Please be quick!' Selina begged the guard in the security booth. 'Our plane – we can just catch it.'

He eyed her clinging T-shirt appreciatively, as she had intended, and waved her through.

Mahmud, just behind her, made as if to offer his small bag for the customary search. Selina tilted her head seductively at the Italian security man and pouted, and at the same moment a stewardess appeared at the entrance to Gate 5 and looked questioningly around. She spotted the four at the security gate and called loudly: 'Flight BA120 to London.'

'Yes!' shouted Selina. 'We're coming.'

The guard passed his hand swiftly through the small bag

and tossed it back to Mahmud. All four ran laughing towards the gate.

With the stewardess in front they hurried across the tarmac to the waiting aircraft, but as they did so Mahmud deliberately lagged behind. For over twenty minutes the driver of a small baggage buggy had been sitting by the terminal building, watching the passengers make their way on to the aircraft and nervously fingering a black bag. Now he saw the man with the big head and stirred himself into action. Speedily he drove the small vehicle between Mahmud and his companions. Mahmud stood still as if to let the vehicle drive past, and as it did so he and the driver swiftly exchanged bags. Then Mahmud ran to catch up the others boarding the aircraft.

The Boeing 727C Europa jet, as the four terrorists were well aware, comprised a first-class compartment for eight passengers, directly behind the flight-deck, and the main economy class, from which it was separated by an internal bulkhead and a curtain across the aisle. The economy section seated one hundred and also accommodated the galley, just behind the bulkhead. The crew consisted of a pilot, a co-pilot and three stewardesses, and now, on the second leg of its journey from Lod Airport, the flight was almost three-quarters full. Among the eighty-four passengers were some Jewish Americans who had been visiting Israel. The rest were mostly British and Italian businessmen making their way to London. The flight time was scheduled as two hours twenty minutes.

As the late arrivals embarked, Mahmud and Selina went to seats 10a and 10b. These, booked months in advance, were the only pair of seats outside the first-class compartment and directly opposite the galley. Leila and Hassan sat three rows back. The plane took off at 12.57, and shortly afterwards the stewardesses began to prepare the in-flight meal. For them the flight was short, and the pretence of in-flight service was best accomplished as quickly as possible. Mahmud knew that they would shortly start their journey down the central aisle, dispensing food. As if in confirmation of this one of the stewardesses appeared pushing a small trolley of drinks.

She passed through the curtains and went forward into the first-class section.

Mentally Mahmud prepared himself. Then he released his seatbelt and motioned Selina to do likewise. 'Now!'

His command sent the adrenalin surging through Selina's body, purging her of fear. Mahmud pulled the small black bag from beneath his feet and placed it on his lap, and as he did so Selina leaned forward to obscure him. Discreetly pulling out a pistol, Mahmud slipped it inside his shirt. Then his hand reached again into the black bag and he passed Selina a grenade and a pistol.

The grenade was of the latest type, consisting of layer upon layer of thick copper wire wrapped around a nucleus of high explosive, the whole thing covered with a smooth layer of olive green plastic. In a confined space such as an aircraft it would be lethal, not just for its explosive capacity but also for the mass fragmentation damage it would cause.

Leaving Selina in her seat Mahmud stood up and turned, making his way to where Hassan and Leila were seated. Hassan nodded as Mahmud placed the black bag on his lap. For a moment Mahmud studied their eyes. Then, finding no hint of fear, he turned and made his way forward to the first-class compartment.

Pushing through the half-drawn curtain that separated first-class from economy, he turned and closed it completely behind him. Some of the passengers looked up, clearly disapproving of his intrusion. Ahead of him stood the stewardess serving drinks. It was obvious to her that this man did not belong here.

'Would you mind taking your seat, please, sir? We're about to serve lunch.' The professional smile barely concealed her annoyance.

Ignoring her, Mahmud suddenly took hold of the drinks trolley and pushed it into the empty space by the toilet door.

Startled, the stewardess dropped a plastic cup and it rolled over the floor, spilling its contents. 'Sir, I really must – ' She stopped in mid-sentence, frozen by the sight of the gun that the man had produced from inside his shirt.

'If you make a sound, any of you, I will kill you. Do you understand?' Mahmud's voice was quiet but distinct.

The passengers, appalled, nodded acquiescence and shrank back into their seats in an effort to make themselves invisible.

'Good. I have friends back there,' he added, waving his hand towards the curtain. Then he reached out, grabbing the stewardess by the wrist. 'What is your name?'

'Jane – Jane Pickering.' The words seem to stick in her throat. 'Please please don't hurt me.'

'I shall not harm you if you do exactly as I say. Now you will come with me to the flight-deck.' With a jerk and sudden twist of his arm he had the woman in front of him and was propelling her towards the small door at the front of the aircraft. Mahmud leaned forward and whispered in her ear: 'Get the door open, but do it naturally – if they suspect anything you will be the first to die.'

She nodded. He was so close that his warm breath washed over her. Then she steadied herself and knocked on the door with her free hand.

'Yes?' came a muffled voice from inside.

'It's Jane. Are you ready for coffee?'

There was a small click from inside as the electronic latch was released. Mahmud pushed the stewardess back towards the galley. At the same time he hit the door with his shoulder, almost falling forward as he burst on to the flight deck to be met with the shocked faces of the two pilots.

'Look to your front!' Mahmud screamed. He thrust the gun into the neck of the co-pilot, 'Believe me, I will kill him – and you too – if I have to.' Mahmud and the pilot looked at each other: their gaze locked for one vital second, and in that time the strength and weakness of each was signalled.

'I am Major Mahmud. I now have control of this aircraft, but the fate of the passengers remains in your hands.' He let this sink in, then continued. 'We are prepared to die, but at that moment everyone on this plane will also die. Do you understand me?'

Captain David Griggs understood only too well. This was no ordinary criminal – he was face-to-face with a professional. He chose not to speak, but his head moved enough to acknowledge Mahmud's words.

Suddenly there were shouts and screams from the rear of the aircraft. As panic set in, the noise rose alarmingly and the aircraft lurched a little.

'What the hell are you doing back there?' Griggs shouted into Mahmud's face. 'If they don't sit down we could lose control of the aircraft!'

In one smooth movement Mahmud swung the pistol from the nape of the co-pilot's neck and slammed it into Griggs's upturned face. His lip burst open as the heavy metal crushed it, and an ugly rip appeared across his left cheek. Captain Griggs's head reeled backwards.

'You will speak only when I ask a question! My people are just moving the first-class passengers to the rear. Now give me the microphone.' Dazed, the pilot shook his head in an attempt to clear it and fumbled for the microphone by his right knee. Blood was pouring from his nose. He handed the microphone to his assailant, then slowly took out a handkerchief and held it to his throbbing face.

'You will all sit down, fasten your safety belts and be quiet,' came the voice over the loudspeaker system. 'My name is Major Mahmud, and I am now in control of this aircraft.' He paused to let the words sink in. 'You have one minute to comply or you will be shot.' Mahmud glanced through the open flight-deck door and down the aisle. The dividing curtain had been removed and he could see almost to the rear of the aircraft. The noise subsided, dropping to a loud whimper punctuated now and then by prayers being recited out loud: 'Hear me, O Israel . . .'

Selina hurried up the aisle towards him, stopping in the flight-deck doorway. 'We are in position and the passengers are all seated,' she reported.

'Good. I shall talk to them, then you will collect the passports.' She nodded, and Mahmud turned his attention back to the two pilots. The microphone was still in his hand and he started speaking again.

'You will notice that two of the freedom fighters are carrying grenades. These are designed to destroy the inside of a battle tank – you understand what they would do to this aircraft.' He paused to look once more down the aisle, where he could see Selina and Leila each holding a grenade above their heads. 'You people are in no danger if you co-operate. You are merely the means to an end. If you co-operate, you will be released safely on the ground in London. One of my officers will now pass down the aisle and collect all your passports. One final warning: anyone not wearing a seat-belt will be shot instantly.'

He was about to put down the microphone when a male voice from among the passengers shouted out: 'You terrorist bastards!'

'Hassan!' Mahmud raised his voice and his accomplice came running. 'Watch these two. If they move, shoot the co-pilot.'

Then with a grim expression on his face he left the flight-deck and walked down the aisle. As he entered the economy section, he stopped and, with a cold smile, surveyed the passengers. Then like lightning his hand shot out, grabbing a small girl of about seven firmly around the throat. As he tugged at the child, only her seat-belt prevented her from being forcibly ripped from the seat. The woman next to her screamed and clung desperately to the little girl. Mahmud moved quickly, thumping the butt of the heavy pistol down hard on the woman's forehead. Her eyes rolled up and she fell back limply into her seat. Mahmud let go of the child.

'*Mamma*!' cried the little girl, and then looked up at Mahmud. Putting her hands together as if in prayer, the small body trembled and shook as large tears welled in her eyes and ran down her cheeks.

Mahmud's face still held that terrible smile. He let his gaze sweep over the passengers before his voice boomed out: 'Who said "terrorist bastards"? You have one minute to stand before me or I shall shoot this child. Believe me! I will do it.'

There was silence for about thirty seconds, then halfway down the aircraft a man stood up and slowly came forward. He looked about fifty, but he stood tall and walked with confidence. Stopping in front of Mahmud, he looked at the Arab with undisguised loathing and hostility. Then the man saw the fanaticism in Mahmud's eyes, and he became afraid.

'Get down on your knees and put your hands behind your head.' The smile was still on Mahmud's face, and his voice sounded almost friendly.

Slowly the man complied.

'Please tell the people who you are.' Mahmud's voice remained buoyant, as if he had just asked the man to repeat a joke.

'My name is Charlie Mandell.' Pride flushed in his voice, covering up his fear. 'I'm an American citizen and proud of it.' He had just spoken his own obituary.

Everyone jumped as the noise thundered throughout the aircraft. Simultaneously the pistol in Mahmud's hand recoiled and Charlie Mandell's head exploded, showering the passengers close by with droplets of blood. Slowly his tall body crumpled to the floor. In the timeless moment that followed, the silence echoed. Then came a faint muffled murmur of sobs from among the passengers.

'You will make sure all the window-blinds are drawn and completely closed,' ordered Mahmud. The passengers nearest to the windows hastily carried out his instructions.

Then he returned to the flight-deck and spoke to his lieutenant. 'Get two of the passengers to put that piece of shit into one of the rear toilets.' Hassan left to carry out the gruesome task.

'You think I am cruel, captain?' Mahmud asked, settling himself against the back of the pilot's seat. He had observed the look of distaste on David Griggs's face.

'Was it necessary?'

'To make them obey, there has to be a lesson. He gave me the perfect excuse, and now he has paid the price for you all. There will be no more trouble from the passengers . . . or from you, captain?' Mahmud let the question hang.

'What are your instructions, Major Mahmud?' David Griggs was taking no chances. This time he would do it by the book.

'I should like you to tell London that you have been hijacked. You will also tell them that there are four of us and that we have weapons and explosives . . . Oh yes, and let them know that we have one dead American. His name is – ' Mahmud corrected himself ' – his name *was* Charlie Mandell.'

David Griggs turned and looked down at the radio by his right knee. He tuned the dial to the correct frequency, then put the head-set on and adjusted the small microphone.

'I'm going to transmit on the emergency channel. They will only transfer me there anyway.'

Mahmud nodded in acknowledgement.

'Hello, London. This is Flight BA120 transmitting on emergency channel. Do you read me? Over.'

There was a pause, then the response came back loud and clear. 'Flight BA120, this is London responding. Do you have a problem? Over.'

'Roger, London control. I call code 7000, repeat 7000. The aircraft has been taken over by . . . freedom fighters. Over.'

Mahmud grinned inwardly at the pilot's choice of words.

'Roger, Flight BA120. Your code 7000 acknowledged. Wait out on this channel.'

The flight-deck was silent for about two minutes, and then the confined space echoed once more.

'British Airways 120, switch on your auto-identifier.'

Again David Griggs looked for Mahmud for confirmation. Again Mahmud gave a slight nod of the head. Flicking a switch above his head, the pilot waited for the response.

There was a new voice talking now, cool and level. 'BA120, we acknowledge. What are your intentions? Over.'

'You will notify them that you have been hijacked and that we shall be landing a little behind time at Heathrow,' Mahmud told the pilot. 'Then you will tell them all about us and the dead American. Once you have finished, inform them that I shall issue further instructions when we are safely on the ground.'

Hereford, 14:50 hours
Karl Leathers stood with three other men by the closed door, poised in the gloom of the long, dark corridor. He and two of the others faced the door, crouched like sprinters on starting-blocks. The fourth man stood to one side, his left hand firmly gripping the door handle. The corridor was wide and windowless, forcing the men to work blind; the noise from the huge extractor fans hummed continuously in their ears.

The Killing House had been designed and built for the express purpose of training men in the skills of close quarter battle. So successful had the concept proved that it had been copied in minute detail by Delta Force in America and anti-terrorist teams in several European countries. For all SAS personnel on anti-terrorist duty shooting in the Killing House was a daily ritual in which each man could easily expend a weekly three thousand rounds of ammunition.

Every conceivable situation was practised, including complex weapon malfunctions, shooting from different positions and at different targets, and, most important of all, the accurate identification of the correct target irrespective of conditions. Realism was often simulated by using as a 'hostage' a live human being in a room full of dummy targets. In the space of a few seconds a team of SAS men would be expected to enter the darkened room, assess the situation, kill the targets and pluck the live hostage to safety. The single drawback against making any kind of mistake was that all ammunition fired in the Killing House was live.

Karl waited, composing himself. Despite the chilly atmosphere of the corridor he was sweating. It was the fourth time they had practised this technique in the last hour. Each time the instructors had modified the internal layout. Karl's black fire-retarding suit fitted him comfortably, as did his Bristol body armour – it was the heavy respirator covering his face that was making him sweat. With a conscious effort he controlled his breathing and listened to the voice in his earpiece.

'Okay, let's do it again, and show me some speed and aggression. And Karl, I want a stun grenade this time!' The instructor's voice had a satirical ring to it.

'Oh, fucking hell – make it easy, why don't you?' Karl murmured the words into his throat mike as his hand dropped from the Heckler & Koch sub-machine gun to his waistband. He felt the smooth black rubber cylinder and unclipped it. Keeping a stable grip on the stun grenade release handle, he swiftly pulled out the arming pin.

'Alpha One, standing by.' Karl balanced once more on the balls of his feet, ready to spring forward the moment the door was opened.

'Alpha One, stand by . . . stand by . . . go, go, go.'

The door flew open and Karl tossed the stun grenade into the room, catapulting his own body after it. Through the blinding light and deafening thunder of the explosion Karl leaped to the centre of the room. His index finger hit the small button on the side of his weapon and instantly a beam of dazzling light pierced the darkness. Like lasers, other beams joined the search, zig-zagging across the room in pursuit of targets. Short bursts of automatic fire filled the air.

'Grab him!' Karl bellowed into his respirator, the throat mike transmitting his command. Two black-clad figures reached for the instructor sitting on the chair and literally threw him out of the door.

'Stop, stop, stop.' Immediately the words finished the room was illuminated by bright overhead lighting. With relief Karl pulled off his respirator and looked around him. The thick smell of cordite filled his nostrils, and he tasted the sweetness of the lead in the back of his throat. He spat the taste out on to the floor and moved forward to examine the target dummies. Deliberately Karl rubbed his hand over their smooth surfaces, checking the accuracy and spread of the hits. He turned back to the others, fairly pleased with the results.

'Well done, lads. That was a big improvement,' he commented. Then he looked up at the instructor, who was just coming into the room again. Seeking confirmation, Karl asked, 'How did it look that time?'

'I've seen better.' The instructor spoke with the authority of a man who had. 'Now let's have a look at – '

Beep-beep-beep – the small black alerter clipped to Karl's waistband sang out, galvanizing them all into action.

'Back to the hangar. Now!' Karl was running even as he spoke.

Two minutes later, as he approached the purpose-built hangar that housed the anti-terrorist teams, Karl slowed down to catch his breath. The main doors were already open, each bay revealing the stub nose of the white Range Rover. At the rear of each vehicle stood a huge flat metal table on wheels. These tables, which held all their specialist equipment, had four small lockers in the side – one for each vehicle crew member. The men dressed hurriedly, throwing the equipment into the back of the Range Rovers.

Karl made directly for the briefing room. 'What have we got, Keith?'

Keith had been left at the office as duty sergeant, and was now busy searching the top drawer of a filing cabinet. 'Just received a tip-off from Heathrow police. Possible hijack coming in, but nothing official yet. It looks like a British Airways 727C Europa jet in-bound from Israel via Italy.'

'Put a BA272C on the screen,' Karl ordered, and the man next to the overhead projector quickly shuffled through the pile of view-foils before switching on the machine. The bright light hit the screen to reveal the outline of a 727 aircraft, its top section cut away to show the seating arrangements. Karl went up to the screen and looked hard at it, slowly tracing his finger over the silhouette. 'It's not going to be easy. Where's the contingency file?'

'The team commander collected it a few minutes ago.' As if

to confirm the man's words, the sound of a helicopter taking off could be heard in the background. In situations like this the colonel and the team commander always flew ahead to make an on-the-spot assessment and, where possible, to set up a control point for the main force when it arrived.

'Keith, find out what the state of play is with the call-in and then give everyone in the hangar a shout. Briefing in five minutes – and one of you move the overhead projector into the briefing room.' As Keith left, Karl picked up the telephone and dialled.

'Hard dog section, Heathrow police.' The voice on the other end was brisk and efficient.

'Can I speak to Burt Simpson, please? It's Karl Leathers.'

'We were half expecting a call from you, Karl – what took you so long? Wait, here's Burt.'

Burt Simpson, responsible for the day-to-day dog patrols in and around the airport, was a professional and knew Karl well. He skipped the small talk and came straight to the point. 'This looks a real one. I've just had a quick word with one of my friends in the control tower and they say the aircraft was hijacked just after take-off from Milan. The terrorists seem to be pretty talkative. And they're dangerous. They've already shot one of the hostages – an American. The plane's due to touch down here in roughly forty-five minutes . . . And that's about it.'

'Thanks, Burt, that's a big help. We don't have the official order to move yet, but the colonel and the team commander are on their way up to Heathrow by chopper. I'm going to request you as police liaison to the team – we need your knowledge of the airport. Hope to see you later, mate.'

In the briefing room all the crews had now reported in and were sitting staring at the view-foil silhouetted on the wall. There were low murmurs of speculation as Karl started to address them. Just at that moment two uniformed policemen appeared in the doorway. They were with the Hereford police escort car and would be responsible for clearing the SAS convoy's route to Heathrow. Karl waved them to a seat.

'Right, lads. We have a hijack in progress, and it's in-bound for Heathrow. As you've seen it's a 727, or more accurately a British Airways 727C. Although it's not officially confirmed, I've just been informed that one of the passengers has been shot dead.' Karl let this sink in. 'I want all crews to load the Range Rovers and be ready for an Immediate Action the moment we get to the airport. Stay in the hangar, with the vehicles ready to move. I'll update you en route as news – ' The shrill sound of the telephone stopped his flow of words.

The duty signaller picked it up, then turned to Karl and said, 'It's a go! High speed request cleared, to Heathrow via the Severn Bridge.'

'You heard the man – let's go!' Karl chased after the rush to the Range Rovers. The escort police car had started to move even before they were in their seats. This was a role they had practised many times, but this time the edge of reality heightened the excitement. Like a sinuous white snake the convoy eased its way out of camp and on to the main Hereford to Ross-on-Wye road, where it gradually gained speed. Soon the vehicles, now escorted front and rear by police cars, stretched out for over half a mile as, with wailing sirens and flashing blue lights, they dominated the fast lane of the M4.

Heathrow, 15.38 hours
David Griggs was applying his full attention to the approach into Heathrow Airport.

'Tower to BA120. You are clear to approach on runway 28 Lima. Wind is ten knots from the west. Call on finals.'

Five miles out and at two thousand feet, Griggs could clearly make out the airport. Below him lay the vast metropolis of London, going about its own business quite unaware of the drama above. He turned to Mahmud: 'Better get yourselves strapped in like the rest of the passengers. We don't want you flying through the window on landing, do we?'

'Thank you for your concern,' replied Mahmud sarcastically.

Griggs used all his concentration as he began the approach.

160

He was now down to five hundred feet, and the end of runway 28 Lima came rushing up to meet him. At the precise moment he cut back the throttles and flared the huge aircraft, touching down smoothly on the tarmac. With a final deafening roar of the engines, British Airways Flight BA120 landed safely. The time was seventeen minutes to four in the afternoon. Almost immediately an airport vehicle drove in front of the flight-deck, its flashing sign reading 'Follow Me'.

'Do exactly as they say,' Mahmud instructed.

The giant jet, unwieldy now that it was out of the sky, followed the truck around to the southern side of the airfield until it came to a lone marshaller standing on pad 05. Gently, with a slight rocking motion, the aircraft came to a complete stop. As if on cue, it started to drizzle.

'Now what?' Griggs enquired.

Mahmud motioned Selina to come to the flight-deck before he replied. 'Now you request a ground power unit and hook it up. I will also need an eight-foot ladder. But they are not to bring them until I give the word. Selina, watch them.' Mahmud turned back into the first-class compartment where Leila was waiting. 'It's time to go. Remember, keep moving around. At the first sign of trouble fire a warning shot and return to the door. We will stay in touch using the radios.' Mahmud studied her face.

'You can trust me. I shall not let them come near.' Leila's eyes shone a little too brightly for Mahmud – she was a fanatic. But she was undeniably good.

He signalled Hassan to remain at the bottom end of the aircraft where he could best observe the passengers, and then returned to the empty first-class section to open the main port side door. Gripping Leila's arm, he gradually lowered her out of the door until she was able to drop safely on to the wet tarmac. 'Bloody English weather,' he swore to himself. Then quickly he returned to the main passenger compartment, where the three stewardesses were now seated.

'I need a coat,' he stated. They looked at him blankly.

Grabbing hold of the nearest stewardess he forced her to the central catering area. 'Your uniform coat – where is it? Show me.'

'In here.' Opening an overhead locker, she removed a neatly folded blue coat.

Mahmud took it from her and made his way back to the open aircraft door. 'Here, put this on,' he called down to Leila. 'It will keep you dry. Call me every fifteen minutes. One of the others will take over from you in about two hours.' Mahmud closed the door and returned to the flight-deck. 'Selina, take the co-pilot and sit him with the other hostages.'

As the two of them left, Mahmud spoke to David Griggs. 'You will now inform them that you want the ground power unit connected. You will also inform them that the person under the aircraft is one of my lieutenants and that she is armed. If any attempt is made to attack the aircraft I will blow it up. Do you understand?'

The pilot Griggs understood perfectly. All doubt had long since left his mind – these were very professional people. He transmitted the demands, then relayed the answer to Mahmud. 'They will not give us a ground power unit unless you agree to release the women and children.'

Without acknowledging him, Mahmud bellowed to Selina. 'Tell Hassan to get two passengers to dump the body of the American on to the tarmac – now!'

Five minutes later, Mahmud picked up the microphone. 'Control tower, you will observe that we have just dumped a body on to the tarmac. It is an American named Charlie Mandell. If we do not receive a ground power unit in the next thirty minutes he will be joined by another.' Then he turned to Hassan. 'Fit the explosives, and let me know the moment it is done.'

Moments later Mahmud received confirmation. 'Captain,' he said to David Griggs. 'I would like you to come with me. I have something to show you.' Slowly the pilot eased himself out of his seat and, with Mahmud's gun at his back, walked down the aisle. 'Stop, look down there.' Mahmud pointed to the floor directly below the starboard wing emergency hatch. 'Two kilos of high explosive, with a timer attached.'

If David Griggs was horrified, it was nothing compared to the look on the faces of the three passengers seated next to the device. Stretching across their laps, he noted the time on the small digital display. It was set for 06:00 hours.

As David Griggs stood up again, he saw that Mahmud's face held a touch of mockery. 'Now you will return to the flight-deck and tell them exactly what you have seen.'

Very calmly, a moment or so later the pilot picked up the microphone. 'Hello, tower. This is BA120. I have a message. Over.'

'Roger. Send your message.'

'I have just been taken by Major Mahmud and shown a bomb in the centre of the aircraft. It is positioned directly above the starboard wing fuel lines, and is fitted with a timing device set for 06.00 hours tomorrow.'

'We copy that, captain. A ground power unit and one eight-foot ladder are on the way. Wait. Switch to frequency 357.5 and remain on that channel.'

Griggs looked up at Mahmud for confirmation.

'Do as they ask – we will now be in touch directly with the people who are dealing with the operation.' Mahmud smiled.

Griggs complied, amazed at Mahmud's correct anticipation of every move. It would be a cold day in hell before they caught this man out, he thought.

16:30 hours

Some forty miles west of Heathrow, one of the three telephones clipped to the dashboard of the Range Rover buzzed. Karl grabbed it.

'It's the Boss. Are you ready to copy?'

'Wait.' Karl reached down by his feet and pulled up a small clipboard. 'Ready.'

'The aircraft has just landed and has taxied to the south end of the airport by runway 05. It's now sitting about 250 metres from the old VIP lounge. Roger so far.'

'I Roger that.'

'Bring the convoy in quietly from the tunnel, use the outside perimeter road to the west, turn off at the south-west island and enter via the cargo gate at 10 Romeo. From here you'll be escorted to the cargo buildings at the back of the VIP lounge. Roger so far.'

'I Roger that.'

'Once in position prepare for Immediate Action. I'll take you for a quick recce the moment you get here. Are you ready for checklist?'

'Wait. Okay – I'll call them off, you answer. Any limitations, deadlines or VIPs on board?'

'A body has been thrown out on the tarmac. Additionally it looks like one of the terrorists – a woman – is positioned outside the aircraft. But the big problem is that we've just been told by the pilot that there's a bomb on board. It's timed to go off at 6 a.m.'

'My God! What have we got here?' Karl was stunned at the news. Then he continued. 'Terrorist numbers and weapons?'

'We are told four, armed with pistols, grenades and explosive.'

'Intentions?'

'Not known.'

Karl knew it would be pointless asking, but at least it would get them into gear. 'Any details on hostages, numbers, nationalities, state of health, etc.?'

'Getting it now. All that information should be here by the time you arrive, as will full details of the internal layout of the aircraft.'

'Who's negotiating and from where? Do we have a direct voice link?'

'There's a trained negotiator working from the old VIP lounge. That's where the police are setting up the forward Alpha Control. The colonel and I will also be situated there. One last thing – the negotiating frequency is 357.5. Over.

'That's excellent, Boss. Can you request Burt Simpson from the hard dog section to act as one of our police liaison officers?'

'Already done. He'll meet you at the holding area in the cargo sheds. Anything else?'

'Negative – oh yes, one last thing. If the hijackers have explosives, make sure a bomb disposal team is on stand-by. See you in about thirty minutes. Out.' Two minutes later he had repeated the information to the rest of the team, and then they were practically at their destination.

'All cars, this is Alpha One. Airport exit coming up. Cut back the speed. Lights and sirens off.' Karl flicked a switch on the radio and spoke again. 'Zulu One, this is Alpha One. In-bound Heathrow, exiting the M4 now. Over.'

Just before the tunnel, a police car pulled off the hard shoulder and took over the lead. Swiftly the convoy of SAS men made its way round the perimeter road to take on the dangerous task they had come to perform.

Downing Street, 16:35 hours
'We have the President on the line, Prime Minister.' The aide looked at the woman seated at the massive ornate desk, wondering where she got her energy from. Her carefully coiffed silvery blonde hair belied her age, he thought, as his words made her look up from the paperwork in which she had been absorbed.

'Thank you, Peter. You had better stay and listen to this – it may help to explain things a little.' She reached out and picked up the red telephone.

'Mr President, how are you?' There was a pause as she listened politely for a few moments. 'We have a problem here that may involve American citizens – correction, *does* involve American citizens.' She stopped once more, listening to the voice from across the Atlantic. 'All the details have already been sent to you by secure means, Mr President, but I thought a quick telephone call from me would help clear the situation. A British Airways 727 was hijacked earlier today. It was flying from Israel to London, via Italy. En route the aircraft was taken over by four terrorists. It would seem that shortly after leaving Italy one of the passengers, an American by the name of Charlie Mandell, was shot and killed.' She let this statement take effect. 'Yes, I agree, Mr President. The aircraft is now on the ground at Heathrow. Operation COBRA has been set in motion. In addition the SAS anti-terrorist teams are now on stand-by. In the normal course of events we should get the situation under control. However, as they have a bomb on board we will have to wait and see what their demands are first. We are checking now to ascertain how many American citizens are on the flight, and you will be notified . . . Yes, of course.' After a brief goodbye she replaced the receiver and sat back in her chair with a worried expression.

'That was very difficult for me to do, Peter. I feel somehow responsible for the man's death. However, now to business – what is the state of COBRA at the moment?' Her manner turned swiftly to one of action.

COBRA, short for Cabinet Office Briefing Room, was a special committee of ministers and officials which had been conceived for just such an emergency. From the moment the hijack had been confirmed, COBRA members had started to assemble. The inner core consisted of fifteen members, with the Home Secretary normally acting as chairman. But in certain situations the Prime Minister could elect to chair the meetings herself. She would need to stamp her style on the proceedings before she could let the main core of the group take over. One thing the Prime Minister was adamant about was that there would be no compromise with the terrorists, no matter what their threats or demands were. If the governments of other countries could adopt a tough line, then so could she.

'The Home Secretary is your link, as you know, Prime Minister, but the chief adviser on this kind of incident is Mr George Jackson from the Security Services.' She raised one eyebrow as her aide mentioned Jackson's name – even she was not wholly happy with his department. Jackson seemed answerable to no one, and she had heard some uncomplimentary rumours lately.

She made a mental note to check up on his department after the present difficulty was over.

'Let me speak to the Home Secretary and to Mr Jackson privately first. Then I will address an emergency meeting of COBRA at five o'clock prompt. I would like you to be in attendance at all times, Peter.'

'Yes, Prime Minister.'

The four of them were seated around the large oval table, the Prime Minister as usual in front of the fireplace with her aide alongside, the Home Secretary and George Jackson facing her. Peter had been paid a brief courtesy nod when the two visitors entered, but was otherwise ignored.

'We are all aware of the present situation,' the Prime Minister opened the conversation, 'but I would like you to clarify it.' Her gaze was firmly fixed on George Jackson.

He cleared his throat and shifted position in his chair. 'Yes, Prime Minister. The pilot has reported that he was shown a bomb placed in the middle of the aircraft. It has a timer attached that is set for 6 a.m. tomorrow.' Jackson paused, letting this news sink in. 'There is a terrorist woman outside the aircraft. She is walking around and seems to be in radio contact with the leader – we are monitoring the conversation, which is in Arabic. They are keeping their conversation brief, giving little away. But both these tactics are new to us, and may prove a major stumbling-block if we try to assault the aircraft.'

'What do they want and why did they kill this American?' The question was direct and blunt. 'And what position are we in with the Security Services?'

'All the normal police cordons are in place, and the incident is being handled from the old VIP lounge about 250 metres from the aircraft. The SAS team should be arriving about now and will take up position to go in immediately should the terrorists start any mass shootings. But in light of the bomb on board, I feel we should be very careful – I fear the hijackers may be prepared to commit suicide. . . . I have the feeling we

167

are being tested.' Immediately he uttered these last few words George Jackson wished he had not said them.

'How do you mean, *tested* – tested by whom?'

Jackson took a deep breath and placed his palms flat on the table in front of him. 'The leader of the group, which we believe consists of two men and two women, is a man calling himself Major Mahmud. His real name is Mahmud al Dhuhoori, also known by his followers as the Lion because of his abnormally large head. You may recall some time ago that we discussed an operation by my department to target this man . . .' Jackson paused and glanced at the aide.

The Prime Minister took his meaning and said softly, 'Peter, would you kindly leave us for the moment.' Once he had left the room the steel came back into her voice. 'Please continue, Mr Jackson.'

As if to bring the Home Secretary into the conversation, Jackson addressed him. 'Sources in the Middle East inform us that Mahmud al Dhuhoori is set to rekindle the spark of terrorism against the Western world – a new Carlos, if you like. For over a year my department has been tracking him.' Jackson did not elaborate any further.

'We are briefly aware of this operation,' the Prime Minister cut in, 'but how does it affect the present situation?'

'To be honest, Prime Minister, I don't know – what we do have, in my opinion, is not a normal hijacking. Mahmud is at present working for Wadi Haddad's PFLP, and Haddad is a man who specializes in terror. His hand, and Mahmud's, can be traced to a number of terrorist incidents in the UK over the past few years – the weapons supplied to the IRA, the murder of the ex-Premier of North Yemen and his family in London. Information from both German and Israeli Intelligence agencies also links him with terrorist activities across Europe. But this time he is out in the open . . .' Jackson stopped suddenly, and waited.

'Go on, please, Mr Jackson.' Both the Prime Minister and the Home Secretary were intrigued by his revelations.

'Haddad is currently operating out of Baghdad. A few days

ago, the Israeli Secret Service reported that one of their agents had been captured and tortured to death. The Israelis had placed the agent in the PFLP camp, in the belief that Haddad was about to carry out another major operation. I conclude we are now witnessing that operation. The worrying thing is that they don't seem to be conforming to the normal-style hijack, and they are very confident. That's why Mahmud has allowed the pilot to reveal so much information about him and the others, plus what weapons they have. He must also be aware that we have anti-terrorist teams close to him by now. To me, all this indicates that they intend to get away with whatever demands he is going to make.'

'There is another possible scenario,' the Home Secretary suggested. 'They could just destroy the aircraft on the ground.'

'You mean a suicide attack?' The Prime Minster looked horrified.

'I don't think so.' Jackson tried to calm their fears. 'If that was the case they would have done it by now, but if 6 a.m. tomorrow is their deadline then – ' Jackson was interrupted by the telephone ringing.

'Yes, what is it?' answered the Prime Minister. Then she handed the phone to Jackson: 'For you.'

'Yes. . . . Wait there,' he told the caller. 'Tell Leathers not to do anything until I arrive.' He put down the phone and stood up. 'It would seem that Mahmud has given permission for us to collect the dead body from underneath the aircraft in exchange for a ground power unit. The SAS would like to use the opportunity to get near the aircraft and have a good look at the woman terrorist on the ground – this may be the break we are looking for. If you will excuse me, Prime Minister, I think I had better be off to Heathrow.'

'Don't hinder the SAS too much, Mr Jackson. They have proved to be very resourceful in the past, and we may need all their skills before this is over.'

'Rest assured, Prime Minister, I am thoroughly aware of how effective the SAS can be!' Outside Number 10 a dark green Jaguar was waiting to convey him speedily to

Battersea heliport, and twenty-five minutes later he landed at Heathrow.

Heathrow, 17:30 hours
'Sierra Four, I have movement on green. The main aircraft door is open and we have two targets.' The voice of the sniper came through the speaker in the Alpha control room crisp and clear. At the same time two red lights changed to green on the small control box that had been set up on the table.

'Roger that, Sierra Four. Keep it coming. All stations listen in. We have movement on green.'

'Sierra Four, the port door is open. Looks like the female has put the ladder up against the aircraft door and is going back inside. . . . Wait – someone else is climbing down the ladder. Looks like a change-over. It's another woman. She has removed the ladder and has placed it by the dead body . . . Now patrolling under the aircraft.'

'Clever bastard,' Karl conceded, as he listened to the sniper's report. 'That's going to make any silent attack very difficult.' Together with the team commander and the colonel, who were standing at the window of the VIP lounge, he had just witnessed the change-over for himself. 'Any chance of checking with COBRA, sir? If we don't go and get that body soon, the terrorists may change their minds.' Then he saw a familiar face enter Alpha Control.

If George Jackson felt uneasy about being in the presence of a man who had once roughly manhandled him, he didn't show it. He joined the three men at the window and said very softly, 'Karl, I think our friend Mahmud is on that aircraft – he's in charge of the hijack.'

Karl was visibly shocked. 'How do you know?'

'The Israelis informed me. So for the moment I think you will agree we have to take things easy. What are your plans?'

'We've delayed their offer to collect the body by asking for assurances of safety for our ambulance crew – in fact it will be me and a colleague,' Karl said, anticipating Jackson's question.

'But if we don't go soon they could start to get a bit suspicious. Who else knows about Mahmud?'

'In this room, just us four. So please don't tell anyone else for the moment.'

The remark irritated Karl. He had no secrets from the boys and was tempted to say something short and to the point, but held back. 'The command for an Immediate Action remains firmly with you, sir. I only hope that if anything violent happens while I'm picking up the body you'll take the correct action and pass control to the colonel – he knows what to do. Now do I have your permission, *sir*?'

'Yes – good luck.' It was obvious to Jackson that Karl had not forgotten the episode in Northern Ireland, nor his swift departure from the E4 course.

Karl walked out of the door to the nearby cargo shed where an ambulance was waiting. A lone figure was sitting behind the wheel: Burt Simpson, like Karl, was dressed as a paramedic.

'Hello, Burt! What's the matter – can't they find a real ambulance man?'

'Sod off – volunteered. Nobody knows this airport better than me. Anyway, why should I miss out on all the action? So tell me, what's the plan?'

'I suggest we head for the control tower first of all, then drive down the service road to the front of the aircraft. When you approach the aircraft reverse up to it – if things get messy and I give you the word, drive off. If it all goes well, we put the body into the ambulance and drive off as normal. Got it?'

'Got it,' said Burt, letting out the clutch with a jolt.

He wove his way carefully around the busy airport, heading roughly south. As the ambulance came in sight of the isolated 727, Karl cautioned him. 'Slow down and pull up alongside, Burt. Then reverse up with the back open to face the aircraft door and flight-deck windows. Leave the engine ticking over. Don't forget, if any shooting starts we leg it out of here – no heroics!' Burt nodded and pulled to a halt, stopping about five metres away from the fuselage and carefully positioning the ambulance so that they could make a rapid getaway if need be.

'OK, Bert. Out we get and open up the back. Let's do it slowly and steadily.' Karl opened the passenger door and stepped down. As he did so he caught sight of the figure standing under the aircraft wing, sheltering from the drifting rain. Even in the shadow Karl could clearly see the young face, and there was no disputing that it was a woman.

He opened the rear doors and Burt assisted him with the stretcher, lowering it on to the ground. Without speaking they wheeled it towards the body that lay crumpled on the wet tarmac. In the lower part of his forehead was a massive hole around which congealed blood glistened. The back of his head had burst open like some giant smashed egg, the cranial fluids running in small rivulets as they mingled with the rain. Karl bent down and placed a blanket over the dead man's face to cover the distorted features.

'He's going to be heavy, Burt – rigor mortis has set in. Come on. At the count of three . . . Eventually, not without effort, they got stretcher and body into the ambulance and Karl closed the doors. As he turned to walk away, he glanced up at the aircraft. A man stood in the open doorway. He was an Arab with a large head, and the head was covered with thick black curly hair that surrounded the face like a lion's mane. There was no doubt, thought Karl in excitement tinged with fear; the man was Mahmud!

For a moment the two of them stared at each other, then Karl turned and got into the ambulance. Minutes later he was back at Alpha Control.

COBRA, 18:00 hours
'So what is the latest situation, gentlemen? And how much room have we to manoeuvre?' The Prime Minister was firmly in command, despite the slight hint of a migraine coming on.

Looking around the Cabinet Office, the Prime Minister studied the faces of the men who made up the COBRA committee. All good men, solid men with purpose, she thought; the country would need their strength in the coming days.

Mentally blotting out the headache, she cleared her mind and listened as George Jackson outlined the latest situation.

'I have just returned from Heathrow and normal air traffic is continuing for the time being. But if there's any serious risk of the aircraft blowing up we have made plans to divert incoming aircraft to Gatwick and Stansted.

'As you know, the SAS have arrived and have positioned snipers around the aircraft, and they are relaying any terrorist movement directly back to Alpha Control in the VIP lounge, where the police negotiators have a direct channel to the aircraft.' Jackson stopped and looked around the room.

'In the event of the terrorists attempting to mass-murder the passengers, the SAS have a simple plan to attack the aircraft. This would only be a last choice solution, and we could expect severe casualties. But given the circumstances it's all we can do for the moment. The SAS are working out a more positive, deliberate plan at this very moment, but with the explosive on board and a terrorist outside it's very difficult.' Jackson paused again before continuing. 'The SAS have been out and collected the body of the American. And I now have it visually confirmed that the man in charge of the terrorists is Mahmud al Dhuhoori.'

The Home Secretary stood up and carried on the briefing. 'The police have managed to contain the press and media, who seem to be content with their present position just outside the wire perimeter about eight hundred metres away. This gives them an excellent viewpoint. However, in the interest of national security I have asked newspaper editors, TV stations and so on not to divulge anything that could jeopardize the operation.' He turned to the Prime Minister and addressed her directly.

'We have also had offers of help from both the West German and French governments. Additionally the American administration has requested that they at least send a Delta team representative over.

'I feel in fact that we can handle this on our own, but it would be politically insensitive if we did not invite a few observers.

The Americans in particular are keen to send people here, and considering that the murdered man was an American I feel it would be beneficial to be seen to co-operate. I have spoken to the SAS colonel who warmly welcomed the idea – these countries have invited the SAS in similar circumstances in the past.' The Home Secretary looked at the Prime Minister for approval.

'I agree with you,' she said. 'For the time being let's keep this strictly a British operation. However, thank all the governments for their continuing support and assure them that we will keep them abreast of developments. With regards to the American Delta force, I have no objection to them sending a couple of observers, and that goes for West Germany and France too – but make it quite plain that they are observers and nothing more. Now,' she added, turning to George Jackson, 'what counter-measures can we put into play?'

'Now here again I must seek your permission, Prime Minister.' Jackson opened the file in front of him. 'We need more information from inside the aircraft. For this sort of eventuality we have perfected a new drug. If the hijackers request more food, and we think they will, one of the meals will be doctored.'

'Is this drug dangerous? Won't the hijackers get suspicious?' The Prime Minister was not at all happy with the idea.

'All our tests have shown that the drug has the same effect as a heart attack. As it will only affect one person the hijackers should not become suspicious. And providing the subject is released within the hour we can easily treat him or her.'

'What if they don't release the person? What happens then?'

'I am assured that only people already suffering from heart conditions are at risk – a healthy person would recover by themselves anyway.' Jackson was inwardly annoyed at what seemed to him petty questions.

'Very well,' the Prime Minister reluctantly acquiesced. 'It seems our only option.'

Heathrow

At 7 p.m. Mahmud had requested food. Forty minutes later a catering truck pulled up with eighty-eight more than welcome hot meals.

'Ladies and gentlemen, we are now going to serve you some hot food. The stewardesses will be passing down the aisle in a few moments.' Mahmud replaced the intercom and surveyed the passengers. Most had spent the last few hours tossing and turning in their seats. Visits to the toilets had been severely restricted, and when they were seated his orders remained that seat-belts had to be fastened at all times on pain of death. Now, eager for any semblance of normality, the passengers appeared calm as they ate, and the listless, apathetic look of the doomed slipped away.

In the first-class area, which the hijackers had converted into their 'office', Selina sat eating her meal. She had just finished her shift outside and had been replaced by Hassan. During her spell the wind had increased, and the drifting rain had made her wet and cold. But the hot food was warming her. As Mahmud approached she looked up and spoke. 'Here – you too must eat.' Swiftly she produced another plastic tray and, removing the foil, presented it to Mahmud with an expression of motherly concern.

Mahmud took the tray. Although he did not feel very hungry, he knew he must eat to keep up his strength – it was vital that he should be fully alert throughout the night. As he ate, he watched Selina and was pleased that she showed no signs of nervousness.

Given time she would become a good fighter, he thought. Mistaking Mahmud's gaze for one of affection, Selina smiled up at him with adoration. He smiled back at her. It was going to be an interesting night. Then he looked at his watch and made his way back to the flight-deck.

As Selina continued to eat she suddenly started to feel very giddy and light-headed. She tried to stand up, but staggered backwards against the seats. Frightened, she groped wildly for something to hang on to. The tray of food slipped from her hand, crashing loudly to the floor.

Mahmud moved the instant he heard the noise, rushing from the flight-deck with his gun at the ready. He stopped abruptly when he saw Selina's body slumped on the floor. 'Leila, is everything all right?' he shouted warningly down the aisle.

'Yes, what's wrong? Are they attacking?' Leila too had heard the crash and was worried.

'No, I don't think so. Cover the passengers.' Mahmud ran back to Selina, at the same time speaking breathlessly into the radio round his neck: 'Hassan, is everything okay out there?'

'Everything is okay. Do you have a problem?'

'No, but keep a sharp look-out for the next few minutes.' Mahmud knelt down beside Selina, gently raising her head and pulling her into a sitting position. Her skin had a peculiar greyish tinge, and her breathing was short and shallow. Suddenly her eyes shot open and with a wild convulsion hot vomit shot from her throat, splashing in a mess between her legs. Mahmud recoiled at the smell, then forced himself to look – it was the food she had just eaten.

Quickly he moved across to where Selina had dropped her tray and scooped up the fallen food. Back on the flight-deck he picked up the microphone. 'I have decided to release any passengers who can convince me they have a heart problem. As I walk up the aircraft they will raise their hands.'

Slowly, still holding the tray with the remnants of Selina's food, he made his way up the aisle. There were several raised hands. At each one Mahmud stopped and assessed the individual; then he stopped by an elderly man. Mahmud thrust the tray in front of the man and said menacingly, 'Eat. Eat it all or I will shoot you.' Frightened and confused, the old man did so. Only when the tray was completely empty did Mahmud remove the pistol from the man's head. Satisfied, he turned and went back to Selina.

She had recovered slightly, and was now sitting in one of the first-class seats. Mahmud saw that the colour was returning to her face.

'I will be okay,' she said uncertainly. 'I don't know how that happened.' Slowly, as her heartbeat steadied and her vision cleared, she began to regain control.

'They poisoned the food – I am sure of it.' Then, as if to confirm Mahmud's words, a thin, sharp cry punctured the air. Mahmud rushed back to see the old man who had eaten the food stagger from his seat clutching at his chest. A passenger next to him undid his seat-belt and rose to help the old man, but Mahmud raised his gun ready and in a rage bellowed, 'No one is to undo their seat-belts without permission!' The would-be helpful passenger quickly sat down again. Mahmud swung round, flustered, surveying the passengers, but they all avoided his gaze. Satisfied there was no further threat, he looked down at the old man, who had collapsed. He had been correct – it was the food. He would wait to see if the man recovered. Yes, it was going to be a very interesting night, he thought.

20:00 hours
'Hello, tower. This is Major Mahmud. I would like to speak to someone in authority.' It was time for a few surprises of his own.

'What is your message, Major Mahmud? Over.'

'First of all we have a passenger who has just suffered a serious heart attack from the drugged food you sent us. I think he will die.'

There was silence for a few moments, and he had to wait for a reply.

'We assure you, Major Mahmud, nothing was put into the food. We would like to request that the sick passenger be released for treatment.' The voice sounded unsure, as if a terrible mistake had been made.

'I will release no one. Do you take me for a fool? Now you will listen to me. I want a two-man television crew to come out to the aircraft – I wish to make a statement. They are to bring with them a portable television so that I can monitor the broadcast. You have one hour to comply.'

'Roger, BA120. We shall pass on your message.'

Mahmud sat and pondered. In a few minutes they would come back with their pathetic counter-demands, such as releasing the women and children. He would be ready.

'Flight BA120, this is the control tower. We will agree to your request if you will release the women and children and allow us to collect the man who has had a heart attack. Over.'

Mahmud ignored the request and spoke to David Griggs. 'Do not answer them if they call again, captain.' With this he left the flight-deck and went to see Selina.

She anticipated his question and assured him, 'I am fine now.'

'Good. You have studied the passports – in which seats are the Zionist pigs?'

Selina pulled out of her pocket a small piece of paper containing nineteen seat numbers. 'Take your pick.'

He made his way down the aisle, stopping now and again at certain seats. As he came to the old man who had suffered a heart attack he looked down. Seeing no signs of life, he casually stepped over him and walked on. Suddenly he snapped at a woman: 'You, on your feet!' It appeared that Mahmud had chosen her at random, for the passengers were unaware that the terrorists knew the seats where those with Israeli passports were sitting.

Shaking, the woman stood up. She was short, with dark, shoulder-length hair. The bright brown eyes that shone out of a kindly face were full of fear. Then, in a loud pleading voice, the man next to her spoke.

'Please, I beg you, take me instead. I am her husband. If you do not, you may as well shoot me where I sit.'

Mahmud stopped, and for a moment there was silence. The woman covered her mouth as if to stifle a scream, frightened even more by her husband's words than by the terrorist threatening her.

It was not in Mahmud's nature to change his mind, and normally he would have taken no notice. But the man had demonstrated the one quality he respected – courage.

'Very well, get up. You, sit down again.'

Tears flooded the woman's eyes. Involuntarily she threw her arms around her husband and clung on to him in desperation. But he pushed her gently back down into her seat and in a stern voice rebuked her: 'Don't be silly, Miriam. Think of the children.' With that he turned and walked down the aisle.

As Mahmud passed Selina he warned her of his intention and cautioned her: 'Keep control of the others.' Then he made for the port-side door and opened it. Turning, he grabbed the Israeli and pushed him forward. 'Kneel down in the doorway where they can see you.' By now the man was shaking violently and Mahmud had to force him into a kneeling position, balanced at the edge of the open door.

As the man made to steady himself, Mahmud placed the pistol behind his right ear and pulled the trigger. The report echoed deafeningly and the man slumped forwards, tipping out of the door and falling to the tarmac below.

A faint wail could be heard from among the passengers. Leaving the door open, Mahmud walked back up the aisle to where the body of the old man had fallen. 'You two, get up and drag him down to the door.' The two male passengers whom Mahmud had indicated quickly unbuckled their seat-belts and did his bidding.

Two minutes later, both bodies lay in a heap beneath the aircraft. For a moment Mahmud looked down at them from the doorway. The night rain drifted into the cabin, wetting his face. Slowly he closed the door . . .

'You have less than forty minutes to send the television crew here. Otherwise I will shoot another hostage.' Mahmud's voice was calm as he spoke to the control tower. That would teach them, he thought. From now on they would act instantly.

20:10 hours

Lying on top of the cargo building 200 metres away, both SAS men had an uninterrupted view of the aircraft. Disregarding the drifting rain, Bobby Dunhill gazed through the Schmidt & Bender telescopic sight fitted to his sniper rifle. The rifle itself was a 7.62mm bolt-action manufactured by Accuracy International of Great Britain. In Bobby's hands it was guaranteed to hit a moving target the size of a man's head at 600 metres.

The marksman listened to the continuous radio commentary via his miniature earpiece. Should he need to acknowledge any command, he could murmur into his throat mike. If he had access to a target, all he had to do was press a small button on the rifle with his middle finger.

'What do you reckon, Bobby – think the crazy bastards are going to blow up the aircraft?' his number two enquired casually.

'I don't know, if you ask – ' Bobby stopped in mid-sentence as he saw the front port door open.

'Sierra Four, I have movement on green. The main aircraft door is open and we have two targets.' The voice came through the speaker in the Alpha control room crisp and clear. At the same time two red lights changed to green on the control box.

'Roger that, Sierra Four. Keep it coming. All stations listen in – we have movement. Assault teams, stand by the IA.'

'Alpha One standing by. Immediate Action ready to roll.'

'Alpha Control, Sierra Four. Looks like one male kneeling down in – shot, we have a shot. I confirm we have one hostage shot . . . fallen from the door, now lying on the tarmac. . . . Doorway is clear. Roger that.'

'Alpha Control. I Roger that, Sierra Four. I now have mass movement in the open door . . . Wait. Second body has now been thrown out, repeat thrown out. Cannot identify Blackbirds . . . Wait,' he added as Mahmud appeared briefly. 'I have Blackbird in door. Roger that.' Bobby pressed the small button on the side of his rifle just as the man disappeared and the door closed. 'Alpha Control, Sierra Four. I confirm two bodies on the ground. Neither are moving, both look dead. Roger that.'

'Bastards! We have to do something, Alastair – we really must.' As he spoke to the team commander Colonel McLean turned away from the window, and was surprised to see that most of the faces in the control room were looking at him. Yes, he thought, they expect the SAS to do something. But first we need to find a television crew – and quick.

As news of the hijack spread, the media circus had started to establish itself. They had dug themselves in and around the perimeter wire where they had good visual contact with the aircraft. Already a clutter of vans and transmission vehicles were settling in for the duration. Two large mobile towers were under rapid construction, which would enable the press and TV crews to see over the wire. Around the accumulation of media vehicles, hundreds of feet of black cable lay confusedly over the ground, and in the background several generators hummed noisily away.

On top of one of the scaffolds, now hastily covered with canvas, photographers jostled for position, fumbling about and fitting long-range lenses to their equipment. Once established they would patiently keep their vigil in the hope of catching a piece of dramatic action.

From this gathering the police now had little problem finding cameramen and sound recordists. Several of the crews jumped at the chance of doing a personal interview with the terrorist leader, and one channel even offered to pay for the privilege. In the end a reliable crew from Central Television was selected. A police car whisked them to the control room where they were briefed, and minutes before the deadline they walked the short distance to the hijacked aircraft.

20:48 hours
Mahmud saw them coming and opened the door. When they were still several feet away he spoke. 'That is far enough. Do you have the portable television with you?'

The man holding the microphone came forward, holding up a small set wrapped in protective polythene. Mahmud produced a travel bag and lowered it by its strap. 'Put it in there.' The sound man obeyed and Mahmud hauled the bag back into the aircraft. 'Are you ready to record?'

'Ready when you are,' said the cameraman, who had been

busy focusing his camera on the dead bodies that lay almost at his feet. He looked up at Mahmud standing in the aircraft door, the bright light fitted to his camera illuminating the open doorway.

'We have only two demands.' Mahmud looked directly into the lens. He produced an envelope and took from it a small piece of paper covered in writing. It was in Arabic, and Mahmud slowly translated it into English as he spoke.

'The People's United Army of World Liberation demands that its brothers of the Irish Republican Army, currently held in British concentration camps, are to be released. They are to be taken to Aldergrove Airport and flown here to Heathrow on the next available shuttle.' He paused.

'Secondly, we require fifteen million dollars, this is to be made-up in notes of fifty and one hundred dollar bills. Failure to comply with these demands by 6 a.m. tomorrow will result in the destruction of the aircraft and the deaths of all the passengers. There will be no extension of the deadline. Here are a list of those to be released.'

With difficulty, Mahmud read out the list of Irish names, thirty-two in all.

'Failure not to show this interview on national television by 22:30 hours this evening will result in the following people being shot . . .' Mahmud turned to a second list of names, the one which Selina compiled from the Israeli passport, and read it out. 'Finally, any attempt to attack the aircraft will result in its immediate destruction. We are all prepared to die.'

Putting both sheets of paper back into the envelope, he tossed it down to the two men.

'That is enough filming. Now take this to your government, and make sure they transmit the interview by 10:30 tonight.'

The sound man was about to ask a few questions of his own, but looking down at the two dead bodies thought better of it. Both men walked hastily back in the direction of Alpha Control.

6

Nemesis

COBRA, *21:30 hours*
'They are demanding *what?*' The Prime Minister looked up at the man clutching the fax sheet, her face contorted in anger.

'The release of thirty-two IRA detainees from Long Kesh, and we have until 6 a.m. tomorrow.' Jackson looked worried – he knew the demands were unacceptable.

'Impossible, absolutely impossible. I will not give in to such demands. . . . Gentlemen,' she cast the words like a spear down the long table, 'find me another option!'

Somewhat timidly the Home Secretary essayed a few possibilities. 'We could try to negotiate, but all the signs are that it would be fruitless and delay could result in even more deaths. Secondly, the SAS anti-terrorist team could attack the aircraft. The main problem is the girl under the aircraft, who would see them coming and raise the alarm. That option would almost certainly cause more deaths – possibly the whole aircraft being destroyed, and we know they have explosives in position.' He paused before adding, perhaps unwisely, 'Finally, we could capitulate and give in to the demands.'

The Prime Minister's hands gripped the edge of the table as if trying to rip a piece out of it. As her head thrust forward, her neck muscles strained and her face turned scarlet with fury.

'*Never*! I will not release these murderers, and I will not give in to blackmail. *You* will find me a solution!'

They wilted under the blistering attack.

Only one of the fifteen men seated in the room dared look at her. George Jackson spoke quietly.

'May I suggest that for the moment we comply with their demands, as far as showing the interview on television. Failure to do so will almost certainly result in more passengers being killed, especially as they have a portable television on board to confirm the broadcast.'

The Prime Minister looked at Jackson with displeasure. She did not wholly trust him. The death of the old man had been a direct result of the doctored food ploy. No, she thought, this whole incident wasn't being handled very well at all, but she remained resolute. 'What would we gain, Mr Jackson?'

'Time, nothing more than time. If we carry out the broadcast then we gain some time. Who knows, maybe the SAS will come up with a plan?' Jackson's voice didn't sound over-optimistic.

'Anything else?' She cast her gaze once more around the room.

'Yes, Prime Minister.' The Home Secretary got to his feet in order to make his point. 'If we can find no alternative to the total destruction of the aircraft and the deaths of all aboard by 6 a.m. tomorrow, what do you intend to do?' He remained standing as he waited for her answer.

The Lady of Steel looked at this man who had guided her through many a bad patch. He was right – she had to make some decision. Deliberately she turned to him and said, 'Make preparations for the release of the IRA prisoners, insofar as, if required, we can have them here before 6 a.m. tomorrow. And get the Treasury to start organizing the ransom money.' Then she looked at the representative of the Security Services. 'Mr Jackson, have the broadcast go out before 10.30.' There was quiet as she spoke; then she added, 'Let's hope we don't have to go through with this.'

NEMESIS

Everyone in the control room watched the television broadcast, which was flashed up towards the end of the ten o'clock news. Once it had finished the gathering split into small groups, each discussing the Arab's demands.

'What do you think, Alastair?' The colonel enquired of the team commander.

'I can't see the government giving in to this. In the end they will want to try some kind of assault on the aircraft – it's going to be very difficult,' the team commander replied.

'Difficult – but not impossible.' Karl interrupted the two men, who turned to look at him. He wore a detached expression as he spoke into his radio: 'Keith, could someone find me Burt Simpson – he's hanging around there somewhere – and get him over here? Now.' Karl moved across to the wall where a huge plan of the airport had been pinned up.

'What are you getting at, Karl?

'Well, sir, I came to Heathrow about three months ago with a group of the lads. We spent most of our time crawling over different types of aircraft and getting to know the airport layout. The hijacked plane was put in its present position for the very purpose of allowing our snipers to get as close as possible, yet at the same time remain concealed. We are also in a good position here to carry out an Immediate Action. But there was one thing I'd forgotten until now.

'When we were here, we took a look at the services. Burt Simpson guided us round the miles of service corridors that run beneath the airport. Now the things is, one of those corridors passes directly under the hijacked aircraft – I'm sure of it.'

'But how do you get out?' The colonel was intrigued.

Karl turned back to the window and pointed. 'Just to the rear of the aircraft, on the edge of the runway, can you see a manhole cover? If one of the snipers took out the girl, we might have a chance. She seems to be using the radio to communicate with her fellow terrorists inside roughly every fifteen minutes. Our timing will need to be on the ball, and we'll have to get that explosive charge before they do. But I think we could just do it.'

Two minutes later Burt Simpson arrived in the control room. Karl explained his idea and Burt looked through some binoculars at the manhole cover.

'I think you may just have found a way, Karl, but it would be wise to check first. Shall we go and have a look?' Burt placed considerable emphasis on the 'we'.

'You would have made a good SAS soldier, Burt.' Karl turned to the colonel: 'Best not say anything about this until we are certain, sir. We don't want to get everyone excited.'

'I agree, Karl. You and Burt go and do a recce. Alastair can take over the Immediate Action team. In the meantime I'll start work on a co-ordinated plan of attack.'

'One thing, sir – can you discreetly ask Sierra Four to keep watch on the hatches? We may need to open one a few inches to establish our correct position.'

Quickly Karl and Burt returned to the cargo bay, where they changed into white overalls with 'Airport Services' stencilled on the back. A police car drove them to the main service building at the heart of Heathrow. Minutes later they disappeared down into the maze of corridors.

The passages were well lit and to begin with they moved quickly, using a service map to guide them. Each time they came to a junction, Karl chalked an arrow indicating the way. He also kept note of how long they had been travelling.

Eventually they came to a corridor that lay in darkness, and both men switched on their torches. Although this one was much narrower, there was still plenty of room to move. As they continued, Burt lit the way ahead, while Karl played his torch beam on the roof looking for the hatch. Then abruptly Burt stopped, causing Karl to bump into him.

'Look!' Burt focused his torch on the large service pipes that ran at head height along the corridor wall, and to which every now and then information panels had been attached. The one Burt was lighting up contained a series of numbers and letters, but the last line was very clear: VIP LOUNGE.

'That makes the aircraft about 200 metres straight ahead.' Karl looked again at the service map. 'It also means we should be able to enter the corridor system from near the holding area, close by the cargo sheds. Come on, Burt, we'll step it out from here.' Karl was keen to find the hatch that led to the surface. He had counted just over 170 paces when they came to a small metal ladder set in the concrete wall. 'What do you think – could this be it?'

'It has to be,' said Bert. 'You going to take a look?'

The metal ladder led directly up for about eighteen feet. Slowly Karl climbed until his head was just below the hatch. Quietly he spoke into his throat mike. 'Sierra Four, this is Alpha One. Do you copy?'

'Alpha One. Sierra Four, that's a Roger.'

'Alpha One. I think I am under the hatch two-thirds of the way between the aircraft and Alpha Control. Over.'

'Roger, Alpha One. Do not attempt to lift the hatch, Blackbird is looking your way. No, wait. She is moving around the other side of the aircraft. Over.'

'Alpha One, Roger that. I am going to attempt to lift the hatch a few inches for a look. Keep a close watch on the girl. Wait out.'

Slowly Kark turned the two metal handles that held the heavy hatch cover in place. They were very stiff from lack of use, but eventually they turned. Bracing himself on top of the ladder Karl pushed upwards with all his strength, and with great difficulty managed to raise the head cover about three inches. Instantly he heard the radio whisper in his ear: 'Alpha One, Sierra Four. We can see the hatch lifting.' Karl let it close again slowly and secured it. As he climbed back down the ladder he spoke excitedly: 'On the nose, Burt – but that hatch is bloody heavy. Come on, the one we want is about forty metres further on.'

Quickly they walked on with Karl playing his torch on the ceiling, and suddenly they were standing directly under the hatch. Karl took a small piece of chalk from his pocket and marked a big cross. 'X marks the spot. I'll just climb up and make sure there are no problems in opening it. If it's okay, we're on!'

COBRA 01:10 hours
'The SAS plan is a simple one, Prime Minister. The terrorist leader Mahmud will be kept occupied inside the plane while the SAS snipers shoot the terrorist who is on guard outside. Once this is done, further SAS men will come up from the service tunnels and assault the aircraft. From what we have learnt, the explosive device is only on a timer and is positioned to set off the remaining fuel in the wings. The SAS estimate that they can get into the aircraft via the over-wing emergency hatches and reach the bomb before the terrorists can detonate it.'

'This is marvellous news, but what are the odds?' The lady looked hard at Jackson.

'Now that the broadcast has gone out, the terrorists will probably think that their hard line is working. They should therefore have no immediate plans to destroy the aircraft. Mahmud is the key to all this – he is the dangerous one. From our monitoring, he also seems to be the only one who communicates with the person outside the aircraft – so if he's talking to us he cannot be using the radio. It would all make sense. . . . The SAS estimate a better than 80 per cent chance of success if we do two things.'

'What two things, Mr Jackson?' the Prime Minister demanded.

'Firstly, release the IRA members as requested and fly them here under strict guard. This would be a convincing distraction – while the exchange details were being thrashed out with Mahmud the SAS would have time to assault the aircraft. It is suggested that we put out a late news flash of the event, again as a distraction. This would also, it is hoped, prevent any further deaths. Secondly, we offer them the money.'

'When do the SAS propose to do it?'

Jackson took this as a sign of approval. 'As the aircraft from Belfast arrives with the prisoners, its noise will help cover the shooting of the woman outside. They would like to assault at around 5.30 a.m. – just before dawn tomorrow.' Again George Jackson paused cautiously.

'There is one other thing, Prime Minister. During any assault the SAS will be using stun grenades, but if for any reason the attack goes wrong they would like permission to use the new SR gas. Then they would gas the whole aircraft and attempt to get everyone out as rapidly as possible.' George Jackson eyed the Prime Minister.

'What about the risks involved?' Her euphoria at the possibility of success was quickly dampened. She had been briefed on the various options available, and knew that this gas acted very quickly. But it filled the lungs with a restricting agent which made it impossible to breathe. In a healthy adult the symptoms could be alleviated by putting the victim in the fresh air or giving oxygen, but in young children and old people it could easily kill.

'We would certainly need to get medical aid to the old and young within three minutes, and emergency arrangements have already been made,' Jackson assured her. 'From the passenger list we estimate twelve people would be at serious risk if SR gas were used.'

The Prime Minister bowed her head. 'May God forgive me! Tell Colonel McLean we agree to his plan, and he has my personal authority to use the gas.'

'Thank you, Prime Minister. May I also suggest that for the time being we act as if we really are going to exchange the IRA prisoners? It would help with security.'

'Yes, of course, Mr Jackson. Now we had better get this organized. Home Secretary, would you arrange for the prisoners to be escorted to Heathrow? Do it as quickly as possible, but I want full security in place. Chancellor, I would be obliged if you could arrange to have the money moved to Heathrow – again, I want it under heavy guard. Now let's get to work, gentlemen.'

Almost immediately fresh life appeared to flourish among the COBRA members as they set to their tasks.

'Mr Jackson, I will leave it to you to inform the hijackers that they have beaten the British government, and for the duration of the incident I would suggest you stay at Heathrow as the COBRA liaison.' At least they now had a fighting chance, she thought.

Heathrow, 02:30 hours
Back at Alpha Control George Jackson spoke quietly to Colonel McLean as Alastair and Karl listened. 'The Prime Minister has agreed your plan in outline.'

'Including the SR gas?' the colonel enquired.

Jackson nodded. 'Yes, she has agreed that too. Now it's about time I went and talked to our friend Mahmud.'

Just as the group was about to split up he said, 'You missed Mahmud once, Karl, but now you're going to get a second chance. This time kill him – make sure the Lion is dead!'

'Hello, BA120. I am the official representative of the British government. I would like to speak to Mahmud. Over.'

There was a slight pause before a voice boomed: 'My name is *Major* Mahmud, and you will use my rank when you address me, British fascist representative.'

'My apologies, Major Mahmud. I have a very important message from the British government. It reads, "Providing there is no more killing, the British government has agreed to release all thirty-two IRA prisoners from internment in Northern Ireland. Additionally, we are arranging for the money to be transferred directly here to you. Your demands will be met in full before 6 a.m. The British government humbly begs, in return, that no other passengers or crew are harmed." Over.'

Mahmud was slightly taken aback. Although he had seen the demand broadcast go out on television, it was hard to comprehend that he had won. Wadi Haddad had been right – the secret was no surrender. 'I will consider the British government's proposal. I will call you back.'

Mahmud sat pondering, not at all happy. He knew the British – they would try something. But for the moment he would go along with their offer. He picked up the microphone again. 'This is Major Mahmud. I would like to speak to the British fascist representative.'

George Jackson replied almost immediately, 'This is the British representative. Over.'

'I am prepared to accept your offer, but if this is a trick there will be no more talk and I shall just destroy the aircraft. Do you understand?'

'I assure you, Major Mahmud, there will be no tricks. The freed prisoners will be here at approximately 5.30. At that time we will also deliver the money to you. We would like to exchange the prisoners and money in small groups. At the same time you should release the hostages until the exchange is – '

'Don't tell me what to do! I will tell *you* what will happen – do you understand?' Mahmud's voice boomed out over the speaker.

'Sorry, Major Mahmud. We will follow your instructions.'

'We will do nothing until the aircraft containing our freedom-fighting Irish brothers has landed and is parked where I can see it. I do not trust you, British fascist.' Mahmud's voice sounded bitter. 'While we are waiting I want this aircraft refuelled. Then you may remove the two bodies from under the aircraft. Do you understand?'

'Yes. We will wait for the aircraft to arrive from Ireland before doing anything else. Your aircraft will be refuelled within the next half-hour, and we will send an ambulance to collect the bodies. Please be assured that the British government will co-operate with you in every way, Major Mahmud.' Jackson handed back the microphone to the police negotiator.

Back in the cargo building, Karl gathered the Alpha teams around the small board propped up on the tailgate of one of the Range Rovers and began to outline the plan. All were in sinister black assault gear, to which respirators would be added before they attacked the aircraft. 'The only people who know about this plan are the high-ups in Downing Street and us – not even the police in Alpha Control know, so let's keep it that way.' Karl looked round at the familiar faces, some of whom he had known for years – good solid men, men you could trust.

'Myself and Alpha Two will take the front port door here. Alphas Three and Four will take the rear port door. Alphas Five and Six will take the port wing emergency hatch, with Alphas Seven and Eight going in on the starboard emergency hatch. Okay so far?'

'What about the explosive charge?'

'I'll come to that in a moment. Myself and Alpha Two are to open the front port door and stop the terrorist leader leaving the flight-deck. At the time of the assault he should be talking to Alpha Control about the exchange of hostages for IRA prisoners. In order to control the passengers, we figure they will have to have one person at the rear of the aircraft by the toilets. Alphas Three and Four, that's your job. Five and Six, you go in on the port emergency hatch and find the third terrorist. You will dominate only your own areas – I don't want any cross-shooting inside the aircraft. And while I'm on the subject it's pistols only. Alphas Seven and Eight, you are to open the starboard hatch and find the explosive. I don't care what you do with it, but once you have it get it away from the aircraft quickly. There's a timer on it, so be careful. Any questions so far?'

'What about the terrorist under the aircraft?'

'Sierra Four will deal with that problem. Once that's done we will climb out of the underground corridor and get into position around the aircraft. The hatch is just to the rear of the aircraft, and as the blinds are drawn we shouldn't be seen or have any trouble – but we have to be quick. Now let's go over it again.'

'First, we enter the service corridors just outside the cargo hangar. A large tent is being erected over the cover, and the area around it will be cleared. I will lead the way, but when we reach the ladder Tommy will go up first.' Several sets of eyes looked in Tommy's direction – he had been chosen for his brute strength.

Karl continued to refine the plan until everyone was happy. Finally, he said, 'We move off from here at 05:00 hours. Until then stay alert and ready for any Immediate Action.

05:20 hours
Mentally shutting out the continuous rain, Bobby Dunhill continued to look through the telescopic sight as the first grey of dawn began to appear. The man lying next to him spoke. 'Not long now, Bobby.'

From their commanding position on top of the cargo building the two snipers had seen the British Airways shuttle arrive from Belfast, and now it rolled down the wide runway heading towards the hijacked aircraft. There was little more than a hundred metres between them when the shuttle throttled back on its mighty engines. Bobby heard his call-sign: 'Sierra Four stand by.'

'Take the bitch out, Bobby!' the man next to him anticipated the command.

The marksman took up the first pressure on the trigger, and as if on cue the earpiece whispered: 'Sierra Four, at my command ... wait, wait, stand by, stand by, Sierra Four. *Fire!*'

Bobby squeezed off the shot.

Travelling at 330 metres per second, the bullet entered Leila's forehead two centimetres above her left eye, blowing a hole in her skull and passing straight through her brain. Her nervous system died before the sensation ever reached her muscle drive, and she crumpled to the ground dead.

'Alpha units. Blackbird is down. Move, move, move.' The team commander almost shouted into the microphone.

'Now, Tommy! Push it open.' There had been no need to tell him – like all the others, Tommy had heard the command. With all his immense strength he pushed upwards, using both hands as Karl supported him from below. The warmth of the underground corridors was replaced abruptly by wind and rain. As Tommy crawled out of the hatch above him, Karl could make out the shadowy outline of the aircraft tail silhouetted in the dim glow of the airport lights. Forty-five seconds later, as the last man scrambled out of the hatch, Karl and Tommy had already positioned their padded ladder silently by the front port-side door and were climbing up.

From his precarious position balanced at the top of the ladder Karl hugged the wet metal fuselage, listening intently to the dialogue between Mahmud and the negotiators at Alpha Control. At the same time he watched the rapid progress of his men as they swiftly split into four sub-groups. Each group moved swiftly to its assigned position around the aircraft. Padded ladders were silently placed against the wings where they joined on to the fuselage.

Karl's attention was momentarily captured by the two men who were crawling calmly up on to the wing. Like black ants they stopped and lay flat against the cold wet metal, their heads just below the over-wing emergency door. On command they would stand and punch the small panel on the hatch, and seconds later they would be in the aircraft. Behind them two more black-clad figures stood ready, acting as back-up.

Almost simultaneously a double ladder was placed by the rear entry door and two men climbed quickly side by side into position. The left-hand man, on command, would turn the handle and use his body weight to pull the heavy door open; at the same time the man on the right would enter the aircraft. Here again, two men stood at the bottom of the ladder to act as back-up.

For almost two agonizing minutes Karl stood poised at the top of the assault ladder, his wet body clinging against the plane's smooth metal. Tommy stood next to him, his hands firmly clutching the large metal handle that would open the door.

Abruptly a new voice came through on his earpiece. Karl recognized the team commander and felt the excitement of imminent action engulf him.

'Sierras, confirm Alpha units are in position.'
'Sierra Four, all in position.'
'Sierra Two, all in position.'

05:26 hours
The calmness inside Alpha Control had dramatically changed. One moment the police negotiators, none of whom had been privy to the secret assault, had been acting as if the hostage exchange was about to take place. Now suddenly the female terrorist who had been positioned underneath the aircraft had fallen to the ground and remained still. Seconds later, black-clad figures had mysteriously crawled out of the ground and swarmed around the aircraft. At that point George Jackson had spoken very calmly to them. 'The SAS are about to assault the aircraft. You will continue to negotiate with Mahmud as if nothing has happened. Remember to keep your voices flat and level. It is vital that the terrorists do not know what is going on.'

At the same time a senior police officer gave a handwritten note to Colonel McLean, who in turn passed it to the team commander. 'You have control, Alastair. Go to it.'

'Thank you, colonel.'

The team commander's voice was soft but very distinct. 'All stations, this is Alpha Control. All units are in position. We are talking to the terrorists. Main player is on flight-deck, repeat main player is on flight-deck.' There was silence for about ten seconds, then suddenly the team commander's assured voice stated clearly: 'All units, this is Alpha control. Stand by, stand by. *Go! go, go!*

Tommy's wet hands had been gripping the door handle for so long that they had turned white, but now, as he heard the command, he twisted the handle sharply anti-clockwise. Immediately the huge door swung slightly inwards, opening only slowly at first. Then, using his full body weight, Tommy dropped off the ladder, still holding the handle, and his momentum swung the door outwards.

Even before the door was fully open Karl had reacted. The moment the gap was big enough to get his hand through, Karl lobbed a stun grenade inside the aircraft. As the gap widened even further, Karl stepped from the ladder and leaped into the cabin.

From her position in the first-class compartment Selina watched as the passengers slept or dozed listlessly in their sets. She too was tired, but also very happy. Since Mahmud had told them of the British government's capitulation, she had day-dreamed almost constantly. They had won, and they would return home as heroes. She imagined the praise that would be showered upon her – and all this time she would be close to Mahmud.

A sharp click and a sudden rush of cold air broke into her happy musing and made her turn round suddenly. Then the peace and quiet of the aircraft was shattered by a blinding light and a thunderous sound as, unknown to her, Karl lobbed his stun grenade. She shook her head, and as her vision cleared, she saw what looked like a black beast claw its way into the air-craft. The beast's head had huge eyes, and a round disc where its mouth should be. She made to throw the grenade in her right hand, but the beast pointed his fiery claw and spat flame at her. Then she felt the blow hit her chest like a mighty hammer. Selina fell backwards between the seats and the grenade rolled from her lifeless hand and down the aisle towards Karl.

Instinctively Karl dived. The drab green ball came slowly down to meet him, and as he grabbed at it he saw with disbelief that the pin was still in place. A sickening relief washed over him, but the brief respite was short-lived. Gunfire came from the rear of the aircraft, briefly distracting him, and then Karl heard movement behind him.

It had been five minutes since the shuttle had arrived from Belfast, its jet engines roaring noisily as it had taxied to a position one hundred metres in front of Mahmud. From the flight-deck he had started to talk to the British representative, who informed him that all thirty-two prisoners had been released, albeit under heavy guard. Slowly the doubts had faded within Mahmud's mind. Now, convinced he had won, he concentrated on the details of the exchange.

'You will send five of the Irish freedom fighters at a time. In return I will release ten passengers. The first exchange – '

Then from behind Mahmud came a thunderous roar and the flight-deck was filled with dazzling light. Through the frenzy he heard abrupt bursts of gunfire.

Turning rapidly, he rushed from the flight-deck, stopping suddenly as he saw Selina's bloodstained body and a black-clad man crawling towards her. In that moment the man heard him and rolled over, trapped by the seats. Mahmud saw the man's eyes gape out of a hideous-looking respirator. He fired, hitting the man squarely in the chest.

Karl's chest was on fire, and the pain made him gasp deliberately for breath inside the respirator. Then Mahmud's rage was momentarily diverted by movement in the aircraft doorway – the back-up had arrived. In that brief second Karl raised his pistol and fired twice. Mahmud collapsed in the doorway and fell to the floor. For a moment his legs twitched, and then he lay still.

Agonizingly, Karl crawled forward. As he passed the open door he saw the first back-up man standing there. 'Here, get rid of this.' Karl handed him the grenade. Slowly and with a massive effort he stood up.

As the confusion cleared, the radio echoed to hastily voiced reports. Karl joined in, but the pain in his chest made his words come out in short rasping bursts.

'Alpha Control from Alpha One . . . I have two Blackbirds down at the front of the aircraft . . . One of them is the main player . . . I confirm main player is down.'

'Alpha One, we copy. All Blackbirds down, repeat all Blackbirds are down. Alpha Seven, have you removed the explosive? Over.'

There was a short silence, then a voice cut in. 'Alpha Control, this is Alpha Seven. We have just made the bomb safe. It's clear of the aircraft.'

Suddenly inside the VIP lounge a loud cheer went up.

'Well done, Alpha Seven. Out to you. Alpha One, request permission to evacuate passengers.'

'Wait, Alpha Control . . . I'll call you back.' Karl moved slowly, down the aisle to the rear of the aircraft. As he passed the passengers some of them looked up uncertainly at the men in black, while others still had their heads firmly pressed into their laps. By the rear toilets four black-clad men stood facing him. On the floor at their feet lay a dead terrorist.

'Move him to one side and get the emergency shute down. We're going to evacuate the passengers . . . Two of you to each door. We'll get them all out via the rear.' As Karl spoke, the men hastily pulled the dead terrorist clear of the doorways.

'Alpha Control, this is Alpha One. We will start to evacuate the passengers in a few minutes, all via the rear doors . . . I repeat, evacuation vehicles to the rear doors only. We are inflating the emergency shute now . . . Roger so far.'

'Roger that, Alpha One.'

'The team commander and colonel are clear to come on board . . . no one else. Over.'

'Roger that, Alpha One. We're on our way.'

Karl walked back towards the flight-deck, stepping over Mahmud's body in the doorway.

Like Mahmud, Captain David Griggs and his co-pilot had also watched the Belfast shuttle arrive. Then came the sudden shock of the assault. Thinking that Mahmud might shoot him Griggs had thrown himself forward, adopting the crash position. Explosions and gunfire ripped through the aircraft, and for a brief moment he imagined the explosive charge going off. As the fighting died down he raised his head to see a strange, black-clad figure standing beside him. With a free hand, the figure removed its respirator mask. The face was wet with sweat and the eyes screwed up with pain – still, he was smiling.

'Captain David Griggs, I presume,' he said in a strained voice. 'I wonder if you could kindly ask your crew and passengers to exit the aircraft in an orderly fashion, via the rear doors only. They are free to leave.' The man held out his hand to the pilot.

Griggs was dumbstruck. He gripped the hand firmly and shook it. Then he picked up the microphone.

'Ladies and gentlemen, please stay calm. The terrorists are all dead and there is no immediate danger. I would like you all to exit through the rear doors only, the rear doors only. Cabin crew, to your stations.' As he replaced the microphone he looked up at Karl. 'Thank you, it's nice having my aircraft back.'

'You did one hell of a job, both of you. And now, if you'd like to go back and join the others, I'll clear up some of this mess we've made.' Karl watched as the two brave men walked down the aisle, joining the other passengers now queuing for their turn to leave.

The exit was swift and professional. Karl watched from the first-class section as the stewardesses worked alongside his own men. Guiding the passengers through the rear doors and sending them sliding down the escape shute, they quickly had the aircraft emptied. A quiet hush settled within the aircraft. It was then that Karl heard a faint murmuring sound coming from behind him. Mahmud, it seemed, was still alive.

Karl's pistol was still in his hand and, covering Mahmud, he knelt down beside him. By some bizarre fate the eyes blinked slowly open in the great lion-like head. Mahmud stared up at him, studying Karl's.

'I killed you.' Mahmud's voice was weak.

'You hit me,' said Karl, 'but to kill me you'd have needed something better than a pistol. This is body armour I'm wearing.' As Karl spoke he looked for the last time into Mahmud's face with its features that evoked distant memories.

His thoughts were interrupted as Mahmud demanded, 'Why do you stare at me? Do you think I am some kind of freak?'

'You do not recognize me, but I know you, Mahmud al Dhuhoori. Remember Oman and the Zakhir Tree, during the final battle for the Shershitti caves? I was there – I shot you.'

For a long moment Mahmud did not answer. Then he spoke quietly. 'I was not the enemy – you were. You stole my country, and I will go back there one day.' The fire had returned to his eyes. 'This operation may have failed, but there will be others – soon I will be free again.'

'No!' said Karl, placing his pistol against Mahmud's head. 'You know the rules. Live by the sword, die by the sword.' He pulled the trigger.